'So, Lady Lace, is that your game? Gathering kisses?'

She was not surprised that he knew her alias. She was well on her way to becoming notorious.

He was dark and handsome—strong and commanding—dangerous. She realised what she had to do.

She closed the short distance between them, slipped her arms around his neck and lifted on her toes to reach his mouth. When she pressed her lips to his he wrapped his arms around her and pressed her to the wall. No escape.

No mercy.

LORD LIBERTINE

Gail Ranstrom

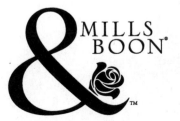

First published in Great Britain 2009
by Mills & Boon, an imprint of Harlequin (UK) Limited.
This edition 2012.
Harlequin (UK) Limited, Eton House, 18-24 Paradise Road,
Richmond, Surrey TW9 1SR

© Gail Ranstrom 2007

ISBN: 978 0 263 22918 9

Harlequin (UK) policy is to use papers that are natural, renewable and recyclable products and made from wood grown in sustainable forests. The logging and manufacturing process conform to the legal environmental regulations of the country of origin.

Printed and bound in Great Britain
by CPI Antony Rowe, Chippenham, Wiltshire

Gail Ranstrom was born and raised in Missoula, Montana, and grew up spending the long winters lost in the pages of books that took her to exotic locales and interesting times. That love of the 'inner voyage' eventually led to her writing. She has three children, Natalie, Jay and Katie, who are her proudest accomplishments. Part of a truly bi-coastal family, she resides in Southern California with her two terriers, Piper and Ally, and has family spread from Alaska to Florida.

Previous novels by the same author:

A WILD JUSTICE
SAVING SARAH
A CHRISTMAS SECRET
  (in *The Christmas Visit* anthology)
THE RAKE'S REVENGE
THE MISSING HEIR
THE COURTESAN'S COURTSHIP
INDISCRETIONS
A LITTLE CHRISTMAS
  (in *Regency Christmas Gifts* anthology)
A RAKE BY MIDNIGHT

**Did you know that some of these novels
are also available as eBooks?
Visit www.millsandboon.co.uk**

Prologue

London, May 25, 1821

Panic licking at her heels, Isabella hurried down the long dingy second-floor corridor of Middlesex Hospital, the man sent by the Home Office leading the way. He indicated a door and she stepped through into a ward with twenty or more beds. The odor, something foul and fetid, hung ominously in the air.

"This way, Miss O'Rourke," her escort said, directing her to a curtain along the far wall.

She slowed, reluctant now, after all their urgency. He'd tried to prepare her, the man from the Home Office—Lord Wycliffe, she thought he'd said. He told her she might not recognize Cora, and that she needed to brace herself and be strong. She glanced up at him again, hoping for reassurance and finding none.

She wished she could have waited for Mama to return from looking for Cora in the park, but Lord Wycliffe had said there was no time to lose. She'd left her sister Eugenia to bring her mother and Lilly to the hospital when they returned. Then Lord Wycliffe had brought her here. To identify Cora. On the way, he'd told Isabella what had been done to her—she'd been beaten, dishonored, disfigured and cast off in a dust heap at the end of a blind lane, where she'd been found by the morning watch. Now, so close, Isabella was afraid of what she'd find.

She swallowed hard.

"Do you need a moment, Miss O'Rourke?"

She shook her head and proceeded slowly. Lord Wycliffe stepped ahead and drew the curtain back for her. He touched her shoulder as she went forward. "I shall wait for you, miss."

Only the meager light able to penetrate a filthy window illuminated the bed, but there was nothing of Cora's in evidence. Where was her cloak? Her gown or slippers?

Isabella stepped closer. The occupant of the bed was swathed in bandages wound around her wrists and neck. Her head was turned away, and Isabella summoned the last of her courage before she touched her shoulder. "Cora?"

Slowly, painfully, her sister turned, and a sob broke free from Isabella's chest. She had thought she was prepared for anything, but she hadn't been prepared for this...this parody of Cora. And it *was* Cora—her honey-blond hair caked with dark, stiff blotches of blood, her forehead missing a large triangle of flesh, her eyes—those sparkling blue eyes—dull now and nearly swollen shut, and her lips cut and distorted.

The tortured lips parted, and a faint sigh emerged. "Bella..."

She took Cora's hand. "I am here, Cora. You will be all right now. I am here and I will take you home."

"Not...going home," she said, and a glistening tear trickled down her puffy cheek.

Isabella nearly choked with the effort to hold her sobs back. "Please, Cora..."

"D-don't pretend."

Isabella could no longer stem the flow of her tears. Her pain and grief welled up and spilled over.

"Be...brave," Cora whispered. "Avenge me, Bella." Cora stopped for a moment when her swollen lip cracked and a fine line of blood appeared. Then she blinked and started again. "He lied about everything...was not who he said."

"Who was not? And how shall I know him?" she asked. "If he lied about his name..."

"A gentleman. Tonnish. Charming, dark hair and dark eyes...taller than Papa was."

"That is not enough, Cora. I need more. You must hold on. You must get well, and we will—"

"His kiss," her sister sighed, closing her eyes as if remembering. "Always…always wets his lips after his kiss. As if tasting…and *he* tastes of…something bitter."

"But—"

Cora opened her eyes again and the sheer intensity of her gaze immobilized Isabella. "*Promise,* Bella."

"I…I promise. I swear it upon my life. Rest now, Cora. Mama will be here soon, and we…we…"

But Cora's hand slackened and her face froze in a concentrated study of Isabella, as if entreating, even in death.

"No…" Isabella moaned as her knees began to buckle. "No…no…"

Lord Wycliffe came forward and braced her. "Come away, Miss O'Rourke. We shall wait for your mother in the matron's office."

But at that very moment, her mother and sisters rushed through the ward toward them. "Bella! Bella! Say it isn't our Cora! Say there has been some awful mistake."

"Mama…"

Isabella tried to stop her mother and sisters from going to Cora's bed, from seeing what had been done to her, but they swept Isabella aside, knocking her back against Lord Wycliffe. A long keening wail broke over the ward as her mother threw herself over Cora's lifeless form. "My baby! Oh, my darling child! Bella, how could you? How could you have let her come to this?"

"I didn't know—"

"It was your *duty* to know!" Mama buried her face against Cora's chest and sobbed, her words barely distinguishable as she said, "It should have been you. Why couldn't it have been you?"

The words, stark in their sincerity, cut into her heart and made it impossible for her to breathe. She turned away from the gruesome scene, and fresh tears rolled down her cheeks. Eugenia and Lilly clutched each other tightly, but Isabella had never felt so alone in her entire life.

Lord Wycliffe, a complete stranger, offered her the only comfort she could find. He slipped an arm around her waist to support her and murmured some indistinct platitude. Grief, anger, pain and loneliness filled her as she silently renewed her promise.

Rest in peace, Cora. I will avenge you.

Chapter One

London, July 2, 1821

"What are we doing cooling our heels at a masquerade when we could be kicking them up at a witches' Sabbath? 'Tis summer, Hunter. There's got to be something better to do. Some prank, some diversion."

What, indeed? Andrew Hunter yawned and scanned the crowded ballroom at the Argyle Rooms. A masquerade, and he and his friends had not bothered to wear costumes or even dominoes. What a sad state of affairs, when he could not think of anything at all to interest him—here or anywhere else. Well, it was bound to have come to this sooner or later. He had not left much undone, untried, untasted.

Henley nudged him again. "There's going to be a black mass in the tombs beneath the chapel at Whitcombe Cemetery. If you know of another…"

Andrew took a deep draught of his brandy and then shook his head. "None better than the Whitcombe Sabbaths. Go on without me, Henley. I think I'll make an early night of it."

"Early night? Are you ailing, Hunter?"

Ailing? Is that what one would call boredom to utter distraction? Aye, then, he had a bloody terminal case of boredom. "It's all hog-wash, Henley. Pretend and make-believe. Witches' Sabbaths, cock fights, bear baiting, whoring…"

His friend gave him a sage appraisal. "We need to find you an interest, Hunter. A cure for the doldrums."

"Lord save me!" Andrew laughed. "You are going to suggest a woman, are you not?"

"Nothing like a willing lass to lighten your cares, eh?"

He considered the suggestion for one brief moment. Then even that palled. How many women had he had in the last year alone? How many assignations and seductions? How many illicit flirtations? God help him, he'd lost his appetite for even that.

When his older brother, the Earl of Lockwood, had married barely four months ago, Andrew had taken a small town house. He had no wish to hang about the family manor and watch Lockwood's domestic bliss—comical as it was. His brothers, James and Charles, had also rented flats to grant the couple their privacy. Whatever restraint had been placed on Andrew by his elder brother's presence was now gone. Perversely, the freedom to indulge his slightest whim had robbed him of the pleasure.

All the same, he felt an odd restlessness tonight, an air of expectancy. Something unusual was in the offing, but he suspected he wouldn't find it in the usual places. "No," he said at length to Henley's suggestion of female companionship. "Think I'll see what's afoot at the club, then stumble my way home."

The look on Henley's face was amusing—as if he could not believe his ears. "Have you become that jaded, Hunter? We used to live for nights like this. Why, look! All around us, men and women are looking for mischief."

Once again, Andrew surveyed the crowd. Spirits were high, it was true. Hiding identities behind costumes and masks gave license to lewd behavior. Or was it summer and the long warm days that loosened one's morals? Whatever it was, it was present at tonight's gathering and would likely be present at the many balls, soirees, musicales, fetes, fairs and pleasure gardens in the days ahead. But…

"None of it is new, Henley. Just the same old thing wearing different guises." Lord, how he wished for something new—anything that would drag him from his constant state of numbness.

"Pshaw! There's plenty of variety. Why, this is the first year Lady Lace has made an appearance."

"Lady *who?*"

Henley inclined his blond head toward a group in one corner. Lively conversation punctuated by laughter carried to them. In the center stood a diminutive woman dressed in black silk and masked by a black lace-edged domino. She was slimmer than he liked, and not nearly as buxom, but she had a certain allure about her. She waved one graceful hand in front of her face in a dismissive gesture, and two fair young men backed away. Two more took their place, including his friend Conrad McPherson.

Andrew narrowed his eyes to peer through the dim candlelight. Yes, she was thin, but not so thin that she could not fill out a gown. And though she lacked a deep cleft between her breasts, milky white swells hinted at what lay beneath the lace ruching that trimmed her décolletage. Chestnut-brown hair tied up in black ribbons would have been drab if not for the gleam and glints of fire in the curls left to dangle down her back.

"Intriguing," he muttered. "Tell me about her."

Henley grinned, no doubt pleased he had snared Andrew's interest. "She is called Lady Lace, always wears black and has, thus far, evaded revealing her true identity. They speculate that she is from the north. Yorkshire, perhaps, or Scotland or Ireland by the faint trace of a Gaelic accent. She has not been long on the scene—a week, perhaps—and some say she is the widow of a country peer. Others swear she is a courtesan looking for her next protector. All we know for certain is that each night she appears, she favors a man with a kiss. And what a kiss! No sisterly peck on the cheek, but one deep and full of promise. Why has she never chosen me, I ask."

Andrew raised an eyebrow. "A device designed to make people talk and men anticipate her arrival. She is nothing if not a very canny businesswoman. Mark me, she will make a choice soon, and the poor devil will pay through the nose for it."

"You are without a mistress at the moment, are you not, Hunter? What say you give it a go?"

"She's not my usual fare. Not enough meat on her bones."

"You might want to try something new, eh? What a coup to make away with the most sought-after woman of the season. Quite a difference between her and the schoolgirls invading town to make their bows."

Did he care about a coup? No. But the thought of revealing what lay beneath the black weeds and lace held a certain appeal. He was not ordinarily competitive, but the idea of claiming a woman who did *not* behave like a schoolgirl and who would not act coy for a marriage proposal was alluring. Pray she was not a courtesan looking for a protector. He had just paid a generous *congé* to the last. "Go on to Whitcombe without me, Henley. I'll catch up to you later."

Isabella O'Rourke fought back her gag of revulsion as the black-haired man kissed her. He had a definite finesse, but the fact remained that she had permitted this intimacy with a stranger. And she knew now all she needed to know.

This was not the man who had killed Cora.

She drew away with a show of reluctance and placed one palm against his chest to keep him at a distance. "La! You quite take my breath away, Mr. McPherson. I shall have to watch myself around you."

He laughed and gave her a crisp bow. "Do not watch yourself, madam. I shall do that for you."

She smiled and drew her closed fan down the side of his right cheek. "I shall think upon it, sir. Now off with you." She made a shooing motion toward the ballroom and waited until he disappeared.

Alone, she exhaled and waited while a bottomless shudder passed through her. She turned to the console table in the alcove and found an abandoned glass of rich amber liquid. Whiskey? Brandy? It didn't matter. With just the slightest hesitation, she lifted it and took a deep drink, holding the liquor in her mouth until it burned. God grant it would burn away the last traces of her humanity so that she could finish what she'd begun.

She swallowed, closed her eyes and leaned her forehead against the wall, waiting for the warmth to spread through her.

"That little shudder of revulsion, madam? Was it for yourself or your partner?"

Myself! She straightened and turned to face the intruder in the alcove. He was watching her, one shoulder propped against the wall and a cynical smile curving his deeply sensual mouth. His eyes, dark and intense, bore into her, and she suspected he saw more than he should. Oh, that would never do!

"You find a kiss revolting, sir?" Her question was not an answer, but she hoped he would not pursue one.

"I do not, but *your* reaction proves different." He bowed, a mere mocking of manners. "Andrew Hunter at your service, madam."

She gave him an equally mocking curtsy but did not volunteer her name. What would he say if he knew she'd only had her first kiss a week ago? "My reaction aside, Mr. Hunter, I do like kissing. That is why I do so much of it." Oh, how smooth her lie was. How convincing.

He grinned as if deriving some satisfaction from her reply. "So, Lady Lace, is that your game? Gathering kisses?"

She was not surprised that he knew her alias. She was well on her way to becoming notorious. She considered lying to him but realized it would be futile. If she was any judge, this man had told enough lies in his life that he would surely recognize hers. "Perhaps I am too countrified, sir, but I am always amazed when I realize the degree to which complete strangers in the city feel they are entitled to the intimate details of one's life."

He gave her a slight nod. "I gather I am not the first to inquire into your background. But a name is hardly intimate, madam."

"There is no need to grant anyone permission to use it, since I do not plan on being long in London."

He reached out and lifted the domino from her face, dropping it on the console table. "Do I look like the sort of man who needs permission?"

No, he certainly did not. His very presence unnerved her. He was strong and commanding. He was dangerous. He was a man just like the one who had killed Cora. And then she realized what she had to do. She would come to it sooner or later, so it was best to have it over and done with now.

She closed the short distance between them, slipped her arms around his neck and lifted on her toes to reach his mouth. She felt his little shock of surprise in the sudden stiffening of his spine, but when she pressed her lips to his, he softened, wrapping his arms around her and turning with her until her back was pressed to the wall. No escape.

No mercy.

His kiss was consuming and powerful. It was undeniable, making her head swim and her senses reel. And then, when her resistance weakened, it turned coaxing, teasing with little flicks of fire at the edges. Her breasts, flattened to his chest, began tingling and aching, quite unlike anything she'd experienced before. Somewhere in the back of her mind it registered that she was losing herself to this kiss— losing her very will to resist.

Oh, dear Lord, she'd lost control of this situation! She summoned the few senses remaining to her and fought to regain that tenuous hold. Alas, Andrew Hunter had no intention of relinquishing it. His tongue met hers and merged with a hot demand. She wanted to retreat, but there was nowhere for her to go. With the wall at her back and Mr. Hunter at her front, she was trapped as effectively as if she'd been caged. And in another minute, she would crave captivity. She slid her fingers up his neck and stroked the soft wave of dark hair at his nape and arched against him, wanting more of the breathless feelings he elicited.

And then he went still and stiff. He surrendered her mouth with a low growl and reached up to disentangle her arms from around him and turned away. Had she disgusted him?

"You have bewitched me, Lady Lace," he said as he turned back. "But I prefer to conduct such activities in private."

She realized that she had somehow wandered from her original purpose, but she didn't know how. She could only stand there, looking at him, unable to speak.

"Name your price. And please do not disappoint me by asking me what I mean."

Oh, that much, at least, was clear. She could only hope he thought she was a courtesan rather than a common whore. "I understand, sir, but I fear you have misread me. I am not for sale. Not at any price."

"Then you are looking for a husband."

"No."

"Just as well, my sweet, since no *respectable* man would marry a woman who'd kissed half his friends and more."

She gave him a self-deprecating laugh and looked away, wondering if there was another abandoned glass of liquor nearby. "Perhaps the man I am seeking is not respectable."

"Then you and I are ideally suited, madam, since I am not the least bit respectable."

She might have thought he was teasing or cajoling, if his tone had not been completely serious. Oh, she could believe him. One could not kiss like that without years of practice and miles of experience. But there was something darker in his voice, something frightening. She glanced back to find him uncomfortably close. She raised one hand to hold him apart.

"No words of affection? No declaration of fidelity or undying love? No pretty manners or promises? What sort of courtship is this, sir?"

"Have I not said you've bewitched me? I could tell you lies, Lace, but I hoped you were not the sort to require such twaddle. How could I love you when I barely know you? How could I swear fidelity when we will both be on to the next lover as soon as our affair palls? But if that is what you need, I shall give it to you, though be warned—I won't mean a word of it, and I won't have you crying 'foul' afterward."

He was honest, at least. Of the four similar proposals she'd garnered, not one of them had been honest enough to tell the truth. "N-nevertheless, Mr. Hunter. I am not for sale."

"If not money or marriage, name your terms."

Searching for words, she shrugged. "When…when I know them, sir, I shall tell you."

"Please do. When I want something, I am not a very patient man."

"Thank you for the warning."

He grinned, bowed and took his leave. When he was halfway across the ballroom, he turned to look at her again. She could feel his gaze sweep her from head to toe. His admiration was clear, but the open sexuality of his gaze unnerved her.

She glanced at her domino on the console table. How would she ever hold him at bay? She had better find her quarry soon.

Lady Lace. Ah, yes. This *was* going to be interesting. How long had it been since a woman had denied him? Well, *that* sort of woman, at any rate.

Andrew took his hat and walking stick from the footman at the door and stepped into the darkened street. The distance to Whitcombe

Cemetery was scarcely twenty minutes, and he waved a coach away, deciding the exercise would expend a measure of his restless energy.

And banish the memory of the most remarkable kiss he'd ever indulged.

To be kissed in so sudden and forward a manner, to be consumed by that kiss to the point of instant and painful arousal, was unprecedented for him.

Lady Lace was definitely a witch. That kiss—how had she known the very thing that would set him back on his heels and make him lose his self-possession? And how had she managed to accomplish the very thing no woman ever had—meet him on his own terms, without demurring or pretense?

How had he thought her drab at first sight? Lace definitely improved with proximity. At close hand, she was perfectly proportioned. Her breasts were soft and ample enough to burn their impression against his chest. And her hair was not dull at all, but alive with multicolored strands of chocolate, chestnut, caramel and copper. And her eyes—the most soulful greenish hazel he'd ever seen. But her mouth—dear Lord—that mouth! It was all his favorites wrapped into one. The hint of a saucy lilt in her voice and the soft, lush lips accented by a small mole above one corner beckoned him. Straight, even teeth and a sweet, almost shy, tongue replete with intoxicating brew completed the spell.

Ah, but what could he do about her? Clearly, she had her own plan. Just as clearly, he was not a part of it. But that knowledge did not satisfy his lust for her or engender any soft romantic notions in him. He wanted her, and he fully intended to have her.

He felt his blood rising again and quickened his pace. He hadn't intended to go to the witches' Sabbath tonight, but now he felt the need to slake an indefinable thirst for excitement and fulfillment. Aye, he'd go to meet Henley and the others and they'd find sin of some sort.

Isabella closed the door of the rented town house on James Street and braced herself. As awful as the night had been, coming home to the guilt and pain was worse. She dropped her cloak where she stood, kicked her slippers off and tiptoed into the salon. A soft sigh from the sofa told her that Eugenia had waited up for her.

Her sister sat up, rubbing her eyes. "Bella?"

"Gina, I told you not to wait up. Go along to bed, dear. Mama will need you in the morning." She went to the sideboard and poured herself a small glass of port to help her sleep.

"She's had a bad night, Bella. She'll sleep late. But she may want to see you tomorrow."

Isabella gave her sister a sad smile. How dear of Gina to hold out that hope. In truth, their mother was the sort who needed to fix the blame for any disaster on anyone but herself. This time it was Bella's turn to be the scapegoat.

And the awful truth was that Bella blamed herself, too. If only she'd paid more attention to Cora's absences. A short walk in the park, indeed! Her sister had been meeting a murderer. If only she'd gone with Cora. If only she'd raised an alarm sooner when Cora had been late coming home.

"Mr. Franklin came by at suppertime," Gina said. "He wants to know if we intend to honor the lease through September. I did not know what to tell him."

A lump formed in Isabella's throat and she sighed. "If I am gone next time he comes, tell him yes. We cannot leave London until Mama is well enough to travel, but that may not be for a while. Nevertheless, we shall pay, even if we leave the place vacant. Mama signed the contract, and we shall honor it. 'Tisn't as if we are destitute."

Gina nodded. "The sooner we leave, the better, say I. Not only has London killed Cora, but it is stealing you away, too."

"Hush, sweet," Bella soothed. "London is not stealing me away. I am simply seeking Cora's murderer. He shan't get away with it. I promised."

"But, Bella, you have changed. You…you are drinking too much strong spirits, you are going out without a chaperone and staying out late. You will be ruined."

She gave a choked laugh. Will be? If Eugenia found out about the kisses… "Cora is dead. *Dead.* The scandal will ruin us all—you, Lilly and me. I only hope we can leave London before the news filters to the ton, which it is sure to do when Lord and Lady Vandecamp arrive in London. They will withdraw their sponsorship in quick order. When Mama is well enough, we will return to Belfast, likely never to return." She sighed. "So, do you really think I care what a bunch of London popinjays think of me? We are already ruined."

"That isn't fair. It wasn't our fault. And, no matter what society will think, it was not Cora's fault, either."

"That will not matter. 'Tis always the girl who is blamed. *What fast behavior! Why was she unescorted? What was she doing there?* Somehow it will be twisted to be Cora's fault. Now go on to bed, dear. I am home safe now, and I shall come up presently. I just want to look in on Mama and Lilly."

Gina stood and gathered her robe around her. "Do not fall asleep on the sofa again. Cook will find you when she comes down to prepare breakfast. She'll tell Nancy, and Nancy will tell Mama."

Bella nodded absently. Nothing was secret from the servants. When Gina was gone, she returned to the bottle on the sideboard. A sip? Just a tiny dram? Enough to let her sleep without dreaming? Or was Nancy reporting her drinking habits, too? Measuring the level of liquid in the bottles?

What was wrong with her? She'd never even tasted anything stronger than watered wine before Cora died, and now she was using it liberally and undiluted. To forget the pain. To sleep without dreams. To wash away her self-loathing and the taste of too many kisses, too many strange men.

She went back to the sofa, leaving the decanter untouched. She just needed a moment to close her eyes and make plans for tomorrow, and to rest.

First, she'd rise early, with her sisters. With Mama unable to cope with even the slightest unpleasantness, Lilly and Gina needed guidance. She could not have them wandering off alone as Cora had done.

Cora. Tragic, beautiful Cora.

How she wished she could remember Cora beautiful now—with her honey-blond hair and blue eyes so like Lilly's, and so unlike Gina and Bella in coloring and temperament. But she could only remember Cora as she'd last seen her in Middlesex Hospital—a grotesque parody of what she had been. And, dear Lord, how could she ever forget Cora's sightless eyes entreating her beyond death? *Be brave. Avenge me, Bella.*

In the weeks following Cora's death, she'd made daily visits to the

Home Office and begged for information. But in the end, there had been no leads, and the case had been put aside. Lord Wycliffe had been too busy, she'd been told, and was working on "other things." They'd sworn they had done all they could, but admitted that Cora's killer might never be brought to justice.

But Bella couldn't accept that. *His kiss,* Cora had said. *Always... always wets his lips after his kiss. As if tasting...and* he *tastes of... something bitter.* So, for the last week, she'd gone out in society, found men who matched Cora's description and urged a kiss—the only avenue the authorities had not pursued. The only one left to her.

That man tonight—Mr. Hunter—had turned away after their kiss. Had that quirk simply been a reaction to her catching him by surprise? But she couldn't recall if he tasted bitter.

The mere thought propelled her to her feet and sent her back to the sideboard. No small dram would do, but a full half-glass. She drank it standing there, and did not move until the little trails of fire tingled all the way to her toes.

Which dream did she most dread? Those of Cora, or a new one of that one impossible kiss?

Chapter Two

Garish sunbeams pierced the heavy draperies around Andrew's bed. It must be afternoon. He winced, his head throbbing in concert with his heartbeat. His tongue felt glued to the roof of his mouth and he could not rid himself of the foul taste. What had he partaken of last night? Sulfur?

Ah, yes. The witches' Sabbath, sans witches. A chalice containing wine laced with brimstone had been passed from hand to hand as the robed and hooded group stood around the altar where Lady Elwood had lain naked in voluntary submission. She'd giggled when Throckmorton poured wine in her navel and proceeded to lap it away. Rather than finding the scene arousing, Andrew had only wondered where Lord Elwood was.

He sat up and rubbed the grit from his eyes, trying to remember the rest of last night. Henley, Throckmorton and Booth had abandoned themselves to the sexual excess of the orgy following the Sabbath, and Andrew had left them in favor of prowling the taverns, looking for carousing friends. He hadn't wanted to go home after all. His encounter with Lady Lace had left him restless and unsettled. He was not ready for sleep, and neither his valet nor his cook were particularly good company in the wee hours.

He snapped the bed curtains back and stumbled to his washstand. The cold water he splashed on his face brought him fully awake. This business of being a libertine was rather more taxing than he'd first imagined, but he'd thrown himself into it with enthusiasm.

As the second son of an earl, he was not heir to the title, had few familial responsibilities and had enough wealth to render him independent. After Oxford, when he'd still been trying to find his way, he'd bought a commission in the Light Dragoons, been sent to Spain to rout Boney, been decorated for bravery and then been spit out again on the shores of Britain.

By the time he'd returned to England, there was no corner of his soul left untouched, unsullied. He'd tried to drown his memories at first, then realized they'd always be a part of him. He should have changed, should have recognized his debauchery and stopped. Ah, but it was years and years too late to turn back now. There was no redemption for Andrew Hunter, Lord Libertine.

He dried his face, threw his towel down and dragged his fingers through his hair. He'd go to a barber today and then to his fencing master for exercise. And tonight, one more time, he'd go through the motions of polite society. At least the arrival of Lady Lace on the scene had broken the monotony. Yes, she'd be a fine, if temporary, distraction.

Bella slipped into the midst of a large group of revelers entering Marlborough House for a ball, wrapping her paisley shawl more closely around her. She edged closer as the men presented engraved invitations, knowing it would be assumed that she was included in the group, then followed them into the hallowed halls.

As unobtrusively as possible, she separated herself from the group and wandered away. She returned a hesitant wave from Mr. McPherson. He would not come talk to her tonight. He was in the midst of a group of women, and she knew full well that her behavior had put her beyond the pale of polite introductions.

She took her bearings, feeling a bit like a country mouse surrounded by such splendor. Marlborough House literally glittered with crystal and candlelight. The richness of the furnishings and decor took her breath away. Before she could turn around, she had a glass of champagne in her hand and was caught in a stream of guests entering the ballroom.

All the gaily colored gowns she and her sisters had ordered would remain in their boxes, and Bella, the most reserved of the sisters, was wending her way through the ton as a wanton. Not precisely the figure the O'Rourke girls had hoped to cut.

She put her melancholy aside and tried to look serene and approachable. If she looked helpless enough, some gentleman was bound to take pity on her. And once that was done, she could manage a few introductions.

She gazed quickly over the sea of people. So many dark-haired men! Before she could take another step forward, she was struck by the sudden, crushing realization that she'd never kiss them all. She had to find a better way to narrow the possibilities.

Bile rose in her throat and she whirled back toward the foyer, her instinct to flee nearly overwhelming her. She needed a moment alone to control her racing heart. She could not think what was behind these sudden bouts of panic, but she could not allow them to control her.

Finding her way blocked by the flow of arriving guests, she turned down a corridor, praying there would be a ladies' retiring room or private sitting room where she could collect herself.

Arriving at Marlborough House, Andrew caught a glimpse of his quarry. Fortune had favored him quickly. Lady Lace. Again, she had dressed in black. A black silk sheath with a black lace overdress and a décolletage that dipped scandalously low. Stunning. He glanced toward the reception line and back down the corridor where she'd disappeared. He'd pay his respects to his host later. But first...

He hadn't taken more than a few steps when he was brought around by a hand on his shoulder. Lord Wycliffe, his former commanding officer and a close friend of his older brother, gave him a canny smile.

"You have the look of a man on the prowl, Hunter. Is some luckless lass in for a run?"

Andrew grinned. "How did I give myself away?"

"The eagerness in your step," Wycliffe told him. "I hoped I would see you here tonight, though it would have been easy to miss you in the crush. I've been meaning to have a talk with you. No time like the present, eh?"

"Actually—"

Wycliffe shook his head and turned Andrew toward the library, where men were clustered in low conversation. "She will not get away from you, Hunter." He went to a tea table where bottles of liquor were waiting, poured them both a small draught and handed one glass to Andrew.

He took the glass and narrowed his eyes. What had he done to put Wycliffe in a mood? "Make it quick, sir. I wouldn't want to give her too much of a lead."

Lord Wycliffe laughed. He edged toward the far side of the room, nearer the fireplace and away from the possibility of being overheard. "Now then, when your brother retired from the Home Office, it left a bit of a hole. And I thought—"

"I'm not Home Office material, Wycliffe. I might have helped Lockwood out once or twice, but if you think I can fill the hole he left, you are mistaken."

"Come, now. Do you forget that I know just how well you work and how discreet you can be? Your service in Spain proved that. It is, in fact, because I know you so well that your name came to mind. After all, who better to catch a scoundrel than another scoundrel?"

Andrew grinned in spite of the veiled insult. "Scoundrel, eh? How are you thinking I can help?"

"We have a case that is rather troubling. We are stymied at the moment and thought you might have an insight."

"You mean, I gather, that you wonder if I know anything."

"It is not a stretch, Hunter, to think that you might have knowledge of a crime. Not that you committed it, mind you, but that you might have heard or seen something. This particular case is the sort of thing that is in keeping with your...er, wide range of interests."

A polite way of saying that he had a reputation for wallowing in the dregs of London society? A fair enough assessment, he supposed. He took a long drink from his glass before answering. "Which particular interest are you speaking of, Wycliffe?"

The man glanced over his shoulder, ostensibly to make certain they were not being overheard. "The religious underworld, so to speak."

Andrew blinked. What interest could the Home Office have in religion—underworld or otherwise? His doubt must have shown, because Wycliffe leaned forward and lowered his voice.

"Black Sabbaths, witches' Sabbaths, covens, satanic rituals. That sort of thing."

"They are absolute hogwash. Frivolity. Grown men looking for an excuse to behave like naughty lads."

"Grown men who have gone too far." Wycliffe cocked an eyebrow. "Perhaps men in your stratum, Hunter. Men with a nasty streak."

He recalled last night. Lapping wine from Lady Elwood's navel could be considered by some to be naughty, even nasty, but why would the Home Office care about that? "Gone how far?"

"You may as well be warned, Drew. Rape. Ritual sacrifice. That sort of thing."

Andrew grimaced. Nasty, indeed.

Wycliffe reached into his jacket and brought forth a small scrap of paper. He unfolded it and passed it to Andrew. "Have you ever seen this before, Hunter?"

Crudely drawn, the figure appeared to be an inverted triangle. On the paper below that was sketched a crude dragon—a wyvern, if he recalled his mythology correctly. "You associate these patterns with dark religions?" he asked.

"We haven't a single notion what they suggest. This is new to us, and completely unprecedented."

"Where did you find it? And why is the Home Office involved?"

"The triangle was carved into a young woman's forehead some weeks ago. The flesh had been removed and we did not find it. The dragon had been painted in blood on her lower belly. *Her* blood. She'd been raped, beaten and left for dead."

"Human sacrifice, then?" A freezing cold invaded him clear to the bone. Wycliffe was right. This had gone too far. He'd seen savagery like this in the war, but never in London. Civilized London.

"There were other, ah, indications that she'd been used as a ritual sacrifice. We found puncture wounds on her wrists, as if her blood had been drained into some sort of vessel. Yet the girl survived for several hours afterward and expired of her wounds at hospital."

"Who was the girl? Is there anything in her background that would give you a lead?"

Wycliffe shook his head. "Fresh into town for the season and had never been here before. Good family. And the evidence would indicate that she'd been virgin before the ritual. According to her family, she had no acquaintances."

"What is it you want me to do?"

"Keep your eyes and ears open. Say nothing, not even to your friends. We cannot have the public in a panic over ritualistic murders. You see, this was not the first body we've found with such markings."

Andrew refrained from asking just how many bodies they'd found. All that mattered now was that, if the killer was not stopped, there would be more. "What do you want me to do?"

"Keep your nose to the ground, Hunter. Eventually you will catch wind of the stench." Wycliffe paused and met Andrew's gaze. "Do not take it upon yourself to handle this on your own. If you hear anything, see anything, bring it to me."

He nodded, thinking of a few of his acquaintances who were capable of such monstrous acts. There were some who, quite literally, knew no boundaries. But this went beyond anything Andrew had ever done, and he could not say that about much.

Wycliffe stood and clapped him on the shoulder. "I knew you would not turn me down, Hunter. And I know I can trust your discretion."

The outcome had never been in doubt. He would always agree to anything Wycliffe asked of him. His guilt over the events in Spain would see to that. He nodded and put his glass down.

At least this would give him another interest this season. Another break from the tedium. Meantime, Lace was waiting.

Bella found herself in a small sitting room and spun to close the door behind her. Alas, Mr. McPherson had followed her. He must have thought she was summoning him by their shared glance in the ballroom. She would correct that notion at once.

She put one hand up, palm outward. "Heavens, Mr. McPherson! You should not be here."

He advanced on her, despite her words. "I have not thought of anything but you since last night. You have enchanted me, and—"

"You have misunderstood me, sir."

"Canny little minx! I want more, and I'm willing to pay for it. Willing, in fact, to set you up in your own place. Name it, and 'tis yours."

He stepped closer. She stepped back, her hand still in front of her. "I have heard it said, sir, that one will know their true love by his kiss.

I am simply trying to find…the right man. I regret, Mr. McPherson, you are not the right man."

"Come now. Give me another chance. Was I not commanding enough?"

"Sir, that is not the point."

"Then what is?"

"That I did not feel that you were, ah, the man I am looking for."

"Balderdash! That's a bunch of feminine nonsense!" McPherson closed the distance between them and jerked her against his chest.

"Stop!" she squeaked as one of her hands became caught between them.

On the contrary, Mr. McPherson crushed his mouth against hers in a bruising kiss. He used one arm to hold her so close against him that she could not gain leverage for her trapped hand to wedge him away. His other hand cupped the back of her head, preventing her from turning away from his mouth.

She tried to protest, but all that came out was a muffled, *"Mmm-ph…"*

She wasn't aware of the door opening until she heard the clearing of a throat. She staggered backward and caught her hip on the corner of a chair when Mr. McPherson released her.

"I say, Hunter, rather bad timing of you."

With a sinking feeling, she turned toward the door. Yes, her rescuer was the man from last night. The one who'd stolen her wits and whose kiss had been open to doubt. He was studying them both, a glass of something amber in his hand, his dark eyes judging and assessing.

"McPherson," he acknowledged. "Should I excuse myself?"

Heavens! She could not decide if it would be safer to remain with Mr. McPherson or make her escape with Mr. Hunter. She glanced away and wiped her mouth on the back of her hand. She thought she tasted blood from the way Mr. McPherson's teeth had mashed against her closed lips.

"Yes, damn it," Mr. McPherson said. "And close the door on your way out."

She turned back and saw that Mr. Hunter had his hand on the door-knob. He met her gaze and stopped. With a lazy smile, he dropped his hand to his side and shook his head. "Actually, McPherson, I like the quiet here. Why don't we all sit down and have a chat?"

Mr. McPherson's face suffused with color. He seized her wrist and pulled her toward the door.

"Leave the lady here, McPherson."

She held her breath while the two men faced each other down. In the end, Mr. McPherson made the decision she would have. He left, slamming the door behind him.

"You are welcome," Mr. Hunter said, the hint of a smile in his voice.

Was he pleased to see her discomfort? She chafed her wrist and refused to look at him. "Thank you," she grumbled. "I do not know what got into him."

"Truly?" His laugh was a low, warm rumble. "I have a few ideas, madam. Allow me to indulge them. Perhaps he did not appreciate the promise you made with your lips that you later recanted. Or perhaps you have so enchanted him that he could not help himself. Or—and this is just conjecture, you understand—perhaps he did not realize you were just making sport of him."

"I did not intend...that is, I did not know he would follow me tonight. I did not mean to encourage him in the least."

"For many men, once is enough."

She rubbed her hip to still her trembling hands. "Is that why you are here, sir? To renew your offer? Will you, too, devil my every step?"

His glance dropped to her hands, then moved back up to her eyes. A flicker of emotion passed over his features, but she could not tell what he was thinking.

He came forward and pressed his glass into her hand. "Drink," he said. "It will calm your nerves."

He stepped away from her, as if he were uncomfortable being close. "As for me, I may devil your footsteps, but set your mind at ease—I will never force myself upon you. I have already said, have I not, that I will wait for your answer?"

She frowned. What an odd blend of concern and anger he possessed, that he could both assist and insult her in the same moment. And she did not care for the touch of antagonism in his voice. "You confuse me, Mr. Hunter. One moment you are pursuing me most ardently, and the next you sound as if you do not even like me. You have taken great care to warn me against you. Is this sport? Are you trying to make your conquest of me more difficult, so the winning will be sweeter?" She lifted his glass, took a swallow and winced as the whiskey stung a little cut on the inside of her lip.

"I think you drink that whiskey a wee bit too eagerly for a lady. Do you have a drinking problem, madam?"

"Not yet, Mr. Hunter, but I am working on it."

He chuckled and shook his head. "I daresay you will get there. You appear to be deucedly determined. But I should warn you that a drunken woman loses her attraction."

She looked up and studied the handsome face. No. Whatever concern he might have had for her was gone. Now there was just a challenge. "What would I have to do to make you go away, sir?"

"Come clean. Tell me what you are about. Or say, 'Yes, Mr. Hunter, I will be delighted to take you to my bed.'"

Bella was discomfited to learn that she could still blush—if the heat in her cheeks was any indication. She covered it with an extra measure of defiance. "Then would you go away? Truly?"

But he only shrugged—not that she would have told him the truth anyway. "Money, then?" she asked. "If I paid you, would you go away?"

He looked surprised, then a little insulted. "This is a first for me. How droll. No one has ever attempted to buy me off before."

"Really? Your company is so tedious that I would have thought you could make a rather nice living from it."

He took his glass from her and raised it as he gave her a crooked grin. "It would seem you've taken my measure, madam."

Heavens! Was there no discouraging the man? She sighed and started to push past him on her way to the door. He caught her arm when she was beside him and leaned sideways to whisper in her ear. "Have a care, Lace. I may not always be around to save you, and the way you are heading, you are going to need saving."

Tears of frustration sprang to her eyes and she blinked them back quickly. "What business is it of yours what I do? Do you devil everyone you dislike? Everyone who has ever done something of which you do not approve?"

He gave her that slow smile again. "Did I say that I dislike you, Lady Lace? I do not recall that. On the contrary, it is my devotion to you that will keep me at your heels."

Chapter Three

Drew's hand tightened around his glass as he watched Lady Lace wind through the crowds when she returned to the ballroom. He wished he could call her graceless or gauche, but she held her own with a quiet dignity that belied her apparent purpose—to kiss every eligible male in society. He eased his grip on the glass before he could break the stem, but his stomach began to tighten.

How many times had he pitied men who'd fallen victim to Cupid's arrow? Who followed their ladylove's every move and sigh? God save him that indignity. Lace was a slow burn in his blood, and as soon as he satisfied his need, he would be himself again. And now, to make matters worse, he'd have to find McPherson and make amends. He'd be damned if he'd lose a friend over a skirt.

"My! Such a dark look, Hunter."

He turned and found Viscount Bryon Daschel and Percy Throckmorton standing behind him. "Then my look matches my thoughts."

Daschel, whose good looks accounted for his nickname, "Dash," followed the line of his gaze and nodded. "Ah, yes. Lady Lace. Quite the comer, that one."

"You do not seriously believe she will be a force in society?"

"Male society, at least." Daschel grinned. Throckmorton sniggered and nudged him.

For some unaccountable reason, Drew wanted to put his fist down Daschel's throat. Lace was *his* new obsession, and his interest had become proprietary. He took a deep breath and assumed a look of unconcern. "She is trouble, Dash. You'd do well to stay away from her."

"No doubt." Daschel gave him a rakish grin. "But when has that ever stopped me? And why do I have the feeling that you intend to disregard your own advice?"

"You know me, Dash. As a…connoisseur of beautiful women, I am immune to her charms. My interest in the woman is…shall we say, more cerebral."

Daschel laughed. "And here I was thinking it was located in another region entirely."

Again Throckmorton sniggered. "I say, Hunter, we all ought to have a go at her. Only fair, wouldn't you think?"

"No. I wouldn't." In fact, if Throckmorton wanted to have a go at Lace, he'd have to "go" through Drew.

"Come, now. Let's not quarrel," Daschel soothed. "Let Hunter indulge his fascination. 'Tisn't as if the chit is in danger of losing her reputation, is it? That, I gather, is too far gone for retrieval, though I haven't spoken to anyone who has made her a conquest yet. Give Hunter a chance to break her in for the rest of us, eh? I warrant he'll do as good a job of it as he always does."

Break her in? Lace might be unfettered, but he was beginning to suspect she was not quite a tart. There'd be no profit in debating the fine points with Daschel and Throckmorton, however. He decided a change of subject was the safest course of action. "Did you come to discuss the woman in question, or did you have other business with me?"

"Thought you might like to come along on a jaunt tonight," Daschel said.

Jaunt. That was the word Daschel always used for an excursion into the opium dens near the wharves. Last year, when Drew had been searching for a solution to his ennui, and for a way to feel anything at all, he'd spent a considerable amount of time and money as a lotus eater. The only thing he'd gained was the knowledge that he did not like being in a helpless state and at the mercy of others.

"Thank you, but no, Dash. Not for me."

"Last year—"

"Was *last* year. This year I prefer a different poison."

"Do tell."

Drew lifted his glass with a self-mocking smile. "Mundane, perhaps, but steadier. Easier to control."

Daschel nodded. "As you will. But you must come with us tomorrow. Throckmorton has arranged a private tour of Bedlam. Should be quite amusing."

"Amusing?" Drew doubted observing the unfortunate inmates of an asylum could provide entertainment. He shrugged. "Perhaps. Where and when?"

"Outside the entrance at midnight. Bring your ready. There's bound to be wagering."

"If I'm not there, do not wait for me."

Daschel gave him a puzzled smile. "Sooner or later, Hunter, I shall think of something to pique your interest."

"I hope you will, Dash," he said honestly. "It is a sorry state of affairs when there is nothing remaining to engage my notice."

Gazing at Lace, Daschel murmured, "I would not call her 'nothing,' Hunter. Finish with her quickly, will you? I fancy I'm next."

Drew gave his friend a rueful smile. He doubted there'd be anything quick about Lace and, unless he was wrong, she'd be worth the wait.

He left Daschel and Throckmorton and moved to the perimeter of the room, keeping Lace in view. She wandered slowly through the crowds, and he saw her decline an invitation to dance with Lord Entwhistle, then move on. After a short conversation, she took the arm of a man Drew did not know and strolled toward an alcove. He knew what would happen there and fought the urge to interrupt them. And failed.

As it happened, he did not have time to interrupt. As soon as he edged closer, Lace pushed past the column and drapery that shielded the alcove from view. She passed him without realizing he was there, her head down and a dark look of consternation furrowing her brow.

Again he followed her through the crowds, to the foyer and down the steps to the street. He was surprised to see that no carriage or coach awaited her and that she simply drew her shawl up around her shoulders and turned toward the Mall.

The Mall? The bridle path after dark? Alone? That was foolhardy at best. At this time of night she could run afoul of brigands of all sorts—cutpurses, cut*throats,* debauchers…. Satanists?

She'd just made a deucedly bad decision. He hurried after her, keeping at a distance. She had made it clear that she did not desire his company tonight but, to be perfectly honest, he was curious to see where she would go. Odd that he hadn't wondered before where she lived, or how. This might well be an opportunity to discover her background. Heaven—or maybe hell—knew Drew was never one to pass up an opportunity.

Bella wrestled with her self-contempt as she turned into the Mall and hurried toward Wards Row. The evening had turned chilly and mist swirled around the hem of her gown, just beginning to rise. Fog would not be far behind.

Her evening had been a complete waste. Even Mr. McPherson's behavior had been boorish, though she had to accept part of the blame for that. Had she never kissed him to begin with… And then she'd gone on to kiss yet another man. To no avail. All for naught.

No, that was not entirely true. There had been Mr. Andrew Hunter to teach her what a kiss *should* be. And to remind her of what she was becoming. She pushed that unhappy thought aside and took note of her surroundings.

Lamplight made her feel exposed in the middle of the inky night. Tall trees lined the bridle path and stirred in the light breeze. Shadows shifted through the leaves. A hint of malice pervaded the air tonight. A hint of something evil. She glanced over her shoulder, certain that she'd heard a footfall.

No. Only the breath of the wind.

The sudden image of Cora creeping out to meet her beau at night rose before her. Had she come here and sat on one of the benches in the light, waiting for him? Had he wooed her until she had willingly gone with him? Was it here that he had swept her away to her death?

Fear and fatigue, grief and guilt—all filled Bella to the bursting point. How had she been so blind to what her sister had been doing? Her eyes brimmed with tears, and she fumbled to fish a handkerchief from her reticule. As she dabbed at her eyes, a faint whisper carried on the breeze and raised the fine hairs on the back of her neck. *Avenge me, Bella.*

No. 'Twas just her imagination. She shivered, realizing for the first time that she'd be safer in the darkness than on the lighted path where she made an easy target. The shadows offered safety, anonymity. They would not frighten her if she became a part of them.

She veered off the bridle path and found sanctuary behind a row of oak trees. All she need do was follow the course of the path in the dimness until she could cut across St. James Park and thence home.

Clever girl! Andrew watched as Lace slipped seamlessly into the darkness. She had good instincts. It had not taken her long to realize the danger she had put herself in. With the slightest hiss of her hem against the grass, she was gone. If he tried to find her and follow her now, he'd give himself away, and he wasn't ready to do that just yet. No, he couldn't let her think she had the upper hand.

She must not have realized that in her haste, she had dropped her handkerchief. He went forward, all reason for stealth gone now, and bent to retrieve the item. The dainty square was of fine Irish linen with a tatted lace edging of the same sort that had been on her gown tonight and the domino the night before.

The little piece of linen was damp. From the dew, or from tears? Why the thought of her tears upset him, he couldn't say. Women cried. It was a natural state of affairs. Nevertheless, he lifted the article to his face and inhaled the faint floral scent. Not quite the same as she'd worn tonight, but similar.

A corner thickened with embroidery threads drew his attention. The letters *C O* in an elaborate script were formed from pale-blue silk thread. *CO?* So, was Lace's real name something as mundane at Caroline? Charlotte? Catherine?

Whatever her name was, she would be his. Once, for a week or a month, or until the novelty wore off—the length of time did not matter. The simple fact was that he would know her in the biblical sense. And she would know him. She might think she was in control of the situation. She might even think she had a choice. But she had no idea who she was dealing with.

Bella closed the door with a soft click and turned the lock. She leaned her forehead against the panel and sighed, vowing she'd take enough money to hire a carriage next time. She hadn't been able to shake the feeling of being watched, and it had followed her all the way home.

She dropped her reticule and shawl on the foyer table before tiptoeing to the sitting room sideboard and pouring herself just the smallest amount of brandy.

"I thought that was you," Gina said behind her.

She gasped in surprise and turned to see her sister rising from a chair in the corner of the room. "*Must* you wait up every night?" she sighed.

"What do you expect, Bella? I've already lost one sister, and my mother might as well be gone. You refuse to tell me what you are doing, where you are going or when you'll return. You refuse my help. And then you wonder that I am waiting up? Please, Bella. Give me credit for common sense. Should something happen to you, I will be responsible for Mama and Lilly. I have a right to know what you are doing."

Poor Gina. She was right. At least Mama and Lilly had the luxury of not knowing that she was sneaking out at night. She drank her brandy and sat on the brocade settee, patting the seat next to her. "You have always been sensible, Gina. I…I just thought it would be easier for you if you did not know the particulars."

"Nothing about this has been easy." She sniffed and swiped at her eyes with the back of her hand. "I want to help. I want to be doing something. But, day after day, we just sit here with the curtains drawn, hushing our conversations so Mama can rest. Even Lilly is feeling the strain. We sigh and cry, and no one actually *does* anything. Except for you. Let me help, Bella. Please."

She sighed. Should she tell her sister what she was doing and risk her scorn? Or lie to her and do even more damage to her conscience?

If she could find some way for Gina to help—some way that would not put her at risk….

"Tell me, Bella. What is it you do every night when you go out? You say you are looking for Cora's murderer, and yet you do not say how. Do you know him?"

"No," she confessed. "I only know that he has dark hair and eyes."

Gina gave her a disbelieving laugh. "Dark? Oh, that must make the search easy, indeed. I am certain you will find him anyday now."

"There's more," Bella admitted, staring down at the floor, unwilling to meet Gina's eyes. "Cora said he was taller than Papa, and that he…he licked his lips after he kissed her as if she were some tasty treat. And that he was a gentleman. A member of the ton. You know our Cora would never have dallied with someone beneath her."

"Cora kissed him?" Gina's green eyes widened, but she collected herself quickly. "A dark man above six feet tall? Well, that is a bit more to work with. But how would you ever discover if a man licks his lips…*Bella!* You are not kissing every dark man you meet?"

She took a deep breath and turned away. "What other choice do I have?"

"Oh! Then this is why you are so insistent that you haven't a future in the ton? That your reputation is sullied? You poor thing! No wonder you are drinking." Her sister jumped to her feet and began pacing. "We must think of another way. Even narrowing the possibilities to tall dark men, there must be more. Think, Bella. What else did Cora say?"

She shook her head. "That he tasted bitter, then nothing more before…"

Gina said, "I have wrestled the thought this way and that for the past week. Cora was beaten. Mutilated. What sort of man kills a woman he has vowed he loved? Further, what sort of man betrays that trust in such a foul, cruel manner? What sort of *monster?*"

"A man who is tall, dark, charming and cunning. One who cajoled and cozened our sister into trusting him. A man who is a part of society and yet keeps his true nature secret. A rake and a rogue of the very worst kind."

"Barely human," Gina agreed.

Bella nodded and went back to the sideboard. "You have not told Mama and Lilly the details of Cora's murder, have you?"

Gina joined her and poured a very small dram of brandy for herself. "Never. That would surely be the end of Mama's sanity."

They raised their glasses in unison and drank. Gina grimaced and her eyes watered, but she sighed deeply when the liquor settled. "There is one thing you have not considered in your search, Bella. The killer is all those things Cora said but, most important, though he hides his true character, it must reveal itself on occasion. His closest friends will be like-minded. Rakes, rogues and villains."

How had she overlooked that detail? She'd known enough to look in the ton, but she hadn't narrowed her search to the very dregs of it. "So, to find him, I should kiss only rakes, rogues and scoundrels?" she mused. "Yes. They become apparent fairly quickly, and they tend to flock together. So in order to find him, I shall have to go where rogues and scoundrels go. G-gambling dens and other unsavory places."

"No! That is too dangerous. You mustn't imperil yourself." Gina's widened eyes filled with tears.

Bella sighed. "In the past week, I have forfeited something of my soul. But I have my promise to Cora to keep. If I do anything less, I will not be able to sleep at night. No, I intend to do whatever I must and I would advise you to keep out of my way."

Gina opened her mouth as if she would argue, then closed it again and shook her head.

"Try to understand," Bella pleaded. "The only other choice I have is to let our sister's murderer go free."

"Oh, I understand," Gina said, determined lines settling around her narrowed eyes. "I feel the need for justice, too, and I know the getting of it can be dangerous. I am only trying to think how to help you."

"I will not take you with me."

"I did not expect that you would. But I can help ensure that Mama and Lilly will not find out. I can keep them occupied."

"How? We are in mourning and will be for another six weeks. Social events are forbidden. They cannot call on neighbors or attend teas. We are trapped in this house until Mama is better and we can go home."

"Lilly is becoming restless. She needs outings. I think short walks and a trip to Hatchard's bookstore for reading materials might be in order. She has been asking for another of Miss Austen's books. And a little shopping for mourning apparel would be appropriate. Yes, and a healthy glass of undiluted wine with supper will keep her soundly asleep at night. We needn't worry much about Mama, yet. She is barely coherent from the laudanum she is taking in the evening. She is bound to make an effort soon, and when she does, I shall be ready."

Amazed, Bella watched as Gina began pacing, tapping one finger against her right cheek in an attitude of thoughtfulness. "And we shall have to concoct some story about what keeps you out evenings, should they discover you gone. Companion to a dowager? Reading to a blind neighbor? Caring for an ill friend?"

"Gina, you are truly diabolical."

"I know I cannot stop you, but I do not mean to lose another sister, Bella. You are about to enter a dragon's den. And where you will be going, you will need all the help you can muster."

A little shiver shot through her at the fierce expression on her sister's face. Just how far would Gina go to help her?

Chapter Four

The soft click of his brother's library door closing behind him was somehow comforting to Andrew. Being in the house he'd grown up in made him feel a part of the family again.

His brother looked up from his desk, gave him a slight smile and gestured to an overstuffed chair by a tea table.

"Pour a cup of tea, Drew. I'll be with you in a moment."

Tea? He glanced at the clock in one corner of the room, the swing of the heavy brass pendulum measuring the seconds. Two o'clock. He glanced at the decanters on the sideboard, then sighed, poured himself a stout cup of tea, laced it with sugar and sat to wait quietly.

Lockwood scribbled a few lines, then pushed the paper aside, stood and stretched. "Good to see you, Drew," he said as he poured his own tea and sat across from him. "I do not run into you as much anymore."

"You'd have to leave your house to do that, Lockwood. I gather this means you are still wallowing in wedded bliss?"

Lockwood grinned. "Have you come to mock me? Or is there another reason?"

"Wanted to know if you set Wycliffe on my heels."

"Ah, Wycliffe." His brother lifted his teacup and regarded him with a speculative gleam in his eyes. "No, actually. *He* came to *me,* Drew, after he'd already made up his mind. He said he was going to ask you for some help and a bit of expertise in the less-savory side of society activities. Is it any wonder your name came to his mind?"

The logic was inescapable. "I suppose not."

"And Wycliffe said he needs discretion. Though your *behavior* is somewhat less than discreet, I have never known you to discuss your women or your affairs with others. I agreed that you were the ideal candidate. Do you have some objection to helping the Home Office?"

"I suppose not," he said again, disliking his own churlish attitude. There was, in fact, not much he did like about himself these days.

"Then what is the problem?"

"I do not like having others depend upon me."

"Drew..." Lockwood began, putting his teacup aside. "It has been a long time since the war. Do you not think it is time to talk about it? I am your brother. No matter what it is, you can trust me."

Not with this. Never with this. "Who said it has anything to do with the war?"

"You were changed when you came home."

"War is not an experience that leaves one untouched. If I recall, even you took a few years to put things in perspective."

"But you were in—"

"I do not need you to remind me where and how I served. And I did not come here to talk about my service to the crown," he interrupted. Blast! Why did Lockwood have to hound him on this? Did he think confession was good for the soul? Not in this case. *Never* in this case. Only Dash knew. And only because Dash had been there.

"So you just came to complain about doing something constructive?"

Andrew took his teacup to the sideboard and poured himself a glass of sherry. To hell with sobriety. "I came to ask if you set Wycliffe on me or if using me was his idea," he reminded Lockwood. "And I need information. Do you recall a scandal that took place years ago? Before we were born? Something back in the 1760s?"

"The Hellfire Club?" Lockwood's eyebrows rose. "The scandal that almost brought the government down?"

He nodded. "Were they Satanists?"

"They were reprobates of the worst sort, Drew. Scoundrels and wastrels to a man. They liked to think of themselves as dedicated Satanists, but they were more interested in sexual licentiousness and excess than any real worship. The pity of it was that they were men of influence, not ignorant superstitious bumpkins."

"And what do you know of witchcraft, Lockwood?"

"I know it's balderdash. Casting spells. Laying curses. Child's play."

"Some take it seriously."

"What have you gotten into, Drew?"

He took a bracing swallow of his sherry. "Don't know. Just that something nasty is going on right under our noses. Wycliffe suspects a cult of some sort and I am inclined to agree. But it's not my business. I'm just to keep my eyes and ears open and report what I learn to Wycliffe."

"Can you leave it at that?"

"Why not? You know how I dislike getting involved."

"Because you're here asking questions, not just keeping your eyes and ears open. The problem has engaged your interest, has it not?"

Andrew considered the question. Yes, he supposed it had. Between Wycliffe's assignment and Lady Lace, this was turning out to be a banner season. He shrugged. "Aye, 'tis mildly interesting. More for the oddity than anything else. But do not get your hopes up, brother. One sparrow does not make a summer."

"Ah, but I do hope that one day you will turn the corner and step back into your life."

Andrew tossed off the last of his sherry and stood, giving Lockwood a cynical smile. "I wouldn't take wagers on it."

"Now you've engaged *my* interest, Drew. This is quite intriguing. Satanists, witchcraft and some sort of problem that involves the Home Office? 'Tis enough to draw me out of retirement."

That was the last thing Andrew needed. If something should happen to Lockwood now that he had settled down and had an heir on the way… "Keep out of it, Lockwood. I can handle this without you."

"I know you can, Drew. I've never known you to shy away from doing what had to be done."

"Hate to dash your hopes, sir, but I am what I am."

"What you are is a good man, Drew."

He couldn't contain his snort of laughter as he closed the library door behind him.

* * *

Martha O'Rourke waved her hand listlessly in front of her face. "Take them wherever you want, Bella, as long as you keep your eye on them."

"Couldn't you come, too, Mama? We will wait while you dress. The fresh air will do you good," Bella said, without any real hope that her mother would agree.

"Fresh air? Is that what you think I need? As if *that* would change anything." She dropped her hand into her lap and gathered her dressing gown tighter at the neck. She glanced at Gina and Lilly, hovering behind Bella. "You should be in proper mourning. 'Tis disrespectful of Cora to have you prancing all over London as if nothing were wrong."

"No one is 'prancing,' Mama." Well, except for her, and she was wearing proper mourning. She tried again. "Lilly and Gina have barely been out at all."

"Nor should they be. Why, in my day, ladies did not leave the house for months. *Months,* Bella."

But her mother had not allowed *her* that luxury. Someone had to deal with the details, and with Mama unable to cope with even the smallest matters, that task had fallen to Bella. "I…I will take Gina and Lilly to a dressmaker for mourning clothes, Mama. Will three each be enough? A walking gown, tea gown and dinner gown?"

"Yes. Yes, three each. And you too, Bella. You look absurd in my cut-downs."

Bella glanced down at herself. Was it true? Had people been laughing behind her back? Mr. Hunter hadn't seemed put off by her appearance, and she would imagine he'd be a severe critic. "Yes, Mama. We shall be home before tea."

Martha collapsed against the chaise cushions again. "Mind you, do not let them out of your sight. Cora would be alive if only you'd paid attention."

Bella winced. Guilt had become her bosom companion without Mama's frequent reminders. She turned and followed her sisters from their mother's private parlor.

"…wish it had been Bella," she heard her mother tell Nancy, the maid. "Cora was always so sweet."

The quick stab in the pit of her stomach was back again. That was happening more and more frequently these days. Tears stung the backs of her eyes and a thick lump formed in her throat. She would not cry again. She would *not*. Oh, but in a deep, secret part of her, Bella wished it had been her, too. Anything would be better than this constant purgatory she was living in.

"She didn't mean it, Bella," Gina whispered as they left the town house, Lilly trailing as she tugged at the ribbons of her bonnet.

"Yes, she did. She'd rather it had been any of us but Cora. She was always Mama's favorite. That is why she thought she could do as she pleased. And now Mama can scarcely bear to be in the same room with me."

"She has always been harsher with you, Bella. I think it is because you are like Papa—smarter than she, and stronger, even though you are her daughter. And yet, what would she do without you? We'd still be moldering behind closed doors after Papa's death if you hadn't coaxed her from her bed and pushed her back into society—and that was seven years ago!"

"What would she do without me? Why she'd have you, Gina. I fear you and I have all the sense in the family, and that Lilly and Cora... well, they were gifted with charm and beauty."

Gina sniffed. "We are not lacking in charm or beauty. More than one lad has said so."

"And I shall hope you will have a chance to prove that. For myself... I am only charming when it suits me. A monumental shortcoming, but there it is."

"I have seen you charm birds from the trees, Bella."

"When it suits me," Bella reminded her. "I am brash and unpleasant the rest of the time."

Gina laughed, and Lilly caught up to them as they entered the promenade beside the bridle path along the Mall. She said yet another silent prayer that no one would recognize her from her nightly excursions into the ton. She hated taking the risk, and yet there was no other way to keep her sisters occupied during the day.

A little farther along, they crossed the path and emerged on the street at their dressmaker's shop. Madame Marie had made their presentation gowns, and now she'd make their mourning gowns.

* * *

Lockwood's voice still ringing in his ears, Andrew had run into Daschel at Angelo's, his fencing master's salon. According to their tutor, he and Dash were equally matched, so they'd been paired for practice. They'd foregone masks and gloves in favor of unimpaired vision and grip. Neither of them were inclined to give quarter, so the bouts were arduous, with frequent lunges and parries.

Other students had gathered to watch them, and Dash was playing to the crowd. Truth to tell, Andrew knew his friend was a better swordsman, but he was apt to let overconfidence cloud his judgment. It was his one weakness, and one that Andrew occasionally exploited.

Daschel scored the last hit of the bout and Andrew gave him a flourishing bow. With a grin and a clap on his shoulder, Dash suggested a ride through the park before they went their separate ways. It only took them a minute to hang up their swords and collect their horses.

"Are you joining us at Bedlam tonight, Drew?" Daschel asked as they turned their mounts onto the path.

"Depends," he hedged.

"On whether you find Lady Lace? Egads, man. If you really want her, we can arrange something."

"Make a business agreement?"

"Or something more straightforward."

"No. I am enjoying the chase. I cannot remember the last time I've had such a challenge."

"How long do you intend to play your little game? And what if, in the meanwhile, she chooses another?" Dash asked. "I do not think you have long to claim her. In fact, I just might try my hand at capturing the lady."

A sick feeling of jealousy settled in Andrew's stomach, and he glanced sideways to see if his friend was jesting. There was a flicker of something he couldn't identify in Dash's dark eyes. Mirth? Or was it something more daring? "Are you suggesting a competition, Dash?"

"One hundred guineas to whoever beds her first."

"Pistols at dawn first," Andrew murmured.

Dash guffawed. "That bad, eh? Well, I suppose I must wait until you've finished with her, then."

Choosing to ignore Dash's comment, Andrew broached the subject that had been on his mind since his conversation with Lockwood. "D'you ever think of…Spain?"

Dash was silent so long that Andrew wondered if he'd heard the question. "I've done my damnedest to forget," he said after a moment. "But, yes. I think of it from time to time. Why?"

"The subject came up with Lockwood earlier."

"Is he still after you to tell him what our unit did? What we saw?"

"I think he knows. Lockwood knows everything, but he believes confession is good for the soul. What do you believe, Dash?"

"Confession? Surely—if you want to hang. But there's no need for that."

Andrew doubted his friend's conclusion that there was no need for him to hang. The secret was like acid eating through what was left of his soul. His conscience was already calloused, and he feared he didn't know right from wrong anymore. "I was in command. I should have—"

"You can't spend your life second-guessing your decisions, Drew. For Christ's sake! There were five of us under your comment. None of us knew what to do. You, at least, contained the situation and kept it from the reports."

Andrew dismounted and started leading his horse. And remembering. Of the six of them assigned to covert duty, only he and Dash were left. Three had been killed in Spain, and Richard Farron had been killed in a duel within a week of his return to England. Richard had been hell-bound for destruction. And there were still days when Andrew wondered why he and Dash hadn't met a similar fate.

"I will never tell. You have my word upon that, Drew." Dash dismounted and joined Andrew.

"And I appreciate your loyalty, but I've increasingly begun to wonder if Lockwood isn't right. The worst that could happen is that I'd hang. And some days that prospect does not trouble me at all. 'Tis probably what I deserve. It is only the thought of what the scandal would do to my family that has kept me silent this long. God knows the world does not have much to offer anymore."

"Stay a little longer." Dash grinned. "I swear, we shall find something to perk you up. I know of things I think I could… interest you in, but I've feared you might balk."

Andrew laughed and shook his head. He knew Dash through and through. He was every bit as much a rake as Andrew, but he had a slightly keener edge—hence the excursion to Bedlam. Was the invitation to Bedlam a test of his stomach for such things?

Dash glanced ahead and narrowed his eyes. "Say, there! Is that not Charlie and Jamie coming our way?"

Drew would not be surprised to find his brothers on Rotten Row on a fine afternoon. He followed the direction of Dash's pointing finger and grinned. James caught sight of them first and rode for them at breakneck speed. He and Charles reined in, stopping barely a foot from Andrew's right boot.

"Well met!" Charlie laughed as they dismounted. "We were hoping to find you, Drew. Jamie and I are looking for trouble tonight. What do you recommend?"

Andrew grinned at Dash. "There's to be an expedition to Bedlam tonight. Fancy a trip into madness?"

Jamie looked interested but Charlie frowned. "What? Do they lock you up with the inmates so you can play at being mad?"

"I rather think they make sport of them, Charlie," Jamie said. "And who's to say we're not as mad as them?"

"Make sport of the unfortunates? But what is sporting about that?"

Dash grinned. "Observation of human nature can be enlightening, Charlie. Indeed, we can learn much from them. They have so few… inhibitions. I warrant their actions sometimes make more sense than ours."

Charlie gave them an uncertain grin, and Andrew knew his wayward brothers would be going to Bedlam tonight. He supposed he'd have to go along to keep an eye on them, though it was not their first venture into the seamy side of London.

"Look smart, fellows! Here come those new bits o' muslin we saw earlier," Jamie said. "Come to town for the season, no doubt."

"Wish we could get an introduction," Charlie agreed as his gaze fixed on a point behind Andrew. "I'd be pleased to know any of them, but especially the one with dark hair and fine eyes. The taller one."

Andrew turned to see three women coming along the walking path. He recognized one immediately—Lady Lace, dressed in her signature black. How interesting to see her by daylight. They were all carrying bandboxes and talking quietly.

Lace smiled at something the taller girl said and looked up. Her eyes met his, and she stiffened and quickened her pace as she recognized him. Why, she intended to give him the cut! How amusing.

He stepped out of his group, nearly in their path, and removed his hat, impossible to ignore now. "Madame," he said with a sharp bow.

A flash of panic lit those lovely hazel eyes, a bit more greenish in the light of day. Her full lips parted and he could see she was struggling for composure as her cheeks tinted a delicate rose. What was wrong with her? He'd seen none of this girlishness before.

He thought for a moment that she would step around him and ignore him altogether, but her quick sideways glance at her companions told him that she was more worried about what they would think than about giving him the cut direct. Interesting.

"M-Mr. Hunter," she acknowledged reluctantly.

He could feel his brothers at his back and knew they would never let the ladies escape without an introduction. "Allow me to introduce my companions." He stood aside to indicate each of them in turn, now with their hats in their hands. "My brothers, James and Charles Hunter, and my friend, Bryon Daschel, Lord Humphries."

The ladies inclined their heads with a slight nod at each introduction and murmured polite responses. Andrew studied them. The taller dark one, as Charles had called her, was lovely and lush looking and bore a faint family resemblance to Lace. His experienced eye detected a sensual nature to that one. The other, slightly younger by the look of her, was fair with sparkling blue eyes. She was, as yet, unformed in her nature and he thought she could go either way—soft and compliant or demanding and imperious.

"A fine day for a walk, is it not?" Dash commented, filling the awkward silence that should have been filled with Lace's introductions of her companions.

"Yes, a lovely day," she conceded.

"Have you been shopping?" Jamie asked with a glance at their bandboxes.

The younger one answered with a flirtatious smile. "Bella thought we could use the outing. I vow, I feel better already."

Bella? Ah, so Lady Lace was actually "Bella." Was that a pet name, shortened from a longer name, or her actual given name? Her dark brows drew together as she shot the younger girl a quelling look.

Jamie glanced around at their surroundings. "Fresh air is good for the constitution, I am told."

"Do you walk here often?" Charlie asked the taller one.

She shot a sideways glance at "Bella." "Not as often as we wish, sir. But we make do."

Jamie fiddled with the rim of his hat. "If the exercise is too demanding for you, I'd be happy to make a loan of my cabriolet."

Andrew frowned. That was going a little too far for a covey of women whose names they still didn't know. And that fact was still the most disconcerting of all. He glanced pointedly at "Bella."

"We have been gone overlong, Mr. Hunter. I am certain you will excuse us. We really must be getting back."

"May we escort you?" Though he knew she'd refuse, just as she'd refused to introduce her companions, he asked just to annoy her. She really was lovely when she had her ire up. Ah, and there it was, the deepening flush tinting her cheeks with indignation.

"No!" She paused and took a deep breath. "I mean, thank you, but no. It is not far and we would not want to interrupt your ride."

He'd almost forgotten the horses. "Perhaps we shall meet again," he said. "Soon."

Her eyes widened and she glanced at her companions once more, then pushed them ahead of her with a hand on the small of the younger girl's back.

They watched the ladies' departure, appreciating the sway of their skirts as they hustled away.

Dash was the first to speak, a smile twitching at the corners of his mouth as he glanced skyward. "I say! Is it snowing? I feel a decided chill."

"Gads!" Charlie glanced at their departing backs and then at Drew. "She appears not to like you much. 'Tis one thing to cut you, and another to cut the rest of us."

Jamie chuckled. "There you have it—the very reason we should learn manners, Charlie. We never want a beautiful woman finding us unworthy of a common introduction. Or judging our companions by our own bad behavior."

Despite their words, Andrew's companions burst out laughing at his discomfort. *Bella* would pay for this. Oh, so sweetly.

Dash glanced between Bella's stiff back and Andrew's own bemusement. "What did you do to her, Drew?"

"Nothing," he said. "Yet."

Chapter Five

Bella tightened the laces at the top of her chemise and tucked the strings into her bodice. "Keeping Mama and Lilly occupied is more important than you can know, Gina. But if there is ever anything I cannot handle alone, I swear I shall enlist you. I *swear* it."

Gina frowned, suspicion narrowing her eyes. "See that you do, or I shall take matters into my own hands."

"Just what do you think I am keeping from you?" She smoothed the fabric of her gown over her hips.

"Many things, Bella. For instance, who was that man today? The one you addressed as Mr. Hunter, who attempted the introductions? Surely you have not forgotten such a handsome man?"

How much could she tell her sister without inciting her horror? "How could I introduce you without giving myself away to Lilly? And no one knows me by my name."

"Really?" Gina tilted her head to one side. "What do they call you, then?"

"Lady Lace." She tried not to notice Gina's giggling as she stuffed a handkerchief in her reticule. "And I am not altogether certain Mr. Hunter is the sort of man one ought to introduce to one's sisters."

"I gathered as much," Gina said. "But I think I would not care. He is far too handsome. And the others, as well."

The slightly stubborn jut to Gina's chin warned her that her sister would need better answers. Which of the Hunter brothers did she have her eye on? Or was it Lord Humphries? She supposed it did not matter—any of them could break her heart.

"Why are you hiding your name, Bella? I thought you did not give a whit for your reputation now that Cora is dead."

"I do not care in the least, but I thought it better if no one knew where to find me. The last thing I want is for Mama to get word of what I'm doing. How ghastly it would be to have some man turn up on our doorstep asking for an audience."

Gina sank onto the bed in feigned distress. "Oh! That would be dreadful, indeed. Awful even under the best circumstances. Mama is enough to frighten all but the most ardent suitors away."

She smiled at Gina's teasing. "And anyway, Gina, when we return to Belfast and our mourning ends, there is still a chance that you and Lilly will find husbands among the gentry."

"You, too, Bella."

"That is quite impossible. My face is now known in London. How could I tell my future husband that he could never take me beyond Belfast lest I be recognized as a...a..." She shrugged and gave a self-deprecating laugh as she pinched her cheeks to bring her color up. "I am not blameless. I have now kissed more men than any collective dozen of my friends."

"As to that, Bella, was Mr. Hunter—the one who spoke to you—one of the men you kissed?"

Heat crept into her cheeks and she busied herself with fastening a jet necklace around her throat. "Really, Gina! I do not see what difference that would make."

"Well, if you are not keeping track, someone should."

"Yes, then. Which is all the more reason I wish to keep you and Lilly away."

"Was he that dreadful?"

No! Lord, no. In point of fact, he'd been the best of the lot. "I fear that he would think you and Lilly are likewise...loose. He could have reason enough to believe that, since we were together. Would you really want to defend yourself against an ardent swain?"

"Yes, if he looked like Lord Humphries or any of the Hunter brothers. I am assuming, of course, that you have cleared them of any suspicion of having killed our Cora."

"I, ah, of that group, I have only kissed Mr. Andrew Hunter."

"And you have acquitted him?"

"Not entirely."

Gina tilted her head to one side. "Not entirely? But how is that possible?"

"I…it was rather sudden and he turned away immediately afterward, so I fear I must do it again before I can eliminate him."

The corners of Gina's mouth twitched. "Ah. I see. Well, yes. I suppose you must. And then move on to the other Hunter brothers? And Lord Humphries?"

"Eventually," she admitted. "If I do not find the murderer first."

"But tonight?"

She swept up her cloak and turned toward the door. "Tonight I am not likely to see them. Remember, I am going where scoundrels and rakes go."

Andrew leaned over Charlie's shoulder. "Seen enough?"

"We've only just begun. Do you suppose it is all like this?"

"I haven't a single notion, Charlie. This is my first visit, as well." When they had arrived at Bethlehem Hospital and paid the keeper for entry, Andrew hadn't known what to expect, though he gathered he would not find it entertaining. Thus far he'd been right.

They'd been led past cells where unfortunates were either cowering in corners or reciting nonsensical words in sing-song voices. Here a man played in his own filth, and there a woman exposed her breasts and cackled. Yet another man screamed and shouted curses, pounding the door separating patients from visitors. And everywhere the odor of unwashed bodies and rancid food assailed them.

The keeper, their guide, told stories of how this one had been abandoned by a lover, or that one had lost his entire family in a fire and had fallen into deep melancholy. But how, Andrew wondered again, could such misery be entertaining? Was it all just a matter of taste?

As much as he wanted to leave, he also wanted to find out what purpose Dash had for this outing, because it was not like his friend to arrange something like this without a reason.

Charlie shrugged and echoed Andrew's own thoughts. "I cannot see the purpose of this, Drew. It tickles none of my senses. I am not amused, entertained, titillated or curious. Surely there's more?"

"Observation of human nature, I believe Dash said," Andrew whispered.

"An' now, gents, 'ere we are at the commons, or the gallery as some calls it," the keeper announced. "These 'uns is harmless. You can 'ave a bit o' fun with them if you wants. Cost you extra, though."

Another group of visitors had arrived before them and stood in a far corner, their laughter overriding the sound of shouts and curses. Andrew turned in the direction of their pointing fingers to find a group of men scrambling over what looked to be a hunk of nearly raw meat. The scene reminded him of a pack of dogs behind a butcher shop. This, he assumed, was what the keeper had meant by "a bit o' fun."

Dash, who had gone ahead with Henley, Jamie and Throckmorton, glanced over his shoulder to look at Andrew. Waiting for a reaction, no doubt. But Andrew had none to give him. Whatever response Dash had been looking for, he could muster neither outrage nor amusement. He'd seen enough in the war to make him numb to human suffering and to realize that there was no limit to man's inhumanity. He turned back to the activities in the common room, trying to keep track of the shifting tableaus as they were incited by the "visitors."

Money changed hands, and then one of the inmates approached a woman dressed in a mobcap and a low-cut dress. He whispered in her ear and she glanced at the group that had sent him. A manic smile exposed gaps where teeth should have been, and she began to hitch her skirts up around her hips. Lord! Were the visitors such immature idiots themselves that they derived pleasure from seeing an unfortunate expose herself?

But it did not stop at that. The payment had been for something else entirely. There, for all to see, the male inmate dropped his trousers and the pair of them began to copulate to the enthusiastic encouragement of the onlookers. On some base level, Andrew realized that watching such activities was arousing for a good many people—that it awakened a hunger, at the very least. He'd known courtesans and the owners of private clubs to arrange such performances. But here and now, at the expense of those who either did not comprehend their actions or appreciate that they were being made sport of, it seemed intrinsically wrong.

"Amazing, is it not, what one will do for money?" Dash asked. "I daresay we could make this lot do damn near anything we chose."

Andrew blinked and turned to his friend. "For a crust of bread or a cut of meat?"

"Aye. Does it remind you of the war, Drew?"

This echo of his own thoughts caused the hair on the back of Andrew's neck to prickle. Was this why Dash had brought him here? "The madness? Or the depravity?"

"Both. And the power. Bedlam is as close to Valle del Fuego as I've found since our return."

That godforsaken village! "Why would you want to be reminded, Dash? God knows I've spent years trying to forget."

"Aye, but there was something there—something lacking in London. Some tiny primal spark. You must feel it. Something so... so fundamental that it has no name."

There was more Dash was trying to tell him, something he would not put into words and was pleading with Andrew to understand. "Uncivilized," he admitted. "Not altogether comfortable."

"Precisely!" Dash's expression was somber. "It pulls at one, does it not?"

Andrew glanced again at the copulating couple. Yes, it pulled at him, that urge to shed everything civilized. This was the part of Bedlam that appealed to Dash—primeval man, stripped of morality, propriety and law.

A chill crept down his spine, and his throat clogged with the heavy atmosphere. He wanted to *feel* again. Anything. To have some part of him awakened to ordinary senses. What would that take? The pull grew stronger, almost impossible to resist. He wanted it, craved it, and yet the last shred of decency he possessed resisted. He spun back down the passageway. "I need a drink."

Belmonde's! Ah, thank God for ordinary debauchery. Andrew's tension eased as he downed his second brandy. Tonight he'd come dangerously close to the abyss. He'd flirted with it for so long that he was mildly surprised he'd even recognized the line. And some fatalistic part of him knew it was coming—the day he could no longer resist the pull. The day he would cross that line.

He was on his way back to the salon from changing coins for counters when he passed the foyer. Ah, the night was full of surprises. There stood Bella, even lovelier than usual, in earnest conversation with the doorman. And he knew why. The little chit did not have entrée.

He went forward. "Ah, here you are, my dear. Don't dawdle." He removed her cloak and handed it to a waiting footman, then turned to the doorman. "Biddle, see to it that she is admitted without delay in the future, would you?"

"Why, yes, sir. I'd have done so ere now, but she did not mention your name."

He grinned down at the speechless woman as he took her arm. "Ah, she is shy, Biddle. Very shy. But you will use my name in the future, will you not, my dear?"

Her eyes widened and she nodded.

He slipped Biddle a few counters and winked as he led her away. "How nice to see you again, Bella. Dare I hope you were looking for me?"

"You…you may hope anything you wish, sir. But I had no idea you'd be here. I thought you and your ilk would be at some aristocratic soiree."

His ilk? He laughed. If she only knew what "his ilk" had been up to tonight! "You're more likely to see me here or at some other tasteless entertainment than at a soiree. But tell me, what is *your* business here?"

"I was looking for…for…"

"Yes. The right man, I believe you said the other night." He shook his head and gave her a rakish grin. "I believe you've gone astray, Bella. The only men here are the *wrong* men."

"Yourself included?"

"Myself at the top of the list."

"I see." She looked down pensively and a stray curl tumbled over her shoulder. "Well, I suppose I should at least thank you for not exposing me this afternoon."

His conscience tweaked him when he recalled how very close he'd come to doing just that. He still wasn't certain why he hadn't. "My companions were much amused by your snub. I think you owe me something for that. I can tell you that I was made to bear some rather cutting rebukes, which I'd have cheerfully done had I but known the reason."

She made no reply as he captured a glass of wine from a passing footman's tray. He presented it to her with a slight bow. "I believe you are still pressing forward with your ambition to become a lush?"

She looked confused for a moment and then laughed. "Not quite so diligently as last night, but yes. I have become a great believer in bottled courage."

What an odd phrase. Did she actually need to fortify herself to come out, or to kiss men? A sudden suspicion tweaked his pride. "Are you meeting someone here, Bella? Or are you on your own?"

"A-alone."

Just the word he had been hoping to hear. "Not any longer, my dear."

"A-about my name, sir."

"If you would like proper address, madam, you will have to give me your entire name."

"I haven't had to give it until now, sir."

"Then how *would* you like me to address you? And should the occasion for an introduction arise? Then what, madam?"

She heaved a deep sigh and glanced around. "Could we not just ignore it? Or 'madam' will do. In any event, it will not matter much longer."

Disappointment sharpened his response. "Oh? Then shall I assume you are near to making your choice?"

"There is not much choice about it, Mr. Hunter. I have yet to find…"

"Yes, the right man. So I gathered. And I also gather that I fall short of your requirements?"

"I…suppose that would be for the best," she said, though her tone was uncertain.

He found encouragement in her hesitation. "Then what is your purpose here tonight? You've said you are not meeting someone, so…?"

"I thought I might see a familiar face."

"You have, madam. Mine."

"Oh, dear."

Her chagrin was almost comical and he grinned at her confusion. "Not quite the response I was hoping for, but at least you are honest."

"Actually, I thought this would be an establishment frequented by, well, by men who did not often attend ton events."

"Looking for fresh hunting grounds, my dear Bella?"

"No. Yes." She shook her head and glanced up at him. The look in those captivating hazel eyes warned him that she was about to lie. He waited, quite breathlessly, for what she was about to say. "I wanted to learn how to gamble."

Ah, diversion. Excellent ploy. So much more inventive than a bald lie. Too bad she didn't know who she was playing with. "Allow me. I would recommend beginning with *rouge et noir* or *vingte et un*. The rules are simpler than the other popular games, and the play is easier to follow."

He led her toward a *rouge et noir* table and explained the rudiments of the game. When she nodded, he handed her a counter. "Try it, madam. There's nothing like risk to make one feel the excitement, is there?"

She held his counter up and smiled. "*I* have nothing at risk. Does that make it more exciting for *you?*"

He laughed. Lord, but she was breathtaking when she smiled. He wished she would do more of that. "I am feeling the excitement even now, Bella." And he was.

She turned back to the table and gave him her glass, but not before he noted the flush that swept up her cheeks. He watched her as she studied the play. After three rounds she placed the counter on red and stood back.

Red won the count, and she grabbed his sleeve in her delight. "Now what do I do?"

"Wager again or collect your winnings and leave the table."

"What do you think I should do?"

"Nothing ventured, nothing gained, Bella." He wondered if caution or risk would win her imagination.

She left the counters on the spot. And again, red won. She clapped her hands and turned to him. "Again?"

"And again, and again, if you wish."

The tip of her tongue made a brief appearance to moisten her lips as she thought this over. Finally she nodded to the croupier to let her wager stand. Andrew leaned close to her ear and asked, "How does it feel, Bella, to have your fortune riding on the turn of a card?"

"*Your* fortune," she reminded him in a whisper. "And it makes me tingle all over."

He groaned at the mere thought. God, what he'd like to do to her to make her tingle! She turned to him at the sound and her eyes widened. "Oh! I should have paid you back, shouldn't I?"

"*Noir!*" the croupier called.

He shrugged. "Too late. All gone. And now how do you feel?"

She watched the croupier scoop her pile of counters away. "Determined to win it back."

"I fear I've done you no favor, Bella. You have all the makings of an incorrigible gambler. Soon you will be impoverished, and 'twill be all my fault."

"Truly?"

"Aye, but I could show you other ways to take a risk. Ways to find that same thrill and more."

"You could?"

Ah! How telling. If she were truly a courtesan, she would not have missed that innuendo. Perhaps she was an adventuress, or an ingenue seeking a protector. And again his curiosity was piqued. Who was she, really? And what was her game? She intrigued him more than any woman he'd ever known. He took her hand and led her toward the dim end of the huge salon and one of the many curtained alcoves reserved for private play.

Whirling her into one of the empty niches, he snapped the draperies closed. Darkness surrounded them, intimate and dangerous. He found her narrow waist and pulled her against his chest. Instinct led him to her mouth, and the merest brush of his lips stifled her little gasp of surprise. Oh, but he would not claim his kiss so soon. He paused to nibble at her full lower lip and slide his hand down the length of her spine, pressing her closer. Her lips parted in anticipation, and he answered with a soft tantalizing touch, still not a proper kiss. Her arms circled his neck and she tried to deepen the contact. Yes, just a few more moments and she would be his for the taking.

He kissed the line of her jaw up to her earlobe and paused there, running his tongue along the curve of her ear until she shivered.

"What price, sweet Bella?" he whispered in that delicate opening, not wanting to cheat her of her due, nor willing to wait much longer. "Name your terms."

She moaned and he was lost. Whatever she wanted, she'd have it. He was no schoolboy, but she made him feel like one, caught up in the wonder of a first kiss. All he could think of was the way she felt against him, the way she tasted, the sweetness of her response and the heart-wrenching sound of her yearning whimper.

He returned to her mouth and hovered there. She would have to come up on her toes to make the final contact. The choice would be hers. Ah, but he knew his women, and Bella lifted toward him. The last rational fragment of his brain worked feverishly. Could he take her here, on the banquette behind this velvet curtain? Should he whisk her home to his bed? Or was there somewhere she'd rather go? To her rooms, perhaps?

The curtain snapped back and the spell was broken.

Chapter Six

"Damn!" Bella heard someone say.

She blinked and came back to herself with a start. Andrew Hunter steadied her with an arm around her waist as she found his brothers, Lord Humphries, Mr. McPherson and a blondish man she did not know staring at them with rapt interest.

Mr. McPherson, who had uttered the curse, frowned, looking for all the world like a scorned lover. "I say! What the deuce do you think you're doing, Hunter?"

Mr. Hunter sighed and released his hold on her. "I would think that is obvious, McPherson. A better question might be what the deuce you are doing *here,*" he challenged.

"Come now, good fellows. Shall we all be friends again?" Lord Humphries—Dash, she thought they called him—made a conciliatory gesture. "'Tisn't as if she is anyone's wife."

Mr. Hunter glanced at her and gave her a reassuring smile. "Nor anyone's mistress," he allowed. "And therefore, open to…proposals of any sort."

"Whatever he proposed, I will double it," Mr. McPherson said. He fastened her with a look so possessive that she wondered if he was in his right mind.

And then she realized they were bidding on her like some sort of horse at auction. They thought she was for sale. Well, why not? Her behavior had favored such speculation. She felt the heat rising in her cheeks.

"Mr. McPherson, you do not have enough to buy me, nor do you, Mr. Hunter. I'd have told you so if any of you had asked. Kindly refrain from addressing me in the future."

And with that, she lifted her chin and swept past the men with what she prayed was an air of aristocratic self-possession.

And found herself confronted with the stark reality of her position. Alone. In a gambling hall. With two men determined to have her. Mr. McPherson was brutish in pursuing his goal, but Mr. Hunter was even more dangerous in his own way. *He* had nearly seduced her with something less than a kiss.

But, worst of all, she still didn't know the truth. Mr. Hunter's near kiss had been utterly confusing. He had played with her, brushing his lips across hers, nibbling, kissing a path to her ear, where his breath had been hot and moist, then returned to her mouth, this time hovering, waiting, savoring his victory over her senses. At some point he had moistened his lips, but when? And then they'd been interrupted, and they hadn't had time to deepen the kiss.

If Andrew Hunter had been Cora's beau, wouldn't she have mentioned more than that particular trait? His seduction was transcending enough to have enthralled Cora, but of all the things she might have been able to say about him, would she have thought about him moistening his lips or tasting bitter? What of his bottomless, enigmatic eyes? What of his self-mocking smile or his wit?

She shuddered and came back to herself. Such silly musing! The moment had meant nothing to Andrew Hunter and even less to her, and she had more important things to worry about. She would simply get a straightforward kiss from him next time they were together. She scanned the people in the crowd, standing at tables, sitting in front of croupiers, talking in groups, and realized she could not bear the thought of kissing any of them tonight. Or ever. Her stomach twisted and she stumbled, nearly doubling over with the pain. *Avenge me, Bella.*

Mr. Hunter was at her elbow, steadying her and turning her toward the foyer. "Do you need assistance, madam?"

"No!" She jerked her elbow away from him. "I believe you've done enough, sir. Go back to your friends."

He gave her that infuriating grin when he should have been mum-

bling an apology. "If I cannot escort you, allow me to have Biddle
hail you a coach."

With a snap of his fingers, her cloak appeared and he draped it
around her shoulders. At his nod, Biddle hurried ahead of them and
stepped into the street with a raised hand to summon a coach. And
before she could protest, he was handing her up and asking her address. She opened her mouth to reply when she realized what he'd
done.

"Tell the driver to turn right on Whitehall and I shall call to him
where to stop."

Again came that infuriating grin. "'Twas worth a try, Bella."

She was saved the trouble of a reply when the coach lurched into
motion.

Edwards cleared his throat for the third time, and Andrew realized the valet was not going away. He sat up and pushed his fingers
through his snarled hair—testament to a restless night. "What is it,
Edwards?"

"A note, sir. 'Tis urgent."

He pushed the bed curtains back and winced at the midmorning
sunlight, then swung his legs over the side of his bed and took the
letter from Edwards. He recognized the handwriting and the seal.
Bryon Daschel, Lord Humphries. What could have gotten him up so
damn early? He broke the seal and read the short letter.

Whatever cobwebs remained from his sleep were wiped clean.
He stood and went to the basin to splash water on his face. "Tell His
Lordship I will be down when I've dressed, Edwards. Have Cook
make coffee."

"Coffee, sir?"

"Yes, coffee." For once, it was too early to start drinking. And too
damned important.

Edwards bowed and closed the door behind him with a mercifully
soft click.

Andrew dried his face on the soft cotton towel and regarded his
reflection with disgust. No time to shave. He ran a comb through
his hair and stepped into the trousers that Edwards had laid out for

him the night before. He was dressed in record time and hurried to the library.

"Tell me you're jesting, Dash." He crossed the room to the coffeepot that Edwards had just delivered and poured them both a cup. Disdaining cream or sugar, he took his cup to his desk and sat, looking for a sheet of paper and a pen.

Dash brought his cup to sit across from Andrew. "Not jesting, Drew. And I believe I've already notified all our mutual friends," he said in a quiet voice.

Andrew stilled and sat back in his chair. "What happened?"

"After you left us last night, Jamie and Charlie decided to go to Thackery's and see what ladybirds might be available. McPherson and I went looking for friends down by the docks. You know McPherson's fondness for opium dens."

"I thought he'd given that up."

"Aye, well, not entirely, it seems. Or at least not last night. He wanted to go to one of his old cribs and have a pipe. I watched over him, let him sleep some of it off, then took him home. I managed to get him to his room, then stopped on my way out to help myself to a brandy in his parlor. And then… then, when I was at the door, I heard the shot."

"But how do you know it was suicide? It could have been someone breaking in. Could have been an accident."

Dash gave a sad smile and looked down into his coffee. "He left a note, Drew. And his pistol was by his side."

Andrew's mind refused to grasp the notion. Dead? Conrad McPherson? They'd been friends since Eton. They'd played on the same cricket team. They'd joined the Light Dragoons together, though they hadn't been assigned the same unit. They'd been in and out of difficult situations and covered each other's indiscretions. And, until Lady Lace came on the scene, they'd scarce passed a cross word.

"Why?" he said, more to himself than to Dash.

"Some nonsense about being weary of this life, and of not being able to have the things he most desires."

"That's twaddle. None of us get everything we want. McPherson knew that."

Dash reached into the inside pocket of his jacket and brought out a sealed page. He tossed it across the desk to Drew. "You will see her before I will," he said.

Addressed in McPherson's handwriting was a letter to "She Who Has Bewitched My Heart." He raised an eyebrow at that. "And you think this is meant for...?"

"Lady Lace," Dash confirmed with a nod. "He was obsessed with her. Said he could think of nothing but her day and night. That he looked for her every time he left his house. From the time she kissed him, he was besotted."

"I...didn't know it was that bad."

"I thought not. And I doubt it would have mattered. You have your own plan for the lady."

"Had I known..."

"What? You'd have given her up to McPherson?"

A red haze clouded Andrew's vision for a moment. Given her up? No, to his shame, he wouldn't have given her up no matter what the cost, and that realization was jarring. When had she become more than a passing interest? How had she captivated his interest so thoroughly? How had she become *his* obsession?

"What are you saying, Dash?"

"Read the letter. I have, and I will not apologize."

Andrew looked down at the paper in his hand. "She Who Has Bewitched My Heart" was scrawled in a barely decipherable script. McPherson must have been barely conscious. He had no wish to violate his friend's privacy, and yet he had to know if there was something he should have seen. Something he could have done to avert this awful consequence. He lifted the broken seal and scanned the few brief lines wherein McPherson confessed his undying love, begged forgiveness for his thuggish behavior and swore that he would love her better in the next world than he had in this one.

He looked up and met Dash's dark study. "You think..."

"He could not have her, so he did not want to live."

"Because of her?"

Dash leaned forward in his chair. "Perhaps it was not entirely her fault, but she surely had a hand in it."

"What did the watch report to them?"

Dash glanced down at the floor and shook his head. "I...I lied to them. They did not see the note. I told them Conrad was falling down drunk, and the pistol must have discharged by accident when he was putting it away. The damned note cannot make a difference now. What she did is not punishable by law."

Andrew's head began to pound. "This whole…event is inconceivable. I cannot fathom McPherson falling so hard for her with so little encouragement." The picture of her pushing McPherson away in the sitting room at Marlborough House flashed across his mind. "Indeed, she never encouraged him that I could see."

"Oh, for God's sake, Drew. She *kissed* him. How many women do you know who simply walk up to a man and kiss him?"

And there was no answer to that. Little though it was, it had been enough to besot Conrad McPherson. "I will deliver this letter, Dash. Count on it."

Bella went back to Belmonde's with a little prayer that she would not encounter Andrew Hunter. Despite last night's disaster, she knew she had entrée there. She would have to find a way into the more notorious gambling houses, but until then, she would have to content herself here.

Biddle gave her a small smile and a nod, and she was again struck by the surface gentility of the establishment. A footman took her cloak and she entered the main salon. She was looking for a place to exchange currency for counters when a familiar voice spoke behind her.

"Good evening, madam."

She turned to find Lord Humphries regarding her with an odd expression. Speculative? Challenging? "Lord Humphries. How nice to see you again this evening."

"Is it?"

A mocking smile curved his narrow lips and she suddenly realized she had never kissed him. *He* was dark-haired and dark-eyed. Perhaps she could eliminate him as a suspect tonight. "Why, yes. Despite the unpleasantness last night, I would not shun you for the boorish behavior of your friends."

His face cleared. "Ah, then you have not spoken with Mr. Hunter this evening?"

"I have not encountered him. Why?"

"Oh, no particular reason, madam." He took her elbow and led her deeper into the salon. "What is your game of preference?"

"I have only played *rouge et noir,* though Mr. Hunter instructed me in *vingte et un.*"

He handed her several counters, and she wondered if women were not supposed to buy their own, or if this was a courtesy. "I wish to pay my own way, Lord Humphries. What are these counters worth, so that I may pay you back?"

"Five pounds each, though you needn't worry about paying me back. I can bear the cost of a few counters."

Such high stakes? She was not certain *she* could bear the cost. One would have to be very wealthy to gamble at Belmonde's. Four counters would mean she owed Lord Humphries twenty pounds, and Andrew Hunter another five. She could never account for such a sum in her allowance. Instead, she would have to ask their factor to increase the household budget. Mama had left the accounts to her, so there would be no questions.

Still, she did not like the idea of being indebted to Lord Humphries. She opened her reticule and saw in dismay that she had only brought ten pounds with her, and that would mean she would have to walk home. She handed Lord Humphries her ten pounds and two of his counters back.

"You gamble on a budget, madam?"

"I…I am certain I will engage in deeper play once I am familiar with the games. As a novice—"

"Caution would be advised," he finished with a nod of agreement. "It has occurred to me, madam, that you have me at a disadvantage. We have not had a formal introduction and I am ignorant of your correct form of address."

She smiled. "*Madam* will do." She wondered if she could simply lure him into an alcove, kiss him and then be on her way. "I would not be averse to a glass of wine, Lord Humphries."

"Yes, I think you *should* have a glass of wine, m'dear. You will be needing it."

What an odd statement. She walked with him toward a punch bowl on a sideboard near the alcoves. He filled a cup while she studied their surroundings. The crowd was larger tonight, and louder. Even the play seemed faster, with money exchanging hands quickly. Would she be able to keep pace when she went to the tables?

Lord Humphries came back to her side and handed her a cup. "I did not see any wine, but the rum punch is quite good here. Drink up, m'dear."

He was right. The punch was delicious if just a bit stout. After her second swallow, she glanced toward the alcoves. Would now be a good time to eliminate Lord Humphries as a suspect? He seemed to read her mind when he took her arm and led her toward one with an open curtain. "You look weary, m'dear. Shall we sit whilst we wait?"

Wait? For what? "You are being most mysterious, Lord Humphries. This is not the first time you have alluded to something imminent."

"Drew Hunter should be here any moment. Were you not meeting him?"

The rum punch, stronger than she'd thought, hit her stomach just as she started to sit. "Mr. Hunter…no. We had no plans to meet. In fact, I'd prefer not to see him this evening."

"Indeed?" Humphries seemed amused by her answer. He sat beside her and gave her a wink. "I do not think Drew will let your preferences stop him."

In the few days she'd known him, she had concluded that Andrew Hunter was a man who would do as he pleased in all things. She would not want to cheat him of whatever he desired. Thus she would finish here quickly and be gone before he arrived.

She looked up at Lord Humphries, laid her hand on his sleeve and gave him a coquettish smile. "I think *you* could stop him, My Lord."

He laughed. "For another smile that pretty, I'd be tempted. But are you trying to set me against my friend? It will not work, madam. The last man who went against Drew committed suicide in despair."

She placed her hand on his arm and leaned toward him. "I am certain you are strong enough to withstand Mr. Hunter's formidable will."

Lord Humphries looked tempted but undecided. "Oh, strong enough, no doubt, madam, but I would not care to make an enemy of him."

She tilted her face upward and smiled her most beguiling smile.

If the man did not kiss her now, she would have to take matters into her own hands.

He blinked. His lips parted. He leaned closer.

"And here he comes, madam," he said in a confidential tone. He stood and gave her a polite bow before nodding to Mr. Hunter and departing in the direction of the tables.

She offered Mr. Hunter a faint smile, a frisson of foreboding making her shiver. "Good evening, Mr. Hunter," she said, rising to offer her hand.

He spun her back to the alcove with a hand on her shoulder. "Until now, perhaps, but it will not get any better, madam."

"Is something amiss?"

"Something? Aye. You could say that."

"Is there…anything I can do?"

"You can go back to whatever demon spawned you."

Her eyebrows shot up and she blinked. "What?"

"You heard me, madam. I have finally taken your measure." He could scarcely believe her duplicity. How could she look so innocent and yet be a siren, luring men to their deaths?

"What…what wrong have I done you, Mr. Hunter?"

"The same wrong you've done dozens of other men, madam. Teasing, flirting, leading them astray from good sense and propriety." God! He couldn't believe *he* was lecturing on propriety, and yet this chit had surpassed him for flagrant violation of the rules of polite society.

"I? Did I lead you somewhere you did not want to go, Mr. Hunter? For I could have sworn 'twas you who—"

He glanced around, aware for the first time that they were drawing attention. He gave her a little push that sat her on the banquette and then drew the heavy curtains across the alcove. "If you think you are going to make a fool of me, too, you are woefully mistaken. In fact, madam, I intend to expose you."

"A fool? Expose me? Explain yourself, Mr. Hunter." Her eyes had grown wide and she looked alarmed for the first time.

"Who are you really, Bella, that you masquerade as Lady Lace? What is your game, if it is not to make a fool of every man in London?"

She replied quickly, almost as angry as he now. "They hardly need my help, Mr. Hunter. Most of them manage to be fools all by themselves."

"Was McPherson one of those, madam? Do you count yourself a winner in that skirmish? Had you set your sights on me to be next?"

"Mr. McPherson? What has he got to do with all this?"

He pulled the note from the inside of his jacket and thrust it at her. "Read it, madam, and see if you can decipher it."

He held himself in check as she unfolded the note and read the few lines. Her hand began to shake and her complexion paled by several shades.

"What…what has he done, Mr. Hunter?"

"Killed himself. Over want of you."

Quick tears welled in her eyes, and she blinked them back. Oh, she was a hard little chit if she could master her emotions so quickly. He snatched the note back and replaced it in his waistcoat pocket.

"I am sorry for his death, but I did nothing to encourage him. You know I tried on several occasions—"

"You kissed him, madam. And not a sisterly peck on the cheek, from what I'm told. If you do not call that encouragement, then what is? If you spread your legs for a man? Would that qualify?"

She blanched and closed her eyes for a moment. "What can I do, save say I am sorry?"

"I shall have recompense, madam. In my own way."

"And that is—"

"To expose you and your game. Whoever you are, wherever you came from, whatever your purpose is, I shall lay it bare for London to see. When I am finished, you will be unwelcome in every drawing room, every parlor, every business in London, excepting whatever brothel you came from. Women who play fast and loose with men have a name, and you wear it well."

"'Tis war," she murmured. Then she looked up at him and gave him an invitation that nearly choked him. "Kiss me, then. A proper kiss. Just once, by way of farewell. Then go with my blessings."

"You want a kiss?" Blast the wench! He'd been right. She was no better than a bloody whore! He leaned close to her and she lifted her lips to him, half closing her eyes in anticipation, waiting for him to meet her demand. Mere inches from her lips, he whispered, "Whistle for it, Bella. You'll have none from me."

Chapter Seven

The afternoon was wearing on when Bella stared at herself in her dressing-table mirror. She was still in her chemise. Dark circles made her eyes look sunken and her hair hung loose over her shoulders. Gina had brought her tea and toast and continued to check on her every quarter of an hour.

She was a mess. There was no way around that. Her stomach had ached ever since last night, and she couldn't think straight. She went to her clothes press and tried on one gown after another. Nothing fit. They all looked like rags draped on a sapling. But the new gowns from Madame Marie would arrive tomorrow and there'd be something to fit her. Finally settling on a dull dark gray, she rang for Nancy to help her dress.

The woman came in a rush of excitement. "Thank the Lord that you're comin' down, Miss Bella. Lady Vandecamp has arrived, all fuss and fury. She's been shut up with your mum since she arrived, sayin' she'll be wantin' to see you girls next. I wouldn't put it past her to drag you out of bed if you're not down."

Blast! That was the last thing she needed—more interference with her plans.

"And just look at you! What is happenin' to you, Miss Bella? All skin and bones. We cannot put you in a corset, or you'll look like a stick. Here…"

She stood still while Nancy dropped the gown over her head and fastened the hooks in the back, then sat down so the maid could brush her hair into a little twist at her nape. She barely attended Nancy's chatter as she wrestled with her own problems.

And the greatest of those was that extraordinary scene at Belmonde's last night. Andrew Hunter had gone from persuasive suitor to adversary in the blink of an eye. He held her responsible for Mr. McPherson's suicide. Was he right? Was it her fault? She'd lain awake half the night, trying to think of what she'd said or done that could have incited such a reaction. The kiss? Such a silly, insignificant thing?

And yet a kiss had snared Cora and had been so significant that, as she lay dying, it had been the only thing she could think of to identify her killer. God forgive her—had *her* kiss proved as lethal as the killer's? And if that were so, had she become the very thing she hunted?

Oh, but just as dreadful was Mr. Hunter's promise to expose her to all of London. She'd thought she did not care. She'd believed it would not matter. But now, faced with imminent unmasking, she realized too late that she *did* care. The shame she would bring on her mother and sisters would be monumental—perhaps impossible to live down. And she would be doomed to listen to Mama berating her, reminding her of her shortcomings and inadequacies, for all eternity.

Well, she had to do something about it. She had to prevent Mr. Hunter from discovering who she was. Obviously, the best way to accomplish that was to disappear completely from the London social scene. He could not find her if she did not leave her house or go where he could follow her. London was teeming with people. It would take a miracle to find a small family visiting from Belfast.

She would simply have to find a way to balance the scales—Cora's justice on one side, her sisters' futures on the other. And that would mean finding a way to avoid Mr. Hunter at all costs, and his friends and brothers as well.

"There!" Nancy pronounced. "You look fresh as a spring morn, Miss Bella. Hurry on down to the parlor. Lady Vandecamp said she'd join you all there when she and Mrs. O'Rourke are caught up."

And, true to her word, Bella had barely arrived in the parlor when Lady Vandecamp swept in. "Oh, my dears! I have just heard *everything*. Your poor mama! Well, never mind. I am here now and I will take over her duties."

"Thank you, madam, but there is little to be done."

Lady Vandecamp looked down her nose at Bella. "Isabella, is it not? You were all just tots when Martha last brought you to visit. All of you." Her gaze swept the other girls and she gave a satisfied nod. "Well, you are all presentable, which will make my duty easier."

Bella lifted her chin. She did not like Lady Vandecamp's officious tone. "Madam, we are in mourning. And Mama has said that we are to leave for Belfast the moment she is strong enough."

"That has changed, Isabella. I have talked sense into her. 'Twould be even more scandalous to squander this trip. And wrong to turn tail and run. The clock is ticking, my dears, and none of you is growing younger."

"Mourning," Bella said again for emphasis. How could Lady Vandecamp refute such a reasonable argument?

"My dears, it has been nearly six weeks. In London, mourning for a sister extends three months, but half mourning begins at six weeks. You can shed the blacks. This afternoon, we shall go to my dressmaker and order more becoming things."

"But—" Gina began.

"No, it has been decided. Your mother is most insistent." The woman took a place on the settee between Gina and Lilly and took charge of the teapot, just as she'd taken charge of everything else. After she served herself, she gazed at each of the girls in turn. "Isabella, you shall wear a dark grayish plum. Eugenia, you shall wear a dark grayish mauve, and Lillian, you will dress in…puce, I think. Yes, the deep browns will bring your color up and set off your blond curls."

"But what is the point, Lady Vandecamp, if we are not going out in society?"

"Well, yes. That would be unseemly. But in half mourning it is quite proper to attend private affairs—small dinner parties, musicales and teas. No dancing, of course, nor theater attendance. And you cannot be presented at court in mourning, so that will have to wait another six weeks. But I insist, and your dear mama concurs, that we cannot afford to waste this opportunity. It is past time you girls were introduced, albeit quietly, to society. You must make contacts and begin to create a 'presence' in the correct circles, which will serve you well in the future. You cannot run back to Belfast. Next year will be too late. *Some* of you," she paused to look pointedly at Bella, "will be quite upon the shelf by then."

"Oh, yes!" Lilly sat forward, alive with interest. "It would be a pity to come all the way to London and not meet a single soul. And I believe we are sufficiently recovered for small gatherings, are we not, Bella?"

"Well, I—"

"So does your mother, dear." Lady Vandecamp patted Lilly's hand with an indulgent smile. Lilly had that effect on men and women alike—they always wanted to cosset her.

Bella glanced at Gina for support but found none. Her sisters were bored, and Gina had already declared her intention to assist Bella in her investigation. She sighed in resignation. "Very small gatherings, please. Did Mama say whether she would be accompanying us?"

Lady Vandecamp frowned. "She is much too devastated to go out in public, Isabella. Now, shall we make our plans?"

Bella poured tea for her sisters and sat back while her mother's friend assumed the reins. According to her, they were to select one gown each for her to take home to her laundress to dye an appropriate shade of half mourning. Then, tomorrow, she would call for them and take them to her dressmaker's shop for measurements, and to select fabrics and look at styles in a fashion catalogue. The following evening, she would hostess a small dinner party at her town home for their first introductions and would expect the girls to arrive early to help her greet the guests. Thereafter, they could expect the arrival of like invitations, which Lady Vandecamp would go through to determine suitability. With her tutelage and guidance, she was certain they could salvage the season. By September all restraints would be lifted, and they could go about unfettered in society.

And all Bella could think was that everything had just become more complicated. And much more dangerous. What if Andrew Hunter or one of his friends was one of Lady Vandecamp's guests?

"Good to see you, Hunter," Lord Wycliffe said, looking up from the papers scattered across his desk. "Sit down."

Andrew took the chair opposite Wycliffe. "I know why you asked to see me, sir."

"Ah, then you have heard?"

"Conrad McPherson? Aye, I've heard. The funeral is tomorrow. I just came from paying my respects to his parents."

Wycliffe blinked. "What? McPherson is dead? I cannot believe it. His parents are good friends of mine. I just went to a dinner party at their house last week. Conrad was there and looked well. Seemed in good spirits. What happened?"

Andrew thought of the note now tucked safely in his waistcoat pocket. The truth? Or the whitewashed version? "Accident, sir. He was in his cups. Evidently his pistol misfired when he was undressing. Tragic."

"Good God! Just between us, I never thought Conrad was especially, well, shall we say, brilliant? But I never thought he'd end this way."

Andrew was a little surprised about the guilt he felt for lying. It could not make a difference, but his instinct to protect McPherson's reputation and spare his family shame was stronger than his scruples.

"If this wasn't about McPherson, sir, why did you ask me to come by?"

"I was wondering if you have anything to report. Any progress?" Wycliffe asked.

Andrew hadn't made progress, but he was acutely aware that he'd promised to listen for any whispers of cult activities. "Afraid not. It's not the sort of thing one would overhear at a ball, and you'd mentioned that you wanted me to be discreet. I've been nosing around, but have nothing to give you at the moment."

Wycliffe sighed and sat back in his chair. "There was another incident night before last. Another young girl, same markings. She died before she was found. That makes five, Hunter. And they're coming closer together."

Andrew experienced another twinge of guilt. His problems paled to insignificance when compared to this. He'd seen violence escalate in the war, and it was never a pretty thing. "I wish I had news, but I don't," he murmured. "But sooner or later, I am bound to hear something."

Wycliffe nodded. "I've never had a case that troubled me more than this one. I've put my best men on it again, and we're still stalled. I had hoped by calling you in, we could tap a source of hearsay normally unavailable to us. Now I fear I am in the unenviable position of asking you to risk more than just keeping an ear out. Could you… would you consider taking a more active role? Whoever is doing this is damned clever."

Andrew wanted to refuse. He wasn't a coward, but he did not like having anyone depend upon him. But the mutilation and sacrifice of young women had to stop. "I've been somewhat distracted the last few days, but my head is clearer now. Believe me, sir, if there is something to be found, I will find it."

"Be careful. These monsters have no conscience. They do not recognize the rules of society. If they get wind of someone asking questions…well, I wouldn't give a farthing for your life."

"Probably not worth a farthing," he muttered. "But I will be careful."

"Hunter, if you do not want to do this, tell me now and I will find someone else. But I cannot sit on this or ignore it."

"I said I'd do it, sir, and I will. I'll bring you something within the week."

"I am counting on it." Wycliffe sighed deeply and looked down at his papers, muttering under his breath, "And so is the Home Office."

Bella could not bring herself to go back to Belmonde's. She suspected Andrew Hunter would be waiting for her there. But last night, she'd overheard a conversation discussing a gambling hell called Thackery's. She summoned a coach once she reached Ranelagh Street and simply gave the name, hoping it would not be too far.

Surprisingly close to Belmonde's, Thackery's turned out to have less stringent requirements for admission. In fact, Bella gathered that if one could walk through the doors, one could qualify. The premises were, nonetheless, grand. The decor had been taken beyond the point of quiet good taste and bordered on opulent.

The main salon was large and boasted a wide, curved stairway leading up to a mezzanine with a brass railing that circled the entire salon. A massive chandelier was suspended in the center at the same level as the mezzanine. The effect was dazzling.

She noted that a number of women stood at the railing to watch the activity below, and she concluded that female presence was more common than it was at Belmonde's. She did not feel nearly as out of place until she realized she was drawing a fair amount of attention, and she was not altogether comfortable with the appraising glances that were directed her way.

A footman noted her discomfort and, with a small bow, said, "Perhaps you would be more comfortable above, madam."

Ah, the only women she noted downstairs were escorted. And yet there were a fair number of men visible on the mezzanine, too. She gave the footman a smile and began to climb the stairs.

From her vantage point as she climbed, she could view the salon below. She saw a few faces she recognized from various balls and parties she'd attended. She thought she saw Mr. James Hunter, but he disappeared into the crowd. Just as well. Though James and Charles were both dark-haired, they were also blue-eyed. They did not meet Cora's description.

At the head of the stairs was a large salon with glass doors open to the landing. The sound of raised voices and laughter carried to her and she wondered if this was where she'd find refreshment and a place to change her coins into counters. With all the self-assurance she could muster, she passed through the open doors.

The light was dimmer here, the smoke thicker and the atmosphere… more close. Murals lined the walls, and cushioned benches were placed at intervals, almost as if for better viewing of the murals. A refreshment table stood at the far end of the salon, and a few gambling tables were scattered throughout. But there was something vaguely disquieting about the mood pervading the salon. Was the gaiety too forced? Was the laughter too brittle? Were the men…too familiar?

She watched as one man ran his hand up and down one woman's bare arm, and another's attention seemed riveted on his companion's daring décolletage. Yet another leaned close to his companion's ear and whispered something, which caused her to giggle uncontrollably. She'd never seen such behavior in polite company.

Polite company? Clearly, that was not the case. These women were prostitutes! Courtesans, at best! And worse—the footman had mistaken *her* for one! She took a deep breath as a stranger headed her way.

"I do not believe I have seen you here before. I am pleased to make your acquaintance, Miss…?"

"I…I believe I have made a mistake. I do not think I should be here."

"I can see you're a cut above the ordinary, miss, but—"

"No, I mean…" But he was dark haired and dark-eyed, and it would be a shame to waste the night. With Lady Vandecamp breathing down her back, she did not know how many more nights she would be able to sneak away. "Lace," she said. "Lady Lace."

"Madam," he acknowledged with a grin and a bow. "I am Mr. Johnson. Shall we sit and become better acquainted?" He gestured to one of the benches along the wall.

"As you please, sir."

She allowed him to guide her to the bench farthest from any groups, which was also in the dimmest corner. She could not help but cringe inwardly at her lie. Now she was pretending to be a prostitute in the name of justice. What had happened to her scruples? Her morals? Where had the shy young lady from Belfast gone? Oh, surely there would be a special place in hell for her. She sat facing the wall, a shabby subterfuge but the only one available to her.

Mr. Johnson sat beside her, facing the room and enabling him to face her, as well. "How have I missed you in the crowds, Lady Lace?"

"I have not been here before, sir."

"Ah, then I count myself fortunate to have found you first. Do you have a protector, madam, or are you at liberty for the evening?"

She could feel the heat creep up her cheeks and prayed that would not give her away. "I am at liberty, sir."

"Shall I arrange for a room here? Or would you rather go to yours?"

"I…I do not make arrangements so quickly, sir. I must know if there is true compatibility."

"Ah, you are selective. I can appreciate that, madam. But how shall we know if we are compatible? That could take weeks."

She forced a coy smile and said, "Perhaps…with a kiss?"

"With pleasure, madam," Mr. Johnson said.

With pleasure, madam. Was that not what Mr. McPherson had said? Was Mr. Hunter right? Did she have the right to kiss men and let them think there could be more? Doubt clouded her mind and she fastened her gaze on the mural. She could not look Mr. Johnson in the eyes and say these things.

And then she realized what the mural depicted! Satyrs chasing nude virgins through the countryside! Men overtaking partially clad women! And everywhere she looked, couples copulating in a variety of positions! Good heavens! Before she could voice her amazement, Mr. Johnson lifted her chin on the edge of his hand and lowered his mouth to hers. She blinked and held her breath.

He met her lips in a nice but unremarkable manner as his hand slipped from her chin down to her throat. But he did not moisten his lips. His hand slipped lower still, to find the curve of her breasts. Before she could protest, an angry voice broke the embrace.

"Here you are, madam, the first time I turn my back."

She did not have to look to recognize Andrew Hunter's voice. How had he found her? And with her back to the room?

"You do not own me, Mr. Hunter."

"I believe I do, *Bella.*"

Her blood turned to ice. Clearly, he was not protecting her name any longer. Was he going to expose her here and now? How much had he discovered about her?

"Excuse me, Johnson, but apparently my…*friend* has neglected to mention that we have a previous agreement."

"I—of course, Hunter." Mr. Johnson stood, gave Bella a puzzled bow and went back to his friends.

Mr. Hunter took the place on the bench that Mr. Johnson had vacated. "I warned you not to play your game in London, madam. That you do so openly is a taunt, is it not? You are daring me to carry out my threat?"

"I came here tonight trying to avoid you, sir."

"Do not think you can escape me, Bella. I have friends everywhere. Friends who know I want to be informed of where you are and what you are up to. So you see, wherever you go, whatever you do, I will know. You can't escape me, Bella, unless you leave London."

Ah, yes. She'd seen Mr. Hunter's brother in the main salon when she'd entered. He must have gone straight to Belmonde's to tattle on her. "I could save you the trouble, sir, and give you a report of my doings every morning. Would that satisfy you?"

"You are a brazen wench," he murmured. "I saw you kissing Johnson. I saw your reaction. Be warned, madam. I had better not find you doing so again."

Her reaction? Relief? What had he thought she felt? She glanced down at the toes of her slippers, then at the mural in front of her. Two could play his game. She was safe from *his* attentions, at least, since he'd declared his intention not to be one of her "fools."

"No kisses, Mr. Hunter? Then what shall I do instead? This?" She pointed to the mural where a couple was engaged in the act of sex. "Or this?" She indicated a scene where a satyr had brought a woman down and was entering her from behind. "What is to your taste, sir?"

He turned to see what she was pointing to and he flinched. "You tempt me to teach you a lesson, Bella. You can be certain that if I did such things to you, you would not soon forget them."

She gave him a scornful laugh. "Someone thinks well of himself, does he not? How would you know what I would or would not find memorable?"

He leaned against her, their shoulders in intimate contact. "Shall we find out, Bella?"

He was calling her bluff! Ah, but then he would become one of her fools—and he would never do that. She was safe enough. With utter confidence, she smiled. "If you wish."

"Very well." He stood, took her hand to pull her to her feet and spun her toward the door. "Thackery's keeps rooms for just such occasions."

Chapter Eight

The temptress! Bella had more audacity than sense if she thought she could taunt him with impunity. Andrew could not decide if he was angrier at her for demonstrating how damned much he *did* care what she did, or for offering herself to another man.

He ignored her little gasp as he tugged her upward and toward the glass doors. Paying no heed to the startled looks of those milling about the upper lobby and around the mezzanine, he turned down the nearest corridor, looking for an open door. When he found one safely away from prying ears or eyes, he propelled her through the door and slammed it behind them.

Only one lamp burned on a console table beneath a looking glass. He turned the bolt with a loud click, signaling to Bella that she would now have to pay for her taunt.

She turned and looked at him, her eyes as round as saucers. Her face registered surprise and something else. Fear? No. Not his Bella. She had no lack of courage. Then it must be excitement. Could she really want him? As much as *he* wanted *her*—and hated himself for it?

"What…what are you going to do?"

His gaze shifted to the bed, and he let a little smile curve his lips. He could not wait to see what *she* would do next.

She waited. Very well, then. He'd play her game. He went forward and pulled her roughly into his arms. She looked up at him and parted her lips. Was she waiting for a kiss? Be damned to that. He'd sworn not to kiss her and he would not be foresworn. Ah, but that was all he'd promised. No kisses, then, but...

He leaned toward her and ran his tongue along the rim of her ear and whispered, "Will you undress for me, Bella, or shall I do it for you?"

She caught her breath and shuddered, but she did not answer. Did she think he was bluffing? Silly girl. And yet her full lips were so tempting he could barely think of anything else. A kiss—just one kiss? Of all the things he could do to her, he was most tempted by that one. But there was a way he could enjoy her without being drawn to her mouth.

He led her to the mirror and stood behind her, the only way he knew he would not have access to those lips. The light of the single lamp flickered, casting the bare expanse above her décolletage in a golden glow. Slipping his hands around her waist, he moved them upward until they were tantalizingly close to cupping her breasts. She blinked and drew a long breath, catching his gaze in the mirror.

He pulled her back against him until he knew she could feel his erection. Good heavens, he hadn't been this aroused in years! And when she emitted a tiny gasp, it nearly pushed him over the edge. He leaned lower and nibbled one tempting earlobe, and she tilted her head to one side to accommodate him.

He could feel her heartbeat quicken beneath his palm on her rib cage. The vixen was responding. Ever so slowly, he drew his hands upward until they covered her breasts—breasts that were infinitely soft and warm. Breasts with peaks that firmed and tickled his palms through the light silk. He did not take his eyes from her as he dipped his fingers inside her gown and found the laces of her chemise. He drew them out, untied the knot and loosened the fabric.

Freed of their confines, those rosy buttons peeked above the frail white lawn of her chemise. "Beautiful," he murmured, watching her eyes for any betrayal of anger. But she had lowered her lashes to veil her response. A fevered blush stole up her throat to her cheeks and she sagged against him. He found those firmed nipples and rolled them between his fingers and thumbs. Her eyes flew open and she grasped the edge of the console table to brace herself.

"Steady, Bella," he whispered. "I've got you. I won't let you fall."

Damn! He'd meant to teach her a lesson. To put her in her place. But she'd drawn him into a web of desire so strong that nothing else mattered. Still, he couldn't—he wouldn't—kiss her. It was far too erotic to find other ways to bring her to willing, trembling submission. Far too erotic to watch her in the mirror as he made slow, deliberate love to her. Her head fell back against his chest, a signal that she'd given herself over to the sensation and was no longer fighting her response.

He unlaced her further and pushed the fabric down to free her breasts entirely. They were perfect, those soft swells of ivory flesh. Not large. Not small. And he wondered how they would taste. How they would feel against his lips and tongue. How they would respond to his caresses.

He turned her to face him and lifted her to sit on the edge of the console table, her breasts now closer to his mouth. First he kissed the spot at the hollow of her throat where he could feel her heartbeat against his lips. He nibbled, drawing the soft flesh into his mouth for a tender nip. When her hands trembled on his shoulders, he moved lower, fastening his lips around one puckered aureole. She cried out, tangling her fingers through his hair to hold him close.

He parted her legs to move closer and then regretted it. Enclosed between those heated thighs, he could only think of one thing. No, two. He still longed to kiss her. Longed to search the honeyed sweetness of her mouth, to reach a part of her forbidden to him by his own vow, to find if her tongue was sweeter than her words. And then he longed to join with her between her legs, find her place of deepest intimacy. To drive into her in a primitive ritual claiming, a marking of his territory. *His.*

Holding her fast against him with one arm, he swept her skirts up with the other, finding his way between the layers of cloth to her center. He groaned when he found her hot and ready. She squirmed against his hand, tilting her hips toward him to give him deeper access.

"Andrew…" she moaned.

Hearing his given name on her tongue jolted him from his passion-muddled thinking. It was Lady Lace who toyed with him—the reason for his friend's death. He backed away from her, nearly upsetting the lamp in his haste. He stopped at the door and spoke without turning. "You won't have me, Bella. You won't make me one of your fools."

But once in the corridor, he braced himself against the wall and doubled over with the pain of his arousal until he could catch his breath. Next time, by God, if there was a next time, she would pay for this.

Wherever you go, whatever you do, I will know. You can't escape me, Bella.... Oh, why couldn't she think of anything else? Why did her mind keep returning to that threat? If he would not leave her alone, if her every move was reported to him, how would she ever find Cora's killer? How could she keep her promise?

But there was more and worse that had happened to her last night. There was that private room above Thackery's main salon. Where had her head been? What madness had possessed her to taunt Mr. Hunter so? And what foolish pride had held her immobile while he did those things to her? Had she been trying to prove he could not move her? That he had no effect on her?

Instead he had proved his point—that if he ever did such things to her, she would not soon forget them. And she wouldn't. It was, in fact, all she could think of.

Her hand went up to her throat, to the spot where her collarbones met—the spot that Andrew Hunter *had* kissed. There was a tiny discoloration there now, and she had covered it with rice powder. A faint moan escaped her and she closed her eyes with the memory of the sweetness his mouth had evoked in her.

"Hush, Bella! What is wrong with you?" Gina whispered.

She came back to the present with a start. Lady Vandecamp's voice droned on, instructing the girls on correct forms of address and how to politely ignore men to whom they had not been properly introduced—as if Belfast had been the back of beyond in terms of manners.

"N-nothing," she lied. "I am just a bit fatigued."

"That did not sound like a yawn, Bella. You must stop staying out so late, especially now that Lady V. is here. She has said that she will be going to considerable trouble to arrange suitable evening entertainments for us and she wants us to be most assiduous in attending."

"Then I shall have to be just as insistent that we not stay late. I must have more time, Gina."

"Oh, my dear." Gina sighed and leaned her head against Bella's. "I did not want to be the one to tell you, but you are on a fool's errand. I thought you would have realized it by now. You will never kiss all the dark haired, dark eyed men in London."

"In the *ton,* Gina. Rascals and rakes. I have narrowed it down that much, at least."

"And still it is like finding a needle in a haystack."

"I only have to be lucky once."

"'Tis like asking lightning to strike."

"Then pray for stormy weather."

"What are you chits whispering about?" Lady Vandecamp snapped in a raised voice. "It would serve you well to attend my lecture as closely as Lillian. You will only have one chance to make a good impression."

"Yes, madam," Gina said in a contrite voice.

"Yes, madam." Bella sat straighter and tried to clear her head. As loath as she was to enter society, she was determined to make a success of it for her sisters' sake.

Lady Vandecamp gave a regal nod. "Very well. Now, as I was saying, tomorrow night will be a dinner party at my home. Arrive by seven o'clock sharp. I want you there before the other guests arrive. I sent out invitations yesterday afternoon and have received all acceptances. This is a small but select group of people who can do you good in society. If they approve of you, they can open doors ordinarily closed to all but the haute ton."

Lilly smiled, excitement heightening her color, and Bella was struck again by how much like Cora she was, in beauty and in spontaneity. Lilly had been born for society life. She would cause a ripple on the calm surface of the haute ton. And Gina—well, Gina would win more hearts than she would recognize. Gina had never known her effect on the people around her, most notably men. She was sublimely unaware that she left a wake of broken hearts wherever she went.

Bella, however, would be the shy one. She would hang back and hide in the shadows, lest anyone find her familiar.

"Your remade dresses will be delivered tomorrow afternoon," Lady Vandecamp continued. "'Tis a good thing I brought my seamstress with me. The ones we order today should be ready by Monday if we pay the modiste extra. Oh, and I have hinted that your mourning is for a sister who had been afflicted with a wasting disease. Do not contradict me. A murder scandal would place you under a cloud, and all the dressing up in the world would not make you acceptable again."

Gina dropped her gaze to the floor, but Bella was angry. This was just what she'd expected. Something that was not Cora's fault would be held against the rest of them. She almost despised society in that instant. And she had no regrets about her course of action. Acceptable or not, Cora would have justice.

But it was clear now that she would have to change her plan. With Lady Vandecamp towing them along behind her, Bella would have to find some way to avoid recognition. Her only consolation was that Lady V. was not likely to ask rakes and rogues to her dinner parties and fetes, so she would not have to worry until she was dragged to a public event.

"Bella? Are you attending me?"

"Yes, madam. A wasting disease. Consumption?"

"Good enough, dear. Now, shall we be off to the dressmaker's?"

"Ye gods!" Jamie shook his head and laughed. "'Tis teatime and you are yet sober! And after McPherson's funeral this morning. What is this, Drew? Turning over a new leaf?"

Andrew glanced up from his notes and motioned to a chair across from him. "Shut up and sit down."

"Oh, bad temper. Not a good sign. You'll have us all clamoring to buy you whiskey tonight just to banish this beetle-browed ogre in front of me."

Andrew gestured to the teapot on his desk. "Help yourself. Or have a sherry if it's more to your taste." He finished making his notations and then dropped his pen. In an attempt to keep busy after the funeral, he'd begun organizing his bits of information to see if they formed a pattern yet. They didn't, and he was growing frustrated.

Jamie brought his sherry and took the seat across from Andrew. "Did you find your Lady Lace last night?"

"Yes, and thank you for letting me know where she was."

"Thackery's, by God. Not that there isn't some damn fine female flesh there, but I expected better of Lace."

"So did I, Jamie. Seems as if we've all been deceived."

"Did you send her packing?"

"I do not own Thackery's, so that was not one of my options. But I'm fairly certain I…ruined her evening. If she shows her face at Thackery's again, I will be surprised." And, unexpectedly, that prospect disturbed him. What if she took his warning to heart and he never saw her again?

"What are you doing tonight, Drew? I've got a taste for the exotic. Charlie said he'd be game for something different, too."

"Exotic." Andrew tasted the word on his tongue. He found it interesting, and a bit disconcerting, that he had become the source of exotic entertainments for his brothers. "Define *exotic,* Jamie."

"Different, of course. Something we haven't done to death. Something that titillates the senses and gets the blood pumping. Something…well, risky and a bit wicked."

"Just a *bit* wicked?"

Jamie narrowed his eyes. "What's afoot, Drew?"

"I begin to think I should ask *you* how to spend my evenings. What have you dabbled in whilst my back was turned?"

"What? At Bedlam? That turned ugly and we departed with haste."

"What happened?"

"Someone—I cannot recall who—tossed a few coins to the three men who were huddled by the fire and pointed to a woman who was rocking her shawl as if it were a baby. The men laughed and dragged her closer and assaulted her. 'Twas then that Charlie and I decided to leave."

"Assaulted, you say? Explain, Jamie."

His brother looked away, not a good sign. "They stripped her of her clothes, and when she fought, they…"

"And what did you do, Jamie?"

"To my shame, very little. Charlie stepped forward and said, 'Here, now, chaps, let her be,' but he was pushed aside by someone crowding to get a better look. I shouted for the guard, but he was busy counting his money. After that, we just backed away. There must have been two dozen visitors by that time. Everyone had gathered to watch—and not just watch, but cheer the fellows on. We could not stop it, nor could we take on those odds."

Andrew nodded. He and his brothers had taken on double their number before, but never an entire barroom, let alone a madhouse. Still, if he had stayed, he suspected he would have cracked a few heads before they put him down. Then a suspicion grew in him. "Was it someone from our group who instigated the attack, Jamie?"

"Aye. But he said he didn't mean it to turn into a rape. Just meant to have some fun and see what would happen."

That would be a blatant lie. One did not throw coins and set men on a woman without expecting something of the sort. Dash. It had to have been Dash. Who else had declared an interest to see man at his basest level? "Dash," he said aloud and watched Jamie's face.

"McPherson, actually."

Relief swept through him. He was glad to be wrong. But McPherson? That was not in keeping with what Andrew knew of his character. Had he regretted his part in the woman's victimization and not been able to live with it? Still, he couldn't ignore that damning farewell to Lady Lace.

After last night in that private room at Thackery's, he could not discount the power Bella held over mere mortal men. It had taken every ounce of willpower he possessed to walk away and not to make abandoned love to her. Suddenly, as absurd as it was, it did not seem impossible that McPherson would rather die than spend a lifetime without her.

"Drew?"

He came back to the conversation with a start. "Sorry. I was… thinking."

"Aye, it had me thinking, too. I did not know that McPherson had that sort of meanness in him."

"All men are capable of all things. You know full well about man's inhumanity to man. There is very little that separates us from animals."

"Allowing for war—"

A chill invaded Andrew's stomach. He glanced toward the sherry decanter. "Let us *not* allow for war, Jamie. That is a law unto itself and has nothing to do with civilization."

Jamie sipped his sherry and eyed Andrew over the rim of his glass.

After a moment he said, "The word is out that you've been asking around excitement."

Ah, he hadn't been as subtle as he'd thought. Well, perhaps that would bring him more success than discretion had. He merely shrugged and arched an eyebrow at his brother.

"Why do you chase the next thrill? The next pleasure?" Jamie asked.

"I want something different. Something I haven't found before. I want to *feel,* Jamie. Anything." That much, at least, was the truth. And again, the vision of Bella, flushed and moaning, came to his mind. Could he call that surge of lust a feeling? Or was it what Dash had called 'man at his basest level'?

"And you do not care what it is? Good? Bad? Right or wrong? Dangerous? Self-indulgent?"

"Not in the least." How else could he tell Jamie he was looking for evil when he'd sworn confidentiality to Lord Wycliffe?

Jamie let out a low whistle. "You're sporting the worst case of ennui I've ever encountered, Drew. I'm afraid you're on your own."

"But if you hear of anything…"

"You will be the first to know."

But Andrew knew he was alone in this. He needed to find the very dregs of humanity, and he did not fool himself that they would be found in the working classes.

Chapter Nine

Bella saw Andrew Hunter in a group loitering on the steps of the Royal Opera House and nearly fled. She'd thought a return to Thackery's was not a wise idea, nor a return to Belmonde's, so she had attached herself to group of revelers entering the theater. Heavens! Was there no escape from the man? Who had tattled on her this time?

He caught her eye as she started to turn away. He looked surprised to see her, and not particularly pleased. Well, he did not own London, and he could not keep her from a public place. She had precious little time now, with Lady Vandecamp breathing down her neck, and she could not allow Andrew Hunter to frighten her off.

She felt the heat creep into her cheeks as she remembered last night. All the way home, she had watched over her shoulder to be certain he was not following her. If he knew her entire name and where she lived… He had said, "You won't have me, Bella. You won't make me one of your fools." How did he think she was trying to make a fool of him? It had seemed to her that he was the one making a fool of her.

He came toward her and she looked about for a diversion—some ploy that would spare her his company. Alas, or thank heavens, she did not see a single soul she knew. She fell back from the group as they entered the lobby and prayed he would not cause a scene.

"Looking for an escape, Bella?" he asked, taking her arm.

"Just from you, sir." She allowed him to lead her down the front steps. "I begin to flatter myself that you are following me."

"Not tonight. I had a previous commitment to meet friends here. And I would prefer not to have them subjected to your... presence."

Oh, that was a cruel barb! Her pride would not let her show how he had wounded her. "You have friends with tender sensibilities? Faith, I hadn't noticed. I thought they were all like you."

"One of them, at least, proved tender enough. I buried him today, Bella, thanks to you. Or had you forgotten so soon?"

Her stomach twisted and she winced. Guilt? She still could not think of anything she'd said or done that could have driven Mr. McPherson to suicide. A kiss, and nothing more. And yet, even though he'd been angry with her when last they'd met, he'd left that damning note. She tightened her jaw and lifted her chin. "No, I have not forgotten. But I cannot believe, that is..."

"Whether you believe it or not, it is so."

"Is this your typically subtle way of asking me to leave, Mr. Hunter?"

"Astute of you, Bella."

"I wish you wouldn't call me that."

"Do you think I give a damn about that, m'dear?"

"Please..."

"I will cease when you give me something else to call you. Tell me your name."

"So that you can ruin my entire family?"

"We've never spoken about your family, Bella. I gather the young women I saw you with in St. James's Park were your sisters?"

There was an implied threat in those words, and she shivered in the night air. "Please, they do not know anything about what I have been doing. They are blameless. Would you be so unkind as to ruin them because of something I have done?"

He grinned, and there was nothing gentle in the gesture. His answer was clear. He would not hesitate to use her family to exact his vengeance for Mr. McPherson. Well, in that, at least, they were alike. She would not let Andrew Hunter prevent her from obtaining justice for Cora.

"Very well," she began. "At least now we understand each other, do we not?"

"We do not. You have yet to tell me what your game is. What, precisely, do you hope to accomplish by cutting through the ton, gathering kisses here and there? And do not give me that twaddle about finding the right man."

Damn him! "Then I am trying to find the *wrong* man."

He seized her shoulders and gave her a sharp shake. "Damn you, Bella!"

Oh, they were more alike than he could ever guess—each damning the other and determined to have their own way! "Would it make a difference if you knew?"

"Probably not."

"Then release me and be warned. Public places do not belong to you, Mr. Hunter. I shall go wherever I want, and you will not interfere."

A dangerous glint in his dark eyes warned her she had gone too far. "Did the events at Thackery's not teach you to use caution in challenging me?"

She felt the heat sweep her from head to toe and prayed that he could not read minds. If he but knew it, she would challenge him again and again if he would do to her what he'd done last night.

"How maidenly that you can muster a blush after all you've done," he said in a tone that sent a chill through her. "Now be gone, Bella, or you will pay for it."

She glanced around and noted that they were drawing attention. As desperate as she was to continue her quest, as short as time had grown for her because of Lady V.'s arrival, she could ill afford to draw unwarranted attention and make herself more recognizable to people she might encounter at one of her sponsor's events. She would have to let Mr. Hunter win this one.

She gave him a wilting glance and turned away, praying a brisk walk home would diffuse her anger at the man.

Seething, Andrew returned to his sister and brother-in-law. "Sorry for the delay. I am afraid I must beg off tonight. Something has come up."

Ethan Travis, his brother-in-law, grinned. "So I saw. Something quite pressing, I gather."

His sister, Sarah, nudged him. "Do not tease him, Ethan, or he may decide to forgo his plans. You know how desperate I am to find him a bride. Why, I had tea with Lady Vandecamp this afternoon. She is sponsoring three young ladies from Belfast this season, and I asked if she would introduce Andrew, Charles and James. She refused!" She paused and nodded at Andrew's astonishment. "Yes. She said that, unless I could vow that they'd mended their wicked ways, she would not consider it. So I ask you, if we cannot entice young ladies from out of town, how can we hope to find willing Londoners to trust their daughters to my brothers? Why, even Lockwood had to go to the Caribbean to find a bride."

Ethan laughed and Andrew frowned at him. In truth, he had never given any thought to taking a wife. Since his return from Spain, he'd spent his entire existence trying to forget the war, and he hadn't met a single woman who'd turned his mind to marriage or even engaged his interest for more than a brief affair. Quite sobering, now, to realize he'd squandered his chance to find a suitable miss.

But now he didn't want a suitable miss. He glanced down the street toward the shrinking figure of Bella. No, not suitable at all, but he wanted her with a keen edge he hadn't felt since his first love.

He kissed his sister on the cheek and backed away. "Sorry. Another time, perhaps." Ethan's laughter followed him down the stairs. Would he laugh if he knew what Andrew was really up to?

Keeping a comfortable distance, he followed Bella. This time, he'd find out where she lived. Perhaps he'd knock on her door tomorrow at teatime, just to see her expression.

But, if he were to be honest, he was simply curious. She guarded her privacy so determinedly that the mystery surrounding her only added to her allure. If he could uncover that, perhaps he could stop obsessing about her. Yes, obsessing. He could admit that much to himself. Bella had reached an undeserved status with him, and he wanted to bring her down to human level.

He quickened his step as she turned on Cockspur Street and continued at a brisk pace. He nearly missed her when she veered down a narrow path leading to the Parade Grounds. Did she intend to cut through one of the walks that bordered the canal?

The evening was still early enough that several couples strolled with children scampering around them while groups of revelers on their way to entertainments passed them. Andrew easily blended in when Bella checked over her shoulder before choosing the southwest path toward the Bird Cage Walk on the south side of the canal.

She was easy to follow—either too inexperienced to notice him, or too preoccupied to suspect that she might be followed. Nevertheless, he moved into the shadows at the edge of the walk until she came to an exit on William Street. From there, she turned right on James Street and her pace slowed. She had either tired or was close to home.

At last she stopped. Her shoulders drooped and she took a deep breath before crossing the street to a respectable town house with an excellent view of St. James Park. What business could she have there? He expected her to knock and be turned away, but once on the stoop, she fished in her reticule, withdrew a key and let herself in. *This* was where Bella lived? Why had he been so certain she would reside in a poor neighborhood or in some squalid rooming house? The chit must be doing quite well for herself.

He was about to retrace his steps when he saw a light come on in an upper window. A moment later Bella's silhouette moved across the lace curtain. The sight drew him across the street to stand beneath her open window. Muted feminine voices carried on a brief conversation. Her abbess demanding to know why she'd come home with no coins?

He caught a few words—a gasped *No!* and then a querulous tone demanding *What now?* He recognized the sound of Bella's voice, though could not make out her words. She sounded tired and…sad. On the verge of tears. She moved closer to the window and her words became clearer.

"Go to bed, Gina. An early night will do us both good. I will find a way to make up the lost time. Perhaps tomorrow, after the dinner party, I can…" Her voice faded as she turned away from the window.

Gina. One of the girls who'd accompanied Bella on their walk through the park. He heard the sound of a door closing and then utter silence. He waited another minute or two, watching the silhouette as she removed the pins from her hair and shook it out. He could almost see the warm lengths threaded through with golden red spilling over her shoulders and down her back. An ache began to grow in his middle.

But then he heard a muffled choking. No, *crying.* He narrowed his eyes as if he could look through walls. Why should the prospect of Bella crying trouble him when he'd done his best to cause it? And why had she never shown him any of this tender sensibility?

Good God! What was wrong with him? He was no lovesick pup in the throes of first love. He was a man filled with self-loathing for wasting his time with a lightskirt when he should be about critical business.

And with that thought, he crossed the street and hailed a coach. The rookeries of Whitechapel were calling him.

When Lord Wycliffe had asked him to keep an ear out, Andrew had assumed it was his familiarity with the rakehells and rogues of London that Wycliffe wanted to tap. But after half a week, Andrew knew that was fruitless. If anyone knew anything, they were not talking. But rape and ritual sacrifice were not the exclusive activities of the idle rich. It would not take a leap to connect such things to the criminal element of London. A man capable of killing to steal a man's purse could easily be capable of killing for such abstract reasons as religion or perverse pleasure.

Yes, his reputation made him valuable to Wycliffe. And now that Wycliffe had given him sanction to do more, he would explore his other field of proficiency. He was known and trusted in even the worst rookeries surrounding the city. His reputation for discretion and his appetite for the low life had earned him the confidence of the underworld. They knew who he was and that they had nothing to fear from him.

He was one of them, if not in criminal pursuits, then in the pursuit of pleasure and novelty. And he was known to pay well for them. Yes, these men knew he would not betray them to the charleys. And they'd find him anything for the coins it would bring them.

He waved his coach on when he stepped down at a nameless gin house on Petticoat Lane. This was no neighborhood to draw attention with a waiting coach. The sound of coarse laughter and shouts carried into the street and Andrew knew there would be fights as the night wore on.

The place quieted when he walked in, then the volume resumed.

Most of these men knew him. He went to the bar and nodded to the keeper. As if by magic, a glass of whiskey appeared. He never drank the rotgut gin—it was as likely to kill you as get you drunk.

A man known as Hank came to stand next to Andrew, his back to the barroom. "What you lookin' for tonight, gov'nor?"

"Something new, Hank. Know where I can find it?"

The man laughed. "What's new for one man, ain't for 'nother. What's yer idea of new?"

Andrew sipped his whiskey and pondered the question. Subtlety had gotten him nowhere thus far. And yet, he was not quite ready to raise an alarm. Wycliffe had wanted to avoid that at all costs. He regarded Hank through the smoke-filled gloom. "Give me some choices, Hank. I will know it when I hear it."

"There's a cockfight—"

"*New,* Hank."

"I heard that on the other side of the East India Warehouses, someone's brought in a bear. If you hurry—"

"A dancing bear?"

Hank looked startled and then laughed. "Love ye, no, gov'nor. A bear for baitin'. There'll be all manner of dogs. Plenty o' blood."

Andrew hid his disgust. This, at least, was closer to his search. "I am not averse to blood, Hank, but I'll leave the bears to someone else."

"Aye? What sort o' blood do ye fancy?"

He shrugged and raised an eyebrow.

The man's eyes widened. "'Ere now, gov'nor. We don't see that too often, we don't. Rare as hen's teeth. And if I was to 'ear of somethin', I'd 'ave a care who I told it to."

Andrew jingled a few coins in his waistcoat pocket.

"Well…I 'ave 'eard whispers." The man leaned closer. "But it's all on the hush."

Andrew liberated a few coins from his pocket and dropped them on the bar. They were snatched away before they could stop spinning.

"I'll ask around. Where'll I find ye?"

"I'll be here tomorrow night, Hank. Same time. And do not think you'll get more coin without an answer."

He gave Andrew a gap-toothed grin and a nod and headed for the door.

Returning his attention to his whisky, Andrew marveled at the ease with which that had been done. He'd expected Hank to demur, say he'd never heard of the like and go away. But London was a town that offered anything the human heart could imagine, no matter how dark or twisted.

He should go home and make an early night of it—especially since tomorrow could last long into the wee hours, depending upon what Hank brought him—but he felt restless.

There it was again, that yearning to *feel*. To experience something. To fill the void where his heart and humanity had been. He tossed off the rest of his whiskey and headed for the door. There were hundreds of gin houses in the rookeries. Maybe he'd learn something at one of them.

Andrew heard Jamie's voice before he saw him. What was his brother doing in Whitechapel? He pressed his way through the crowd toward the voice and found Jamie, Dash and Henley sitting around a small table facing two rough-looking longshoremen. Empty tankards were stacked in two crooked columns and Jamie was just adding one to the pile in front of him. Dash and Henley clapped him on the back, added another shilling to a pile of coins and looked expectantly at the longshoremen.

"Come, gentlemen!" Jamie cajoled. "Can you not tell I am near to passing out?"

A hoot of laughter went up and the longshoremen threw another shilling on the pile with begrudging respect.

The barkeeper, identifiable by his soiled apron, brought two more tankards and slapped Jamie on the back. "Never saw a toff 'oo could swill gin like a longshoreman. You sure you ain't from Liverpool?"

Jamie emptied the tankard in three lusty swallows and laughed again. "Why, my skinny little sister could drink these men unconscious."

Andrew winced. Jamie did not sound foxed, but his words were ill-advised in a place like this.

The man with the tankards in front of him began to stand, his hands fisted at his sides.

"'Ere now, laddie," his companion said, pushing him back into his chair with a hand on his shoulder. To Jamie, he added, "'Tain't nice for ye to be tauntin' me boy like that."

"He's a boy, all right," Henley crowed. "Bring us a man if you want to see Hunter do some serious drinking."

That, apparently, was one taunt too many for the longshoremen. The drinker came to his feet again, overturning the table in his haste, and swung one meaty fist at Henley, sending him reeling backward into the jeering crowd.

Jamie muttered, "Damn!" under his breath as he got unsteadily to his feet. The drunken longshoreman swung at Jamie now, and whirled around when he failed to make contact. Jamie had ducked the punch and was laughing. A tactical error.

Now both longshoremen rushed Jamie, and there was nothing for Drew but to wade in. He found himself shoulder-to-shoulder with Dash, taking on the longshoremen and their friends. One lunged at Jamie and they both toppled backward onto the plank floor.

Andrew lost track of Henley, but from the sound of breaking chairs behind him, Henley was holding his own. Jamie, however, was not faring so well. One longshoreman held him down while the other drew back his arm to deliver a knockout punch. Andrew intercepted the man's fist and delivered a punch of his own. In the next moment he was fending off three men who all seemed to want to break his nose.

"Get up, for God's sake!" he shouted at Jamie over the commotion. Lying on the floor, his brother would be stomped to death in the melee. The fight was promising to escalate into a riot within a few minutes. Dash appeared and dragged Jamie to his feet as Andrew held the longshoremen off.

"My winnings!" Jamie shouted, starting to bend over to scrape the shillings off the floor.

"Get him out of here," he yelled at Dash as he swung at a man intent on targeting Jamie.

His opponent on the floor for the moment, Andrew looked around for Henley. Everyone in the gin house was engaged in mayhem.

Henley was swinging wildly, hitting nothing, one eye swollen nearly closed, and two men circled him, looking for an opening. Thankfully, Henley and the men were damn near as drunk as Jamie, and Andrew put them down in quick order.

He tossed Henley over his shoulder and made for the door. But the fight, too, had spilled onto the narrow street. Dash had leaned Jamie against the neighboring building and was thrashing a man soundly. A cursory glance told Andrew that Jamie had suffered no lasting harm, and he dumped Henley beside him.

"Stay put," he told them as he turned to extricate Dash.

But Dash did not want or need Andrew's help. He laid the man out with a powerful upper cut. The man reeled back against the building, cracking his head against the brick, then slid down the length of the wall, his head lolling to one side. Dash kicked him for good measure, then grasped a handful of his hair to hold him steady for another punch. Something unholy lit Dash's dark eyes and Andrew caught his breath. He'd seen that look before in Valle del Fuego. If he didn't stop him...

"Come away," he shouted, trying to penetrate Dash's concentration.

The longshoreman was unconscious, completely defenseless, and his face looked like raw meat. Andrew gripped Dash's shoulder, then ducked when Dash rounded on him.

"Daschel! It's me! Hunter!"

A tenuous sanity returned to Dash's eyes and he dropped his hands. "What..."

Two more men erupted from the gin house, tumbling into the street with the barkeeper behind them, shaking one huge fist. "And don't ye come back! None of ye, d'ye hear?"

Suddenly Dash laughed. "Good God! Now we're getting thrown out of gin houses. Can we sink any lower?"

Andrew laughed, too, partly in relief that Dash was himself again, and partly because the fight was over and they'd all escaped with life and limb intact. "Shall we collect our friends and be off?"

Dash hoisted Henley over his shoulder while Andrew took charge of Jamie. They went back toward Petticoat Lane—the nearest place they'd find a coach for hire.

Dash began to chuckle. "Damn, that was fun."

A month ago, even a week ago, Andrew would have agreed, but tonight had seemed excessive. From Jamie's drinking to Dash's beating of the nameless drunk, there seemed to be no purpose to any of it. Maybe, if he wasn't sober, it would hold more appeal, but now it just bored him to distraction. Had his dissipation finally run its course?

Jamie shrugged Andrew's hand away. "I can walk, Drew. I might have drunk prodigious quantities of gin, but I can still stand on my own."

Andrew gave him a wry smile. "No doubt, brother, but perhaps I need someone to lean on."

"Ah," Jamie nodded, "glad to help, then."

Dash snickered and shifted Henley's weight on his shoulder. "We ought to go back and teach that barkeeper a lesson. He cannot afford to offend his betters."

"You're drunk, Dash. You will thank me in the morning."

"I'm as sober as a spinster," he protested. "What say we go whoring after we're rid of these green cubs?"

Actually, the prospect of his own bed was more alluring, but he'd never make progress with Wycliffe's investigation at home. He smiled at the irony. Whoring for king and country? Surely there was something wrong with that, but he couldn't think what at the moment. And maybe he could purge the memory of Bella. "Aye," he said.

Chapter Ten

Bella was certain she and her sisters looked odd in their muted mourning, but Lady V. had been correct in her color choices. The dark mauve did complement Gina, and Lilly glowed in the midst of a rich puce that set her fair beauty off to advantage. Her own grayish plum infused her complexion with a warmth she did not feel.

"Ah, and here are Lord Lockwood, and his wife, Lady Lockwood," Lady V. proclaimed as a tall man took her hand. "Lockwood, may I present the Misses O'Rourke—Isabella, Eugenia and Lillian."

The earl was tall and darkly handsome with lively deep-blue eyes—Bella always noticed the color of eyes these days—and vaguely familiar. Lady Lockwood was quite lovely and carried herself with an unassuming grace.

Bella curtsied, and her sisters followed suit. When she glanced up again, she noted that Lord Lockwood was watching her rather intently. "Miss Isabella, have we met before?"

Her heart began to pound. She knew she'd never kissed him, but he might have noticed her at one of the affairs she'd sneaked into. A bluff was her only choice. "I must doubt that, Lord Lockwood. Unless... have you been to Belfast in the last several years?"

"Alas, no. I shall be certain to send my bachelor brothers, though. If you and your sisters are examples of what Belfast has to offer, I begin to think I would have them married and settled in no time."

"Is that your ambition for them, Lord Lockwood?" Gina asked.

Lady Lockwood laughed. "He will need more than ambition for that task, I fear."

"Perhaps they will not need to go so far." Lockwood looked at their hostess with a quirked eyebrow. "Would you consider introducing your protégées to my brothers, Lady Vandecamp?"

"Charming rogues, every one of them," Lady V proclaimed with authority. "But, as I told your sister yesterday, Lockwood, I could not do so in good conscience without the reassurance that they have mended their ways."

Lockwood guffawed. "So my sister and I are hawking our brothers to all and sundry? What a sorry state of affairs we've come to."

"A state of affairs that you yourself were also in, not so very long ago," Lady V reminded him. "Reformed rogues and rascals can make the very best of husbands, but not until they've put their scoundrel ways behind them."

"Then, alas, I shall have to decline to recommend my brothers. I am certain they could have benefited from such delightful company."

Bella smiled as he gave every appearance of regret. "Thank you for the compliment, Lord Lockwood. I shall hold hope that there will be others who suit your brothers."

"No doubt, but I cannot help but think you are an opportunity lost for one of them, Miss Isabella."

"Lockwood!" Lady Lockwood feigned shock.

Bella shook her head to deny that she'd been offended by his frankness. "Not I, Lord Lockwood. I think I shall not marry this season."

His smile faded and he lowered his voice. "I am sorry for your family's loss. Such a tragedy. Had she been ill long?"

"C-consumption," she lied. Odd, considering her recent activities, how difficult that falsehood was for her. By now she should be capable of all manner of deceits—and all without blushing. And how convenient for her that Lockwood had assumed her unguarded remark had been due to Cora's demise. "But the end was sudden. Had we known...well, we would not have left Belfast."

"I understand, my dear."

"We should be delighted to have you to dinner," Lady Lockwood said. "Is your mother still in seclusion?"

Bella nodded. "Lady Vandecamp has been so kind as to see to our introductions, but our mother has taken to her bed and we cannot coax her away."

Lady V. steered Lord and Lady Lockwood toward the parlor. "Very kind of you. I shall look at our schedule and see what may be convenient. And, of course, I will want to see the guest list beforehand."

Bella and her sisters trailed behind. The Lockwoods were the last of the guests to arrive, so Lady V. would be leading them into dinner soon.

"Psst, Bella!"

She turned to look at Lilly. "Yes?"

"I thought Lady V. was going to introduce us to some eligible men. Where are they?"

Gina covered her giggle with her fan. "Were you not paying attention, Lilly? There were three, to balance Lady V.'s table, no doubt. At least, I hope so. I would be loath to think she had determined these are our future husbands. You met them all."

Lilly groaned. "Not old Lord Simpson? And Mr. Griffin?"

Gina nodded. "And Sir Cedric Hammersmith."

"But they are so old!"

"Hush!" Bella cautioned them in a lowered voice. "Lady V. finds them eminently suitable. If they are old, then their money is old, too. Do not be so quick to dismiss them. They could be quite nice."

Gina cast a covert glance at the parlor. "Which one do you fancy, Bella?"

She posed a thoughtful look. "Hmm. I think Mr. Griffin would be a possibility. He has children from a previous marriage, so I would not be pressured to produce an heir. And did not Lady V. say he had more money than Midas?"

"Drat! He was my choice, too," Gina teased.

Lilly sighed. "I'd sooner meet one of Lord Lockwood's naughty brothers!"

"Yes, I must say they sound much more interesting than those we've met so far, with the possible exception of the young men you refused to introduce us to in St. James's Park."

That was all Bella needed—Gina or Lilly in a pickle with a rogue! Mama would have her drawn and quartered. "Do not entertain any notions in that direction, or I'll lock you in your rooms." The dinner bell rang, and Bella hurried her sisters along. They would have to follow Lady V. into the dining room like good little children.

Lilly held them back a moment. "Did Lady V. mention Lord Lockwood's family name? I would not fancy one of the brothers if they were named Mackerel or Cod. Or something silly, like Mr. Piggly. I would not like being Mrs. Piggly."

"Lockwood's family name was not mentioned, but it is of little consequence. You will not be meeting any unsuitable men. Lady V. would have vapors."

"But the unsuitable ones are ever so much more interesting."

Bella sighed. How could Lilly know such a thing? She had the sinking feeling that she and her sisters were doomed to poor marriages.

The advantage of being the only sober contestant in a bar fight was that Andrew had easily dodged most of the blows. While Jamie was home nursing a colossal headache and a blackened eye, he had nothing more than some skinned and bruised knuckles to show for his part in the fray last night. Ah, but afterward, when he and Dash had found their way to Miss Alice's finishing school, he'd suffered deeper wounds.

Miss Alice, formerly known as "Naughty Alice," had come up in the world. Her place was still a bawdy house—and still catering to every desire, every sin, known to man—but it had become more acceptable with a fresh coat of paint, new furnishings, cleaner rooms and prettier females.

With one hand around a bottle of whiskey and the other around a buxom wench named Sally, Dash had quickly disappeared into one of the upstairs rooms. Andrew had been left to suffer the attentions of women vying for his business in the salon below.

Alas, one after another, he'd eliminated possible companions for the remainder of the evening. This one was too fleshy, that one too skinny. Another was too blond and colorless, while yet another was too dark. All of them were far too eager. And none of them was Bella.

Dash would have laughed if he'd known Andrew's reluctance to chose a companion last night had been caused by his memories of Bella in the room at Thackery's. None of the women at Alice's came close to Bella's odd blend of insouciance, beauty and self-possession.

He admired her fierce independence and even, in a paradoxical way, her defiance. Yes, he wanted Bella with increasing ferocity, and that was a deeper cut than any he'd suffered at the gin house last night.

And tonight, as he waited for Hank in the gin house on Petticoat Lane, she was still in his mind. Was she kissing some stranger in a room at Thackery's? Waltzing with one at a ball? Had she found the "right" man? Or was she waiting for him?

Dash nudged him. "You know it's balderdash, do you not, Drew? Lace is no more responsible for Conrad's death than she is for the Corn Riots. Conrad was muddled by opium and he was making stupid decisions. Had it not been Lace, it would have been another."

How telling that Dash had guessed the cause of his brooding. "But it *was* Lace, and that is the point."

"There is nothing you can do about it now, Drew. Unless you plan to make her pay for it."

"The thought had occurred to me."

A wide grin split Dash's face. "Ah, and how might you accomplish such a feat?"

"I cannot think of anything fitting."

"Come, lad! Think. Surely two such imaginative Corinthians as we can think of something. What would set her back? Make her pause before flirting so outrageously with another naive man?"

"I would hardly call McPherson naive."

"Naive enough to kill himself."

An uneasy chill went up Andrew's spine. McPherson must have been deep in his cups or smitten beyond reason.

"She made light of his feelings. She dismissed him out of hand once she had what she wanted. Why, she even tried to set me against you the night you found me with her at Belmonde's."

This was unpleasant news. "How so?"

"She tried to persuade me to protect her against you. Stand between you two, so to speak."

"Bloody hell…"

"I told her it wouldn't work. And then, quite conveniently, you arrived."

Andrew remembered that night—the night he had declared war on her. Had it been only three nights ago? He hadn't suspected she could be so duplicitous, and that was even more reason to keep his distance. His frustration grew and darkened in his belly like a roiling storm cloud. "I have been chasing her from public places of late, but perhaps I will play with her, devil her with anticipation and apprehension. I will tell her what I know about her, what I've found out, and then I will tell her I am waiting for the perfect moment to expose her. It could be amusing to watch her squirm."

"I had other ideas, Drew. But this sounds interesting. What have you learned about her?"

"That—"

"Psst, 'ere I am."

Hank's whisper caught him off guard and he turned to the sound. "What have you got for me?" he asked.

The man looked harried and wide-eyed. "An' 'oo might this be?" he asked nodding in Dash's direction.

"Might be a friend of mine."

"What you asked about, gov'nor. I found somethin' might be to yer liking."

Andrew hesitated, aware that his inquiry was to be kept confidential. When Dash had followed him here, he hadn't been able to find a logical reason to send him away. He would have to let Dash think he'd made inquiries for himself. "Then spill it, Hank."

The man shifted his eyes to Dash and then back to Andrew. "There's been talk, gov'nor. Talk about goin's on that you wouldn't speak out loud."

"*You* had better speak them aloud if you want more coin."

"Nothin' sure. Just hints. Blood game, like ye asked for."

Andrew ignored Dash's intake of breath. "I'll need something more than that, Hank."

"Some of the local doxies 'ave disappeared, if ye knows what I mean. Gone, and no one knows where. A couple of 'em before, and more lately. Talk is, they're bein' used."

"Used for what?"

"Games, gov'nor. For some toffs 'oo gots a mean streak. An' the charleys ain't doin' a thing about it. Paid off, they is, or ignorant."

Close. Oh, so close. "How do I get in on the game?"

"Couldn't say." Hank backed away, looking at Andrew as if he'd grown another head.

Andrew took two shillings from his waistcoat pocket and jingled them in his hand. "Bring me a time and place, Hank, and I'll pay for it. Five quid. And here's a token of my promise." He placed the shillings on the bar and waited. Five pounds would keep Hank in gin for a very long time.

Hank licked his lips and fixed his stare on the bar. Andrew could almost see his mind working—weighing moral principles against creature comforts. He snatched the shillings off the bar and had them in his pocket before Andrew could change his mind. "Tomorrow night, gov'nor." He turned and scurried away through the crowd.

Silence stretched out between him and Dash, and he did not know quite what to say. Dash had heard every word of his conversation. He turned his attention to his rotgut whiskey and took a drink.

Dash exhaled and finished his own drink before he spoke. "Care to explain that, Drew?"

"No, actually."

"Shall I collect that your interests have...expanded?"

"Take it however you want."

"Come now, do not be surly. When have I ever judged you? This just...surprised me."

"Why?"

"I've always thought of you as, well, more conventional."

"Conventional?" Andrew laughed. "Tell that to my brother. He thinks I am out of hand."

Dash smiled. "He does not understand men like us, Drew. Our rules were forged by necessity. And when the war was over, we brought them home with us."

"They have no place here. We are not at war, Dash."

"No, but the war is still with us, is it not?"

Andrew did not answer. The question had been rhetorical. He tossed off the rest of his whiskey and slammed the glass down on the bar. "Do not worry about me, Dash. I am just restless."

He nodded. "And that brings us back to Lace, does it not? Take her, Drew. Purge your blood of her the only way you can. She knows you want it. She expects it. Hell, she has provoked it. I daresay *she* wants it. Test her and see."

How persuasive his friend's words were, and how seductive it was to be urged to do what he wanted to do anyway. What would it hurt? *He'd* been the one to call a halt at Thackery's. She'd taunted him, and then held her ground.

Yes, she was fair game, and had been ever since she'd entered society. Who knew how many men might already have succeeded?

"I am relieved to hear that dinner went well," Mama said. "And an invitation from Lord Lockwood and his wife—well, that is somewhat of a coup, according to Eleanor. See that you make the most of it, girls. And you, Isabella, mind you keep an eye on your sisters."

Bella nodded, though she needed no reminding.

"Eleanor—Lacy V., that is," Gina amended, "said that Bella handled herself quite well. She said that she thinks Bella will receive the first offer."

"Humph! Lilly is the prettiest now that Cora…" Mama stopped long enough to sniff and apply a handkerchief to the corners of her eyes. "And you, Gina, are the liveliest and most charming. Bella is too serious and educated to charm a man. Too like her father. Why, some days I see him looking at me through her eyes—those condemning, greenish, all-seeing eyes."

Bella glanced away and put her teacup down. She hated when Mama started speaking of her as if she weren't in the room.

Gina, always sensitive to Bella's discomfort, changed the subject. "Dinner with Lord Lockwood is tomorrow night. He said he would invite his sister and her husband. They are quite a force in society and know all the right people. I warrant there will be invitations in abundance after that."

"These affairs are being kept small, are they not? No more than a dozen or two? We would not want people thinking we are disrespecting Cora's memory."

"Lady V. is being most circumspect," Lilly contributed. "She knows all the rules for mourning and for getting on in society."

Bella stood and smoothed the black taffeta of her gown before turning toward the sitting room door. "I am going out for a walk. I shall be back by suppertime."

"Mind who you speak to. You should take Nancy with you, Bella," her mother called as Bella swept her reticule off the foyer table and opened the door to the street.

Yes, Lady V.'s dinner had been a great success, but she'd been all too aware that she could be unmasked with the arrival of the next guest. Mixing in society, however cautiously, was going to be nerve-racking. This had never been in her plan.

And that was the reason she must see Lord Wycliffe again and urge him to resume his investigations. There had to be a way to honor her promise to Cora without shaming her family, but she could not think what. Tonight could well be her last night free of obligations for a very long time.

She had found no solutions by the time she entered the building where the Home Office was located, only more reasons to be concerned. Though the clerk had bade her to sit while he summoned Lord Wycliffe, she had paced instead, unable to calm her nerves. Would she be turned away as a nuisance?

A moment later Lord Wycliffe arrived and ushered her into his private office. There were stacks of papers on every flat surface, including the floor. A massive desk was cluttered with folders, reports and files, and he had to clear the seat of a chair to accommodate her.

"Please, Miss O'Rourke, sit down. May I offer you a cup of tea? I can have my clerk—"

She glanced at a decanter on a bookshelf behind his desk. "I…I would rather have a glass of sherry, Lord Wycliffe."

If he was surprised, he covered it quickly. "By all means, Miss O'Rourke."

She took the glass from him and waited for him to sit. "I am sorry I did not make an appointment, but I came on the spur of the moment."

"Quite all right. What can I do for you?"

"My sister. Have you made any progress in your investigation?"

He stared at her for a moment and then poured his own sherry. "Miss O'Rourke, I thought I informed you that we had exhausted our leads and that we were moving on to cases we *could* solve."

"Then reconsider, sir. My sister deserves justice."

"I understand and I agree. But we haven't the resources—"

Bella hated herself for begging, and for the tears that rushed to her eyes. "If you do nothing, My Lord, I shall have to do it myself."

The man sat back in his chair and regarded her thoughtfully as he took a sip from his glass. "Are you not already doing so?"

Heat swept up from her toes. "You know?"

"I've heard. You are making quite a splash as Lady Lace."

"You would not reveal me, would you, sir?"

His expression somber, he shook his head. "But I am concerned for your safety."

She closed her eyes and took a deep breath. "If you will not resume your investigation, I really have no choice in the matter, but you must know that I cannot go on much longer. I will be found out, and my family will be shamed."

"I am sorry for that, Miss O'Rourke, but the choice is yours."

The tears she could not shed in front of her mother began to flow now and she rummaged in her reticule to find a handkerchief. "You heard what my sister said to me, Lord Wycliffe. You heard her plea and my promise to her. If you will not find her murderer, then what else am I to do?"

He leaned forward, resting his forearms on his desk. "Have faith, Miss O'Rourke."

She shook her head. "My faith died with Cora."

Lord Wycliffe came around his desk and gave her an awkward pat on her shoulder. "Miss O'Rourke, I have contacts, agents whose job is to ferret out information. If I should hear of anything that could help you, I will send for you."

"Only my sister, Eugenia, is aware of what I am about. My mother is completely ignorant of my doings."

"Yes, Miss O'Rourke. I understand. You can depend upon my discretion. If I find anything, I will be careful that it is delivered into your hands only."

It was little enough, but it was something. Bella squared her shoulders and stood. "I will thank you for whatever help you can give me, Lord Wycliffe."

He opened the door for her and stood aside to let her pass. "Please, Miss O'Rourke, be very careful. The men who did that to your sister are capable of anything."

Chapter Eleven

From his position at the *rouge et noir* table, Andrew saw Bella enter Thackery's main salon. She handed the footman her cloak and lifted her chin a bit defiantly. Did she suspect he was here and would challenge her? As to that, he was still undecided.

She took some coins from her reticule and changed them for counters, then climbed the curved staircase to the mezzanine. He could not keep his gaze from her. This was the first time he'd seen her in anything but her habitual black. She was wearing a charmingly cut gown of sleek plum gray that complemented her complexion. Her gleaming hair had been secured at the crown with matching ribbons. Her dress's small train swept the stairs behind her, teasing him to follow. As if he needed such an inducement.

The croupier called the color and Andrew walked away. Bella hadn't seen him, and that gave him the advantage. He took the stairs two at a time and followed her through the glass doors into the salon, then stepped aside into the shadows. Would she give him a reason to stop her tonight?

The men nearest her moved like moths to her flame. She was immediately surrounded by four of them. Perhaps Johnson had told his friends what an easy mark she was. Or, at least, how easy it was to coax a kiss from her. The anger began to churn in his belly again.

Bella sent two of the men away, fair-haired lads from the country, and linked arms with the other two. She seemed nervous, but she kept an unwaveringly pleasant look on her face. The three of them sat on one of the benches and kept up a lively conversation punctuated by laughter. What a determined little tart she was!

And then, just as he'd suspected, she leaned toward the man on her left, who was peeking down her neckline. She lifted her face to his and dropped her eyelids to mask her gaze. The man accepted the invitation and met her lips with restrained fervor. Andrew's hands curled into fists.

After a scant moment she broke the contact and shook her head. She turned to the man on her right and smiled. Was it his turn now? Yes. He bent to her mouth with a confident grin.

Andrew stepped forward. He'd be damned if he'd stand by and watch her share intimacies with strangers. She was his. He had marked her, laid claim to her, the last time they'd been at Thackery's. Pride held him back. And curiosity.

This man's kiss was longer, and he noted that Bella pushed at his chest as if trying to dislodge him. She turned her head, but her companion cupped hers to hold her immobile.

Cold fury ignited in Andrew's gut—whether at Bella or her over-eager swain, he couldn't say. A few long strides had him behind the man in seconds. He jerked him to his feet and slammed him against the wall, leaning in so that his face was inches away.

"Leave the lady be," he gritted between clenched teeth.

"Lady?" the man asked. "Do you see someone I do not?"

From the corner of his eye, he saw Bella's wince.

"The little whore ought not to be leading men on. She'll give me what I want tonight, or I'll know the reason why." He pushed Andrew away with a rough shove.

"Allow *me* to give you a reason why," Andrew said. He stood his ground and delivered a punishing blow to the man's stomach that brought him to his knees.

"Mr. Hunter! Please!" Bella pulled at his coat sleeve. "You are drawing attention."

"And you, madam? Do you think your behavior is circumspect?"

"I...I have more success when you are not present," she said, her cheeks growing bright pink. "I suspect I am in greater danger from you than from anyone here."

His opponent on his knees, gasping for breath, Andrew turned on her. "You put yourself in this position, Bella. What would have happened to you had I not been here?"

She glanced about as if looking for the answer from a stranger. "You...you had no right to interfere."

"No right?" He reached across the distance between them and ran his knuckles across her collarbone where he'd left his mark. "I *own* you, madam." He glanced around the room, noting the faces turned toward them. "Tomorrow there will not be a man in London who does not know it. Who will you kiss then?"

Andrew's opponent lurched to his feet. "Welcome to her," he muttered under his breath and staggered toward the punch bowl.

The color drained from Bella's cheeks. "Why can you not leave me alone, Mr. Hunter? What have I done to you? You are ruining everything."

"Leaving your first two questions for later, madam, tell me what, exactly, I am ruining? Your opportunity to dupe another man? To make a name for yourself? To find a new protector? Is my cash not as good as anyone else's?"

"If...if you want me, you will have to kiss me."

Good God! Did she think that would stop him? *Take her, Drew. Purge your blood of her the only way you can. She knows you want it. She expects it. Hell, she has provoked it.* Dash was right. Her veiled invitation to a kiss was an invitation to more.

No, he would never kiss her. For some reason, she had discounted their first—and only—kiss. But for that single instance, she was done with a man once she'd gotten a kiss, and he could not risk that. He'd deny them both that little intimacy to be certain she was never done with him.

Without another word he lifted her in his arms and carried her out the glass doors and to the nearest corridor. The gossip in the morning be damned. He went to the room at the end of the passageway, kicked the door open and deposited Bella on the velvet coverlet before returning to lock the door and wedge a chair beneath the knob for good measure.

Bella scrambled to the side of the bed and stood. He had his back to her, securing the door. She glanced around the dimly lit room, hoping to find another door or some manner of escape. None but a single window with a long drop to the alley!

This room was similar to the one he'd taken her to the last time they'd been at Thackery's, but the furnishings were all in deep green rather than red. Plush carpeting muffled her footsteps, and thick walls covered in velvet gave her little hope any cries for help would be heard. The window was open a crack and the light curtain shifted on a night breeze. Oh, if only she weren't afraid of heights!

He turned to her and gave her a smile that chilled her to the bone. There was nothing mirthful there, only confident and satisfied. He knew he was in control and he was relishing her fear. There was nothing for it but to face him down. It had worked last time. It would work now.

She held her ground and lifted her chin. "What now, Mr. Hunter? A repeat of the last time you had me alone?"

"A repeat? Oh, no, Bella. I never repeat."

She swallowed hard as he came slowly toward her. "A…a variation of the same, then? But it will not matter. You will not move me, and you will not stop me."

"Stop you from what? Kissing men? Taking on two at a time? Maybe I do not care beyond getting my share."

"Of kisses? Then I win, Mr. Hunter, since you have sworn never to kiss me again."

"And maybe I do not mean kisses when I say I want my share."

"Were you bluffing when you said that you own me?"

"I never bluff, sweetheart. You will learn that about me soon enough."

Everything sensible inside her called for her to retreat, but pride proved stronger than good sense. He arrived before her and reached out to trace the mark he'd left on her throat, covered now with rice powder. "Maybe I want more of this."

She swallowed and kept her expression neutral as his finger dragged downward to the cleft just barely visible above her neckline. "Or this," he said, his voice lowering to a husky whisper.

She shivered, and gooseflesh rose on her arms.

He laughed. "I must say that I admire your ability to keep an unmoved expression, even as your body betrays you. Which shall I listen to, sweet Bella? Your body or your words?"

"M-my words."

He shook his head. "I think not, love. Your body does not lie, but those luscious lips do."

He moved close enough for her to feel his heat and the soft caress of his breath. She lifted her face to him and parted her lips. "I have never lied to you."

"Nor have you told me the truth." His hands moved down from her shoulders and cupped her breasts in a touch so delicate that she nearly moaned. "But look how sweetly these talk to me, Bella. No curses, no dares or defiance, just a mute request for more."

His thumbnails flicked over her aroused nipples through the fabric of her gown, and her knees weakened. How could she let him do this to her? How could she allow him such intimacy when he so obviously disliked her?

Her arms were leaden at her sides, but her tongue was agile enough. "Are you certain you can tell the difference between loathing and desire, Mr. Hunter?"

He chuckled, a throaty sound that sent a little quiver up her spine. "Oh, my dear, you may be certain I know the difference."

Heavens! She hadn't even given him pause!

His hands moved to the hooks holding her bodice closed and they were undone so quickly and skillfully that she did not have time to frame a rebuke. But when he slipped the laces at the top of her chemise, she found her wits and began to back away.

"There's nowhere to go," he told her, following her pace for pace until her back hit the wall. "Interesting, is it not, that you demur when it is too late?"

"Too late?"

"Far too late. Far, *far* too late. In fact, it became too late when you decided to kiss two men at the same time."

"But..."

"Too late for *buts* as well." He tugged the gathers open and freed her breasts, then pushed the sleeves of her gown down over her arms until it fell to the floor before he took one step back to examine the result.

"Just a chemise? No stays? Dear, oh dear, oh dear! Such a naughty girl."

"I...I..." At last she was freed of her stupor and crossed her arms over her chest. "I could not fasten stays alone."

"What? No help? No lady's maid? No...sister?"

She blinked. Had there been a hint of a threat in that word? What did he know about her sisters?

"Ah, well. Never mind. This just makes my job easier. Come now, Bella, uncross your arms. Too late to play coy."

"Mr. Hunter! I insist—"

"Andrew," he said. "Formality seems absurd under the circumstances, wouldn't you agree?"

"I...no! That would suggest a familiarity we do not share."

He laughed. "Oh, Bella, believe me, you are about to earn the right to call me anything you wish."

She shrank back against the wall again. "I—"

"Well, yes. We can do it here against the wall, if you wish, but I thought the bed might be more comfortable."

She glanced right and left, puzzled. "What?"

"This..." He bent and tilted his head to nibble her earlobe.

She caught her breath, half afraid, half seduced by the sensation. His breath was hot in her ear and his faint groan sent a vibration through her.

"Your flesh is so sweet, Bella. I cannot think when I've tasted sweeter. Are you as sweet all over, I wonder?"

Oh, she hoped so, if it meant he would keep nibbling. She closed her eyes and leaned her head back against the wall as he shifted his attention to the hollow of her throat. Lethargy made her limbs heavy and she wove her fingers through his hair to hold him close. She should fight. She should struggle, or at least protest. He could still be Cora's killer. Oh, but how could she believe that when he was working such magic on her?

He dragged the tapes of her chemise down her arms, baring her flesh as he nudged it lower with his chin, kissing his way downward.

Holding her fast by the waist, he captured one aroused nipple between his teeth and gave it a little tug.

"Oh!" Something deep in her belly tingled and awoke a hunger for more. Her knees threatened to give out, but he held her steady, bearing her weight with no sign of strain. He continued his attention to her breasts, first one and then the other, until she thought she would scream with pleasure.

What was happening to her? Why did she not protest? Cry foul? Why did she just stand here and thrill with anticipation about what he might do next? And, oh, all she could think was that Andrew Hunter had been right all along—she would never forget the things he was doing to her. There could be nothing more distracting in all the world. She flattened her palms against the wall behind her, hoping to support herself.

At last he released the ribbons of her chemise, and it dropped to the floor. She wanted to be good, to beg modesty, but it seemed too late for that now, especially when he returned his attention to her breasts before slipping further downward to her stomach as he knelt in front of her. There he ran his tongue around her navel, causing gooseflesh again.

She came back to reality with a jolt when she realized he was unfastening her drawers. "Stop!"

"Not now, Bella, and not for anytime soon," he mumbled against her stomach. And her silk drawers puddled around her ankles.

She groaned with embarrassment. All she was clad in now were her garters, stockings and slippers. He gripped her hips, holding her immobile as he kissed his way lower still. By the time she realized his intent, she was too late to stop him.

"Andrew!"

He chortled. "And there you have it, Bella. We are finally familiar enough for first names."

He stood and lifted her in his arms, the rough wool of his jacket scratching against her bare skin. Lord! He was still completely dressed and she was completely bare!

Well, not completely. He placed her on the velvet counterpane and removed her slippers, watching her intently as he ran one strong hand up her leg to the garter. "Shall we leave them, Bella? A little naughty, perhaps, but then we've already established that you are a naughty girl. Hmm. Embraced between the silk of your stockings, or the silk of your skin? I cannot think which I crave most."

She used her hands to try to shield herself again, which incited another of his low laughs. She could only think of one thing that would stop him. "Kiss me, Andrew."

He blinked, and then a soft smile curved his mouth and the deep brown of his eyes heated her blood. "Oh, I intend to, sweet Bella." He laid one finger across her mouth. "But not these lips."

She puzzled that for a moment while he shed his jacket, waistcoat and shirt, tossing them aside with no regard to where they landed. His boots followed, and then his trousers, and finally his drawers. The burn of embarrassment washed over her and she closed her eyes. She had been wrong all along. *He wasn't bluffing.* He intended to go through with this dare. This challenge. This absurd war of wills.

"You…you win." She struggled to sit up, hoping her capitulation would satisfy him.

"Yes, I do," he said as he pushed her back and came down beside her. "That much was never in doubt. But I intend to see that you win, too."

He kissed the line of her jaw to her ear and then whispered, "Say my name, Bella. Prove to me that you've surrendered."

"Andrew." She sighed and tangled her fingers through his dark hair as he bent to claim one turgid nipple. Oh, the liar! He'd had no intention of quitting. He was only dragging her deeper into his world.

Get up, her conscience warned her. *Flee. He is too proud to follow you.* But her body would not let her. Andrew Hunter had been right about that, too. Her words were lies, but her body sighed the truth. She *wanted* to stay. She *wanted* this deep magic he was working on her, no matter that she knew it was wrong—that this would make her irrevocably unmarriageable. Oh, yes, she would surrender it all for the things he did to her on that green velvet bed. And that made her as wicked as he.

"Andrew," she moaned as he kissed a blazing path downward.

She twisted on the counterpane, gripping the fabric in her fists because she was afraid that if she didn't hold on to something, she would evaporate like morning mist, rising toward heaven with the sensations he created deep inside her.

She gulped when he found a new place to kiss, a place of intense pleasure, and she could tell that he knew what he was doing to her, and that he was taking pleasure in it himself. She was tingling all over, ready for more. Wanting more. Needing more. "More…" she groaned.

He left that place and moved upward and over her, parting her thighs with his knees and drawing hers up to caress his hips. His voice was strained as he whispered, "You do taste sweet, Bella. A nectar unlike any other. Intoxicating…"

He kissed the little hollow directly beneath her earlobe, licking and nibbling until she shuddered with the delight of it. "Andrew," she said again, because she couldn't think of coherent words. Only of him.

Then he pressed downward, insinuating that wholly male part of himself into that vulnerable pocket he had so recently left. His intruding thickness was both terrifying and titillating. "Hurry," she gasped, afraid she would change her mind in another instant. "Please!"

He cupped her buttocks, lifting and tilting them up to him at the same time he pressed forward. "So snug," he whispered, "barely broken in."

She rose to him as he thrust downward, and a sharp sting erupted through her. She moaned. It was done. Finally and irrevocably done. But Andrew's stillness surprised her. Until that moment he'd been fluid, moving, seducing, caressing, creating a seductive rhythm. She opened her eyes and met his dark unfathomable gaze.

"Bella," he groaned in a voice rife with regret. "Why?"

And, absurdly, tears trickled from the corners of her eyes into the hair at her temples. He regretted making love to her. He was angry that she hadn't told him she was a virgin and not the courtesan he'd thought her. And all she could think was that now she truly was as wicked as she'd ever accused Andrew of being. She should care that she had just surrendered her virginity. Why didn't she care?

She closed her eyes against that look and said, "Finish it, please."

He began moving again, slower now, not as deeply, not as urgently. He smoothed her hair back from her face and kissed her closed eyes, her nose and cheeks, all the while moving within her, building the passion and the pleasure again.

His fingers laced through hers, holding her hands against the pillow, a gesture both innocent and somehow intimate.

She tilted her hips up to him again and adjusted herself to the mild discomfort and the fresh anticipation. Andrew's muscles trembled, as if he held himself back with great effort. Instinctively she met his gentle thrusts. He released her hands and began stroking her again, doing the things he'd done before to make her forget her inhibitions. When the building pressure reached a fever pitch and she arched her head back against the pillow, he took long sure strokes, reaching deep inside her until she shuddered with the warm waves of pleasure sweeping over her, leaving a heavy languor in their wake.

Andrew sat on the windowsill, taking slow, measured breaths of the cool night air. He had to clear his head, had to make sense of the last hour.

What the bloody hell had she been thinking? Why had she not told him? Why had she not stopped him?

Ah, but she had tried, hadn't she? The timid *buts* and little challenges designed to stop him. Her hesitancy. Her lack of sophistication. And, finally, her admission of defeat. All the signs had been there, and he'd ignored every last one in his own eagerness and anger.

And worse, she hadn't screamed at him, hadn't cursed him or struck him—which he richly deserved. But the look in those beautiful hazel eyes as tears rolled down her cheeks had been enough to make him consider castration. The memory of her softly urged, *Hurry,* and *Finish it, please,* ripped through him like a knife. She hadn't been able to make him understand, or to stop him, and so she'd only asked him to be done quickly. God! That he could have done such a thing to her...

He glanced back at the bed and at Bella's still form upon it. She'd been so weak and lethargic that he'd covered her and let her sleep. But he'd vacated the bed, knowing his own ungovernable lust would tempt him to seduce her again if he lay with her there. When she awoke, he'd take her home, but first he'd strip the counterpane and take it with him. He'd leave no evidence of what he'd done to her, and the cost would be discreetly added to his bill tomorrow. Then he would lie without shame to protect her reputation, and swear nothing had happened in this room but an argument and a compromise. Because he, of all the cads and villains in the ton, had been the one to despoil her.

He had to make amends. He would give her anything she wanted. He would compensate her, turn over his fortune, find her a husband she could love and trust. Swear to never importune her again. Anything. Just so he wouldn't have to see those tears again.

But his problem went much deeper than simple remorse. After this event, he was even more confused about Bella's motives. Virgin, by God, and kissing her way through the ton! She had committed social suicide. For what purpose? What significance did a kiss have for her?

He could not stop her. He could not interfere. But how could he stand by, now, and watch her offer those lips to other men? He'd have to find a way or be destroyed by it. And if he could not find a way, he would have to avoid her, forget she existed.

What dark irony! He'd wanted to feel again, to experience some remnant of human emotion, so the gods had smiled and given him guilt. And they'd added affection for good measure, but only after all hope of winning what he'd found was lost. Instead of redemption, he'd found a whole new level of hell.

Chapter Twelve

"Thank God you are home!" Gina whispered theatrically as she closed Bella's bedroom door. "Mama woke up near midnight and went looking for you. She was ready to call the watch when I told her that you were sitting with a sick neighbor. *Who,* she asked. Oh, I am not good at making things up, Bella. I told her it was Mrs. Browne, who lives just around the corner and is a widow. Now Mama says she must meet Mrs. Browne as soon as she is well enough to receive guests. She believed me, but I think Nancy is suspicious."

Bella groaned. "Poor Mrs. Browne is about to die from her illness. Or do you think Mama would want to go to the funeral?"

Gina covered her mouth to stifle a giggle. "That would be like her, would it not? But where have you been, Bella? 'Tis nearly dawn. I was about to raise an alarm, myself. And look at you! Was your hair not done up?"

"It…became tangled and I had to take it down." She did not like lying to Gina, but the truth would never do. *I just gave my virginity to Andrew Hunter—that handsome man in the park—and my hair came down.* She went to the window in time to see the coach pull away. Andrew had waited until she turned the wick of her lamp up. Thoughtful? Or merely making certain that she would stay put for the remainder of the night?

The ride home had been awkward, to say the least. Andrew had seemed at a loss for words, and she was suddenly shy. Heavens! The man had seen her naked! What did she have left to hide? They'd barely spoken and barely touched, the green velvet coverlet stained with a smear of her blood wadded on the seat between them. He'd spirited her out the rear door of Thackery's and into a waiting coach, then swore to her that he would never tell what they'd done. He had instructed her to deny that anything had happened in that room but a private conversation.

She knew that he had nothing at risk. He would not fear the censure of society for sleeping with a…a courtesan, so his concern was for her. A part of her—the rational part—was relieved he was being so pragmatic, but the other part cringed with embarrassment and shame. Had she been so gauche that he could not wait to be rid of her? And now that he'd *known* her, was he done with her? Well, not entirely done with her, since he'd promised to find her again soon and discuss her future.

What future? She had no future. She could not even think beyond finding Cora's killer. And it had not escaped her that Andrew still had not kissed her. Before, and all the way through his seduction, he had kissed nearly everything *but* her lips. Why? Was it still a point of honor with him that he had not joined the ranks of those she had kissed, but for that first aborted attempt? She could not count that first night when he'd turned away.

"Goodness, Bella! Are you certain you are quite all right? You have just gone very pale."

"I am just tired, Gina. Exhausted. I long for my bed."

"Do you need help?"

"No! I mean, I can undress."

"Good. Then we had both best get some rest. We have our final fittings at the dressmaker's this afternoon and we are to be at the Lockwoods' tonight by eight o'clock." Gina blew her a kiss and closed the door behind her.

Drat! The dinner party. How had she forgotten that? She would have to think of an excuse to stay home. There was so much she needed to think about.

Because she loved Andrew Hunter—for no particular reason beyond the look in his eyes and the desolation in his soul. Because she'd made an impossible muddle of their relationship with her lies and secrecy. Because there was nothing she could ever do to make things right.

And because tonight, after the dinner party, she'd sneak back to the ton and kiss tall, dark-eyed strangers again.

Andrew fidgeted as he waited for Wycliffe to finish signing his correspondence. He couldn't imagine the reason for his summons, especially given that they had decided to keep their meetings clandestine to avoid speculation by any of Andrew's less savory friends—the ones they hoped to draw out.

Hank was supposed to bring him a time and place for the next "blood game" tonight. He was close to finding out everything Wycliffe needed to end the slaughter, and he was risking that by being here now. But he suspected that Wycliffe had held back some information.

The man dropped his pen and pushed the pile of papers aside. "Thank you for coming on such short notice, Hunter."

"Doxies," Andrew said without preamble. "My source says doxies are disappearing, but you said it was innocent women. In town for the season, I believe."

Wycliffe looked a bit surprised. "Would it have made a difference?"

"Aye, it would. I've been looking for a connection in the ton. You've misdirected me."

"Not deliberately. Initially we thought we had two separate cases. We did not connect a few missing prostitutes with the other women. Without their bodies, how could we know? They could have just run off, or changed their crib. We have only recently made a possible connection, when a body with the same markings did show up. And we still believe the men who are engaging in this…activity…are part of the ton."

Slightly mollified, Andrew sat back in his chair. "Was this why you sent for me?"

Wycliffe went to his cupboard and brought two glasses and a bottle of brandy. He poured for both of them and handed one glass to Andrew. Oddly enough, he did not want a drink, but he took the glass, guessing that Wycliffe was about to impart some unpleasant information.

"I've been told that you have fixed your attention on a woman known as Lady Lace."

Andrew frowned. "What has she to do with any of this?"

"Quite a lot, actually. And I blame myself for not telling you sooner. I simply thought it would be better that way. My mistake."

The first stirrings of uneasiness began in Andrew's stomach. "You cannot suspect her?"

Wycliffe snorted. "Lord, no. Do you recall when I first approached you to help us? I told you about a young woman who'd been raped and mutilated, then left for dead?"

Andrew nodded.

"That young woman was Lady Lace's sister."

Everything inside Andrew stilled as he assimilated this information. What had Wycliffe said? Fresh into town for the season? Good family? But—

"I went to inform the family, and it was then that I met the woman you know as Lady Lace. As she was the eldest at home at the time, I escorted her to the hospital to identify her sister. It was a heartbreaking scene. I think her sister clung to life just long enough to tell Lady Lace goodbye, and to charge her with finding the murderer. To be precise, 'Avenge me,' was what she said. And Lady Lace gave her vow."

Andrew took a drink of the brandy, trying to imagine Bella at her sister's bedside. This, then, was the reason for her trademark black gowns, but was it the cause of the shadows in her eyes, the sudden moroseness and her determined drinking? Ah, yes. He'd done his own share of drinking to forget. "You did not tell me that you found the victim alive. What else did she say?"

"I had stepped back to give them privacy. We had already questioned the girl to find her family, and she had told us that her abductor had spent several days meeting her in the park and wooing her, but that he had lied to her and she did not know his true name. Only that he was tall and dark. You can imagine how little help that was. But I overheard a fragment that she shared with her sister—something she did not share with us. There was something peculiar about the man's kiss."

Andrew's mind whirled with this information. "Something peculiar about his kiss? What was it?"

"I do not know, and Lady Lace has not said."

This, then, was the reason Bella was kissing her way through the ton. She was looking for the man who killed her sister—identifiable only by his kiss. *The right man.* Good God! And he had thought her a courtesan in search of her next protector. Could he have been more mistaken?

"What else?" he asked, fascinated by the way this skein of deceits was unraveling.

Wycliffe shrugged. "It was after I heard the victim entreat Lady Lace to avenge her that she expired. Before I could question her, her mother and two more sisters arrived at the bedside. The rest was hysterics and general pandemonium. I fear our Lady Lace took the brunt of the mother's grief. I am not often given to sympathy, but she had mine that day.

"From her subsequent visits to my office, I gather Lady Lace has been the backbone of the family since her father died a few years ago. The mother is completely incompetent and it appears that the victim was her favorite. She has been rather hard on Lady Lace and holds her accountable for not supervising her sister properly."

"Lace… What is her true name, Wycliffe?"

"If she has not told you, Hunter, I shan't betray her. I owe her that much, at least."

He shrugged. Sooner or later, he'd find out. "When…when did all this begin?"

"We found her sister near the end of May. Lady Lace haunted my office every day for a month afterward, begging for news, but we had none. In fact, we came to believe she was the key to solving the puzzle, and so I finally resorted to telling her that we'd moved on to other investigations, and that we would do nothing further on her sister's case unless we came into new information."

"But you have not abandoned the investigation, have you? You lied to her." And then the full implication of Wycliffe's admission sank into his muddled mind. "You lured her into her own investigation. You let her think she was the only instrument for her sister's justice."

Wycliffe nodded. "We were finding more bodies by then, Hunter. We were desperate. Still are."

"She could have been killed."

"We have taken every precaution against that. I have one of my best covert operatives keeping an eye on her."

"*I* have been keeping an eye on her and I've seen no trace of this operative."

"You wouldn't. He is good at his job. But you are also my agent. I put you in proximity to Lady Lace for that purpose, among others."

Anger began to boil through his veins. "Your plan was to put the two of us together?"

"Aye. I hoped you might form an alliance. Unfortunately, from my reports, you have become adversaries of sorts instead. I hear that you are trying to force her from the scene."

Andrew groaned. God, what he would have given to have had this information a week—or even a single day—ago.

"Then, yesterday, Lady Lace came back to my office, entreating me to reopen her sister's case. She was desperate—almost frantic. She said that she fears exposure once she and her sisters enter society."

"You allowed her to risk her life and ruin her reputation so that you could use her as *bait?* Bloody hell, Wycliffe! Are you man or monster?"

"Monster, no doubt, and I shall pay for it in the next life. Did I mention we are desperate? And what of you, Hunter? Your confrontations have been remarked upon. Desist. If you cannot help her, at least do not hinder her. I am depending upon her to draw the attention of our villain, and I am depending on you to be a gentleman."

One day too late to be a gentleman now, damn him.

"And do not think to tell her my scheme. She would still honor her promise to her sister, but the knowledge that we have people watching her could make her more reckless. And, for that same reason, I do not want her to know that you are involved."

"Then why have you sent for me? It seems to me that you have set the scene and there is nothing for me to do."

"Do not impede her. Assist her or let her be."

Assist her and subject himself to the sweet torture of her nearness and subject her to the danger of his ungovernable lust? Or shun her and leave her to the monsters of the world? Wycliffe included? Damned to hell either way.

* * *

Something was wrong. Andrew knew it the moment he entered the gin house on Petticoat Lane. The conversation was not as boisterous, half the occupants looked over their shoulders to see who had entered, and the crowd parted to let him through to the bar.

The barkeeper ignored him until he knocked on the bar to draw his attention. He came with a sullen expression, as if he'd rather not have Andrew's patronage. Whatever was going on, it had something to do with him. He'd stake his fortune on it.

"What d'ye want?"

Andrew dropped a shilling on the bar. "Whiskey."

A moment later, a glass in front of him, he caught the barkeeper by the arm as he turned away. "What's going on here?"

The barkeeper curled his upper lip. "As if ye don't know."

"Humor me."

"Hank ain't comin'."

"And why is that?"

He wiped a cloth across the filthy counter. "Dead."

Andrew hid his shock. Whoever had got the better of a man like Hank must be skilled and extremely dangerous. "How did that happen?"

"Murder. Knife in the gut."

"Why would you think I would know about that?"

"He was askin' yer questions."

"How do you know that?"

"Everyone knows. Ain't no secrets in the rookeries."

"But how do you know he was killed because of my questions? He could have been about his own business. Someone might have had it in for him."

The barkeeper gave a humorless laugh. "Aye, more 'n a few. But 'twere the way he was found."

"How was he found?"

"Carved up, like I said, and had the beast on 'im."

Andrew frowned. "Beast? What the hell are you talking about?"

"The blood dragon. That's a warning. It means don't go askin' no questions."

Dragon? What had a dragon to do with...*blast! A wyvern!* According to Wycliffe, Bella's sister was found with a wyvern etched in blood on her abdomen. Yes, that would connect Hank with Andrew's questions. He shook his head in disbelief. There was a degree of sophistication in such a warning that would be lacking in the rookeries. Wycliffe had been right to suspect someone in the ton.

He slipped another shilling across the bar. "You've heard of this before? Using a blood wyvern as a warning?"

"Aye. 'Tis the mark of the Blood Wyvern Brotherhood."

This time Andrew could not hide his surprise. "What in blazes is the Blood Wyvern Brotherhood?"

The barkeeper glanced over his shoulder. "No one knows, gov'nor. The mark just appears, and everyone keeps clear."

Andrew thought quickly. After what had happened to Hank, he would be hard pressed to find another snitch. Whatever questions he had, he'd better ask now. "Hank was going to bring me a time and place. Do you know anything about that?"

The barkeeper gave him a look of utter disbelief and turned away. Andrew caught his arm and held him back. "A name, then. Hank told me some of the local girls had disappeared."

"Talk to a man by the name o' Wilson. They was his girls. An' that's all I'm sayin'."

And the barkeeper went back to the other end of the counter. Andrew gulped his whiskey and turned to find Jamie standing behind him. "What the deuce are you doing here?"

"I've been looking for you. What have you got into, Drew?"

"How much did you hear?"

"Enough to be concerned. What questions are getting people killed?"

He shook his head. "Best keep out of it, Jamie. The less you know, the safer you are."

Jamie gave him a doubtful look. "From the sound of things, you could get killed. Seems to me like you need a friend. Someone you can trust."

Andrew remembered another name. Devlin Farrell, the unofficial king of the Whitechapel rookery. He'd helped Farrell out of a scrape years ago. It might be time to collect on that favor. But not until everything else had failed. It was not a good thing to be in Farrell's debt.

He clapped Jamie on the back. "I think we should go see Lockwood. He has rather extensive experience in these matters. Perhaps he will have some ideas on gathering information."

"He's hosting a dinner party tonight."

"And we were not invited? There must be some mistake." He grinned and Jamie laughed. "I am certain he would not want us to miss meeting his guests. Shall we drop in?"

"To what do I owe this sudden visit?" Lockwood asked as he closed his library door behind him.

Andrew assumed a wounded look. "Just came to see how the landed gentry lives. Now that we've been excluded—"

Lockwood rolled his eyes. "Damn. You've caught me. The truth is that we are hosting and introducing Lady Vandecamp's recent charges, new to London. She specifically asked me to exclude my brothers unless I could vouch that they'd given up their wicked ways."

Andrew propped his elbow on the fireplace mantel while Jamie finished pouring them brandies. "Ah, we are too evil to meet these fresh flowers from the country? Well, I own it. And I confess there is little I would find appealing in a country girl, so Lady V. and I are in complete accord."

"And I am in accord with Drew," Jamie said, handing Andrew a glass.

"Then why have you come?"

"Your previous contacts and experience. Do you recall that problem I told you about? Well, I've run into some difficulties. I am not getting the answers I need, and I wanted to know if you have any advice for me. Any contacts I might use."

"My, this is all so mysterious," Jamie said. "What are you up to, Drew? Gads! Is this about Lady Lace?"

He shook his head. "Just satisfying my curiosity. I've heard some rumors I'd like to put to rest."

Lockwood sighed. "If it were as simple as asking a question, Drew, there'd be no mystery, and no problem. You have an advantage, as you are known and trusted by the right people—or the *wrong* people, as it were—but you are not one of them. They never forget that. Still, this is something different. Something more."

"Aye. Then tell me what you know about a Whitechapel procurer by the name of Wilson."

"Ah, Wilson. Nasty piece of work, that one. He'd sell his own mother for a farthing. Rumor has it that he thinks nothing of inflicting a beating if one of his girls comes up short for the night."

Andrew tried to think what life must be like for such unfortunates—living hand to mouth, giving over their earnings to a man who abused them, nothing to look forward to but their next flagon of gin. He tapped his finger against the side of his glass. "And if some of his girls went missing?"

"I'd wager he had something to do with it. Once he has them under his thumb, they do not get away."

"He's capable of killing them?"

"Easily."

"Would he sell them for..."

"More vile use? Aye, for enough money."

Andrew's mind worked feverishly. Had Wilson sold some of his girls for use in ritual sacrifice? And would anyone go looking for them? Or, in a world where life was cheap and everything was for sale, would anyone even notice? But how could he find out for certain? "What would he do with them afterward?"

"Dust heaps? The river? Carts to the countryside? There are any number of ways for a determined man to shed himself of useless baggage."

"Have I had too much to drink, or are you talking about disposing of bodies?" Jamie asked.

"You are best out of this, Jamie. I'll explain later if you insist."

"Have you talked to Devlin Farrell?" Lockwood asked.

"I'll talk to Wilson first. Failing satisfaction, I shall search out Farrell."

"Excellent plan." Lockwood rubbed his hands together. "Then, if that's all?"

"Anxious to get back to your guests?"

"That would be the polite thing to do."

"My, how marriage has changed you, brother." Andrew put his glass down and crossed to the library door. "Jamie and I know the way out."

Lockwood laughed and followed them anyway. Just as Lockwood's butler was handing them their coats and hats, a spate of conversation carried from the corridor. The dinner guests, evidently sated, were crossing the entry hall on their way to the parlor. A group of women with their heads together in conversation nearly ran directly into them. The look of consternation on his brother's face was almost laughable. These would have to be the fresh ingénues to whom Lady Vandecamp did not want Andrew, Jamie and Charlie introduced.

The scent, the slope of her neck, the rich depth of color in her hair—Lady Lace! Half a second later, she looked up—to beg pardon for not watching where they were going, no doubt—and met his gaze. Her color drained and then bright spots of pink appeared on her cheeks.

"Oh! Sorry," one of the sisters said.

"Not at all," Lockwood said. "I was just showing my brothers out."

"Brothers?" Lady Lace looked from Lockwood to him, then to Jamie. She seemed at a loss for words.

When her gaze came back to him, her color heightened even more. He'd have given a year's income to know what she was thinking at that moment. About last night? Or afraid he'd betray her in front of Lockwood and her sisters? Yesterday he might have, but after his conversation with Wycliffe, she was safe enough. From him, at least.

For his part, he noted a slight warming in his own body. Would *she* betray *him?* What he'd done to her last night was little better than rape. Whatever she did, he would deserve it.

But she did nothing. She just stood there, looking lost and nearly terrified. He shot a warning glance in Jamie's direction, and Jamie gave him a barely perceptible nod of understanding.

The youngest of the three girls giggled and beamed a sunny smile. "Goodness, Lord Lockwood, why have we not been introduced?"

"They were…otherwise engaged this evening, Miss Lillian," he said.

"But they are here now."

"On business, and just leaving."

"What a shame. But surely we shall not be deprived of making their acquaintance."

Lady Vandecamp debouched from the dining room and headed

their way with grim purpose. "Ah, here you are, girls. You leave my sight for scant seconds and you are already in trouble."

"Trouble?" the youngest asked, her blue eyes wide as she looked from Lady Vandecamp to Lockwood and back again. "But what have we done?"

"Did you arrange this 'spontaneous' visit, Lockwood?" Lady Vandecamp asked with a skeptical lift of an eyebrow.

Lockwood shook his head in denial. "Quite unexpected. You have my word upon it."

"Ah, Lady Vandecamp, how nice it is to see you once again," Andrew said, trying to keep his amusement from showing as he took her hand and bowed over it.

Lady Vandecamp sighed with resignation. Given the circumstances, she could not very well forbid an introduction without offending Lockwood. There were so many ironies in the situation that Andrew could not begin to count them.

Lockwood bowed to the inevitable. "It is my pleasure to present the O'Rourke sisters. Miss Isabella," and Bella bobbed a barely discernable curtsy, "Miss Eugenia, and Miss Lillian." The other two followed Bella's example. "They are visiting London from Belfast.

"Ladies, please meet my brothers, Andrew and James Hunter. Were my brother Charles here, you'd have met the entire lot."

Isabella O'Rourke. He liked the sound of that. He bowed and smiled. "Ladies, you are truly an improvement on the season."

Jamie, too, offered a bow and murmured some polite compliment.

"And now that you've met them, get on with you," Lady Vandecamp made a sweeping motion with both hands and the girls resumed their progress toward the parlor.

Only Bella looked over her shoulder, a fact that Lady Vandecamp did not miss, although she did miss the fact that he mouthed the word, *later.*

"Do not be forming any designs on my charges, Mr. Hunter. I intend to keep them far away from the likes of you and your brothers. These girls are too innocent to deal with such rascals."

Jamie snorted and then covered it with a cough.

Andrew gave her a somber nod. "I warrant they will learn well from you, Lady Vandecamp. They will, no doubt, snub us at every opportunity. But, be warned. I intend to win your approval."

The social lioness preened with self-satisfaction. "You have a far way to go, Andrew Hunter. And you, as well, James. Meantime, leave the O'Rourke girls alone."

Chapter Thirteen

Later? What could Andrew Hunter have meant by that single veiled word? Bella pushed her curtain aside and looked down into the darkened street. The clock on the landing struck the midnight hour and she shivered. Was he out there, waiting?

She supposed she should be grateful that he hadn't exposed her during the awkward introductions. On the coach ride home, Lady V. had instructed the sisters to be polite to the Hunter brothers, should they encounter them again, but to give them no openings for familiarity. Familiarity? Heavens! She and Andrew had been much more than merely "familiar." If only she could depend upon him not to interfere with her plan.

A shadow moved in the park across the street, then came into view beneath the streetlamp. Andrew. He looked up at her window and tipped his hat.

She dropped the curtain, turned her lamp down and swept her waiting cloak from the bed. A cautious glance into the passageway told her that the house was abed for the night. A faint light shone beneath Gina's door and she almost knocked to tell her where she was going, but she could ill afford an argument at the moment.

By the time she came down the front steps, Andrew Hunter had come across the street to meet her. "Thank you for not disappointing me, Miss O'Rourke."

She blinked at his odd formality and tried to assume his degree of sophistication. "I could hardly refuse, sir. With your constant threat to expose me, I believe you have assured yourself that I will come whenever you call."

"Blast!" he muttered. "I am sorry for that. I am sorry for almost everything. All that has changed now."

"What has changed?"

"Shall we walk, Miss O'Rourke, or shall we hire a coach and have a drive through Hyde Park?"

The night air was chill and damp for summer, but she did not want to be trapped inside a coach and at the mercy of a man who could steal her wits without so much as a kiss. "Walk," she said.

He offered her his arm and she ignored it. Best not to touch him. Even that much could make her lose her resolve. He shrugged and began walking, leading her toward Stafford Row, and then toward the river.

"Miss O'Rourke, why did you not tell me you were...maiden?"

"I did not think...I was not prepared...that is, I had no reason to think you would believe me. It would have been the first time you did."

He was silent for a moment, then nodded. "You are right. I wouldn't have believed you. Your behavior was not the sort that would lend itself to that conclusion."

"I know. My fault, I fear. You must have been dreadfully disappointed."

"Disappointed?" His voice was raw. "Oh, Bella, I can think of other words to describe what I was. *Shocked* comes immediately to mind. Horrified at my behavior. And sorry that it was too late to take everything back."

She cringed. She had been so awful that he wished he could take it back? "I...I know you expected more skill. I tried to warn you—"

"A fact of which I am painfully aware and that I will carry with me to the grave, Miss O'Rourke. I do not expect you to forgive me, and I will understand if you choose to bring charges against me, but I wished to talk to you first about your options."

She looked down at the toes of her slippers, alternately appearing and disappearing beneath her hem as they walked. "Options?"

"There is no way I can compensate you for the loss of your...that is, there are no provisions for replacement of such an item, but my fortune is at your disposal. Name what you will, whatever you need to assure your future, and I will pay it without quibbling. In addition, I swear my eternal discretion. No one will hear about the events of last night from me. If you prefer to bring charges and expose me for the villain I am, I shall confess it without hesitation. If, for the sake of yourself or your family, you prefer to ignore it and that I never trouble you again, I stand ready to leave any event at which we may both find ourselves. Additionally—"

"Stop!" she finally managed to interject. There were so many layers to his discourse that she hardly knew where to begin. If she could have her way, they would not be discussing this at all. How humiliating to have him scrambling to dust his hands of her and to learn what lengths he would go to just to be quit of her! She tried to organize her thoughts and gather whatever shreds of pride he had left her.

Best to start at the beginning of his charges, she supposed. "I did not tell you of my *condition,* Mr. Hunter, because I did not think it was relevant or of any particular interest to you. And when I realized that you were not bluffing and intended to go through with your seduction...well, by that time I had some complicity and, to be frank, I..." She kept her gaze down as scorching heat filled her cheeks. "I ceased to care."

"Miss O'Rourke, you could not possibly know what lay ahead."

"I am not a simpleton, sir. Of course I knew. And I knew that I should be more vigorous in my protests, but, well, I was not, and that is my fault, is it not?"

"No." His voice was emphatic, as if he insisted upon accepting the entire blame.

She ignored him to finish as quickly as possible—at least before she lost her courage for such forthrightness. "So, you see, you needn't worry about paying me off, buying my silence or spending your days in gaol. As to your other offers, I would be grateful if you could keep our indiscretion to yourself. This is not an attempt on my part to deceive, but a desire to salvage what I can of my family's reputation. If you cannot do it for me, then do it for them. And if you intend to avoid me, sir, you will have to change your habits."

"Me? Avoid you?"

"I...I must continue on as I have been. Please stay out of my way."

"You expect me to stand aside and allow you to continue ruining your reputation?" A note of disbelief tinged his voice.

She nodded. "You cannot stop me, Mr. Hunter. You can only make it more difficult."

He stopped and turned her to face him. He seemed to be struggling for words as he adjusted the hood of her cloak and brushed her hair back from her cheek—such sweet commonplace ministrations for someone as fierce as Andrew Hunter.

He hesitated, then shook his head as if changing his mind about something, dropped his hands to his sides and turned back in the direction they'd come. "I will not try to stop you again, but I will not stay out of your way. Somehow, Miss Isabella O'Rourke from Belfast, you are going to have to find a way to deal with me. Now come. It is time you were home safe in your *own* bed."

When all was said and done, it was a small matter to find a man like Wilson. In the way of the rookeries, one only had to know the right people and the right questions.

After seeing Bella home, Andrew wound his way through a maze of ramshackle buildings to one of the worst, and then down a corridor lined on each side with cribs—rooms where prostitutes serviced their marks. And there, in a room at the end, sitting in an overstuffed chair to accommodate his bulk, was John Wilson, pimp extraordinaire. A small lad led Andrew into the room and announced his name.

Wilson's round ruddy cheeks looked like apples when he smiled at Andrew, but he made no effort to rise from his comfortable chair. "Andrew Hunter! I've 'eard o' ye. I knew 'twas just a matter o' time before ye found yer way to my cribs. We got all ye could imagine 'ere. So what is it ye wants?"

Andrew glanced around. Although living in the middle of squalor, Wilson displayed signs of his wealth, made on the backs of countless women. The expensive upholstered chair, the remains of quail and puddings soiling the fine china on a side table, even the servant girl cowering in a corner were all conspicuous displays of Wilson's superiority over his minions.

"You look to be doing well, Wilson."

"Aye, 'tis easy catering to the likes of ye and yer fellows. Such predictable sods, ye are."

"No surprises?"

"Now an' agin. Rare, though. Takes more than ye're capable of to surprise me. Sit down."

Andrew noted that the only available chair looked to be soiled with something greasy. He shrugged. "No, thanks. I'll stand. This shouldn't take long."

"Out wiv it, then. I know ye didn't come to ol' Wilson for the usual. A couple o' girls at once? Mayhap a mixup of lads and girls? Or do ye just have a taste for the lads? C'mon, Hunter. Surprise me, if ye can."

He'd like to surprise the man with a fist to his gloating face, but that would not get him the answers he needed. "I'm looking for a couple of girls, but I haven't been able to find them. Thought you might know where they'd got to, since they are some of yours."

The smile faded from Wilson's face. "You suggestin' somethin', Hunter?"

"What do you think I'm suggesting?"

"I had somethin' to do wiv my girls disappearin'."

"That would be logical, would it not? After all, they were your girls. They did what you ordered. Went where and with whoever you told them."

"Ye got names?"

"Oh, I hardly think that necessary. You and I both know who I am talking about, do we not?"

Wilson narrowed his red-rimmed eyes. "Think yer bein' clever, do ye? Well, whatever yer lookin' for, ye ain't gettin' it from me."

Andrew took a wad of folded banknotes from his waistcoat pocket and held them up for Wilson's view. "I prefer to let my funds ask the questions."

There was a long, thoughtful pause before Wilson answered. "Why do ye want to know? You workin' for the charleys?"

He managed a laugh. "Come now, John. You said you knew of me. Had been expecting me. What do *you* think?"

"Don't know what to think, but I'd bet yer not workin' for them. Ye got friends. Ye could ask 'em the same thing yer askin' me an' get better answers. All I know is that sometimes they goes out fer a job an' don't come back."

"And you are compensated for that fact, are you not?"

Wilson waved one pudgy hand and the light flashed from a large gold ring. Bought with the payment for the last missing girl? He sniffed. "I miss 'em. Wish they'd come back."

"Hmm. But they cannot, can they? Unless they are like Lazarus."

"What makes ye think that, Hunter?"

"Just an educated guess, judging by your new jewelry."

"I don't think I like what yer hintin' at."

Andrew realized he was not going to get answers from Wilson. He should have been more diplomatic, but the man set his teeth on edge. He took a deep breath and reminded himself that Wycliffe expected him to be discreet and to bring back answers. "Very well. Enough hinting. Shall we say that I am in the market for something exotic? Would you be the man I'd come to?" He waved the banknotes again.

Wilson licked his lips and his fingers twitched on the arms of his chair as if he longed to snatch the cash from Andrew's hand. "May as could be. What would ye mean by *exotic?*"

"The same as you arranged before. Your girl would not be coming back."

Without registering the faintest hint of shock or denial, Wilson considered his words for a moment, his focus still on the wad of banknotes. "Ye *'ave* surprised me, Hunter. Didn't 'ave you figured for the like. Some of yer friends, aye. Should 'ave guessed by the company ye keep."

Friends? But it was too late. He could tell by the look on Wilson's face that he had betrayed his own surprise.

A veil fell over Wilson's eyes and he dropped his hand. "I've got nothin' for ye, Hunter. Get out."

What the hell had he gotten into? What the hell had his *friends* gotten into? And which friends?

Bella haunted the parlor, waiting for Eugenia to come down. Breakfast had come and gone and lunch had just been cleared away. Mama and Lilly had gone to their rooms for a rest. And still there was no sign of Gina.

Dim light had spilled beneath Gina's door last night when Bella had returned from her walk with Andrew. She'd knocked lightly, but when she hadn't gotten an answer, she assumed that Gina must be engrossed in a book. This morning, when she'd tried the latch, it was still locked. Nancy had shrugged and said that Gina was "lounging."

Bella was not so certain. Uneasiness sent a little shiver up her spine. She climbed the stairs for the fifth time, stood at Gina's door and knocked. No answer. She knocked again, louder this time as something akin to panic crept into her heart.

"Gina!" she called, not caring if Mama or Lilly overheard.

She heard a thump and an unsteady stumble toward the door. The lock clicked and turned back to allow the door to open a crack. A small sliver of Gina appeared in the gap. "What?"

She looked dreadful—pale and pinched. Her dark hair hung in listless strands, and dark circles rimmed her eyes. Bella leaned her shoulder into the door and pushed her way in, not caring if Gina protested. The curtains were drawn and the room was shrouded in deep shadows.

"Gina! For heaven's sake! Are you ill? You look dreadful. Did you eat something that disagreed with you?"

Her sister staggered back to her bed and threw herself onto the mattress. She mumbled indistinguishable words into the pillows.

Bella went to the window and drew back the heavy drapes to open the window and let the bracing fresh air in, but Gina moaned something about the draperies. Bella closed them quickly and glanced around again for any clue to Gina's illness.

Her gown from the dinner party last night lay in a heap on the floor. Her garters and stockings were in a wadded lump on the dressing table and her underpinnings were strewn across the floor as if she'd had difficulty removing them.

"Why did you not ring for Nancy? Or I'd have helped you, Gina."

Her sister rolled over and threw her forearm over her eyes. "Not at four in the morning."

Bella paused in the process of lifting Gina's gown. "Four o'clock?"

"I must say, I have new appreciation for your stamina, Bella."

She dropped the gown and hurried to Gina's bed, gripped her shoulders and gave her a hard shake. "What have you done, Gina? Tell me where you've been!"

Gina scooted up and lay against the pillows. "I am doing my share to keep our promise to Cora."

"My promise, Gina. *Mine.* You made no such promise."

"I still think it is unfair that you bear the entire burden of avenging Cora. And I think it is making you ill."

Yes, that burning in her stomach was becoming quite familiar to her. And bless Gina for wanting to help her, but... "Nevertheless, it is my obligation. What would Mama do if she lost you, too, Gina? Now tell me what you have done."

"I...I heard some of the gentlemen at Lockwood's dinner party discussing the Royal Cockpits. There was to be a fight last night, and I knew that would be an ideal place to find rogues and gamblers."

"Gina, you little fool! If they were talking about it, they were likely going! Did any of them recognize you?"

"I did not get there," she said, wincing at Bella's strident voice. "I fell in with a group of people outside a theater. It was somewhere in...in...oh, I don't know. My memory is a bit fuzzy. The ladies—demimondaine, I am certain—thought I was one of them, and the men must have believed the same. No one asked who I was or where I came from."

If anyone should see the resemblance to Cora...but no. Lilly resembled Cora, but Bella and Gina were darker and took after Papa's side of the family. "Well, that is the last time you are venturing out. Never do anything so foolish again. Promise me, Gina."

She gave Bella a querulous look. "When you give me the same promise, Isabella."

"Did you..." She sat on the edge of the bed, almost afraid to frame the question. "Did you kiss anyone?"

Gina closed her eyes. "My courage failed me. I could not think how to invite a kiss, and the only man who seemed intent upon having one did not fit Cora's description. How do you do it, Bella? Night after night..."

"You forfeit something of your soul," she said with a little sigh. "But you will not be so foolish again, Gina. Now tell me, did anyone recognize you? Did you find anything familiar in any of them?"

"I do not think anyone recognized me. And we have not been about in society, so how would I know any of them? The man who tried to kiss me was a Mr. Henley. I do not know why, but I did not like him at all."

"Mr. Henley? Was he blondish?"

Gina nodded, flinging her arm across her eyes again.

Andrew's friend. She recalled him from Belmonde's. Or was it Thackery's? She had barely paid him attention, since he was neither dark nor tall. But if he was one of Andrew's friends, Gina had likely found the right sort of group to ferret out Cora's killer.

She rubbed her temples, hoping to banish her sudden headache. "I am going out tonight, Gina. Lady V. does not have anything scheduled for us, and I fear such nights will be few in the future. Please stay at home in case Mama should need something."

"Oh, yes. After last night...do you know, they were drinking the most foul-tasting wine I have ever encountered? I'd rather drink vinegar. I vow that is what has upset my stomach so dreadfully and caused my thundering headache."

Bella gave her a rueful smile. "Oh, I am certain it had nothing to do with the quantity of wine you consumed."

"No. I swear to you, the wine tasted like...like sulfur."

"Sulfur?" Had Gina stumbled into the very group that Bella had been searching for? In all her kisses, she had never found one that tasted bitter, as Cora had said. Could it have been sulfur Cora had tasted? "Gina, do you recall any of their names? Or where they took you?"

"Mayfair? Oh, I am not even certain it was Mayfair," she confessed. "We took a coach, and one of the men gave the address. I did not recognize it, though."

"How did you get home?"

"I...believe they brought me home. My mind is a bit fuzzy on that."

Good heavens! They knew where she lived! Where they all lived! It would be a small matter for them to find out who Gina was. "How much did you drink, Gina?"

"Not much. Or I thought I hadn't, but if not, why would I have such a colossal headache? Things went muzzy. Out of focus."

"These men from last night…were they from the ton, Gina? Can you remember any of their names aside from Mr. Henley?"

"No. Why are you so angry, Bella? I was only trying to help."

"Anything could have happened to you last night. You say you cannot remember, but who's to say you were not…that is, that someone did not take advantage… And you *are* helping, Gina," she soothed. "What would have happened if you hadn't been here to misdirect Mama the other night? I shudder to think what she might have done."

"Nothing happened to me," Gina snapped. "I would know. Surely there would be signs. But time is growing short. If we do not find Cora's killer soon, you could be recognizable in the ton. Why, last night at Lord Lockwood's, his brothers recognized us from the park."

"That will not be a concern any longer."

"What do you mean?"

"Mr. Hunter—Andrew—has sworn they will not tell." She'd agonized over the possibilities and could think of only one reasonable solution. "But the more people I am introduced to, the more likely I will be recognized as Lady Lace. Therefore, despite Lady V.'s insistence that we all attend the invitations, beginning tomorrow, I am going to plead a persistent malaise and retire from polite society. I shall stay at home with Mama every night until you and Lilly return, and then I shall go about my business while you keep watch here. Once I find the killer, I shall inform Lord Wycliffe of his identity and return to Belfast. It is the only way we can be certain you and Lilly will be safe from scandal."

She turned at the door to look over her shoulder at Gina. "Now wash up, little sister, and if you should recall anything at all about last night, come to me at once."

Andrew found Devlin Farrell in the back room of a prosperous gin house on Petticoat Lane. Farrell's was a popular spot and moderately better than the rest that lined the street. One was less likely to be poisoned by the brew they served and also less likely to be stabbed for one's purse. It was certainly a cut above Wilson's common whorehouse, but that was not saying much.

Farrell sat behind a highly polished desk, looking incongruously more like a businessman than a crime underlord. Though his black hair was longer than was fashionable and a dark stubble lined his jaw, his gray eyes, the color of Damascus steel, were sharp and shrewd. Though the sun had set, his day was just beginning, but he was none the worse for wear, and not looking a day older than the last time Andrew had seen him.

He threw his pen down and pushed the inkwell and paper away as he sat back in his chair. "Andrew Hunter," he said. "As I live and breathe. I wondered when I might see you again."

Andrew smiled.

"What do you want from me?"

Some things never changed. Farrell never bothered with niceties and always cut right to the heart of matters. "Answers if you have them. Suggestions if you do not."

Farrell pulled a bottle from a drawer in his desk and produced two clean glasses. "Whiskey?"

Andrew nodded again.

When they both had a glass in front of them, Farrell said, "It has been a while, Hunter. I thought you might have forgotten I owe you a favor."

Andrew suppressed a smile. "I had, until circumstances required it."

"Interesting. What circumstances?"

"Damned if I know." Andrew took a deep swallow of the smooth whiskey—Farrell's private stock, not the swill served at the bar. "That has been the major problem in finding answers. I am only guessing at the questions."

"Give me your best guess."

"Human sacrifice."

He expected a quirked eyebrow, a grunt or some other indication that he'd surprised Farrell, but the man just sipped his whiskey with a thoughtful frown before he stood and went to shut his door.

"And what has your curiosity piqued about that?" he asked when he sat again.

"Rumors. I've heard things but I cannot credit them."

Farrell leaned back in his chair and propped the heels of his polished brown boots on his desk as he regarded Andrew with a speculative narrowing of his eyes. "There's more to it than that, Hunter, or I'll eat my hat. You do not cross the street out of mere curiosity."

"I thought I knew every perversion in London, but this is one I hadn't known. I could want in on such an exotic entertainment."

Farrell guffawed, a rarity for him. "Now I know you're lying. Some of your friends have very little in the way of scruples, but you have not abandoned all of yours."

"Nevertheless."

"And what makes you think I dabble in such nastiness?"

"Whether you do or not, Farrell, I know that if it has been whispered by the smallest mouse somewhere in the rookeries, you will have heard it."

"Sorry, Hunter."

Farrell had the answer to his question, but had decided, for some obscure reason, not to tell him. "Then what can you tell me of the Blood Wyvern Brotherhood?"

Though his face remained impassive, Farrell's eyes glinted hard lights. "So you know more than you're telling."

"You now have the sum total of my knowledge."

Farrell poured them more whiskey, but Andrew pushed his glass aside. "Knowledge is power, Hunter. Those who have it are envied. Resented. Hated. If you know too much, you become a danger and your life is…at risk. Before you ask any more questions, be certain you want the answers, and that you are willing to deal with the consequences of that knowledge."

"I am prepared."

Farrell stared at him for one long moment and Andrew thought he would refuse again, but he finally blew out a long breath and sat forward. "Brotherhoods are the games and trappings of the ton, Hunter. Here in the rookeries, life is much simpler. We do not need the veil of secret societies and brotherhoods. We simply do and take what we want. The men you're looking for are your kind, not mine."

"I've gathered that much."

"As for their game…yes, I've heard whisperings."

Andrew sat forward now. "I need a time and place for the next one. Get me that much and all debts are canceled."

"There's a reason I haven't involved myself in this, Hunter. You see, it has nothing to do with me or mine. It doesn't involve my people, and it doesn't happen on my ground."

"Now *you're* lying. I already know that several of the local doxies are missing."

"Girls go missing all the time. They go home, back to the shires, run off with some foolish lad, even acquire respectable work." He paused, then shook his head as if changing his mind. "But you are right. The women you have heard about are not missing. They are dead. Some have been found by the watch in the morning. Others… well, their bodies were found and given decent burials without sanction of church or state. Their deaths were horrific, even for the rookeries, and we avoid unwanted attention here. We do not want the charleys poking into places they do not belong. We put the warning out, and no more girls have gone missing."

"Were they…did they have any markings? Any peculiarities about their deaths?"

Farrell nodded. "Triangle cut from their foreheads, bled from their wrists, a wyvern drawn in blood on their bellies, and their private parts mutilated. Entirely likely that they'd been raped first. Or during. Is that what you wanted to know?"

Andrew's stomach churned. "Aye. That's what I needed."

"Your turn, Hunter. What are you going to do with this information?"

"The Brotherhood has turned their attention to different prey. Virgins. Girls from the ton."

"So I've heard. But I've heard that it is just practice thus far. I have heard, in fact, that there is to be some special rite performed Friday after midnight."

"Friday? *This* Friday?"

"The thirteenth," Farrell confirmed.

Two bloody days? So little time to stop it? Andrew's pulse drummed in his ears. He looked back at a calculating Farrell. "Get me the time and place," he said again. "*Before* the thirteenth."

"That sort of information is what got Hank killed. Do you understand what I mean about knowledge being a dangerous thing?"

He nodded. "I'll risk it."

Chapter Fourteen

Devlin Farrell's words still ringing in his ears, Andrew ran into Jamie and Charlie at Thackery's. They had come to tell him that Bella had arrived at Belmonde's. He'd been a fool to think she might come back to Thackery's. After what he'd done to her, she'd likely never go there again.

Dash was waiting in the lobby of Belmonde's when he arrived. "Should I congratulate you on chasing Lady Lace from Thackery's? Or should I take wagers on how you'll banish her from here?"

"Do not take wagers, Dash. I will not be making a scene tonight."

"I heard about the events at Thackery's night before last, Drew. You must have set her back on her heels if you can rest on your laurels tonight."

"That won't be necessary. She and I have…come to an agreement."

Dash stopped and gave him a puzzled look. "Agreement. Hmm. Would that agreement include her favors?"

"Do not be absurd. We can barely tolerate each other."

"Indeed? How have I misread you so completely? I'd have sworn you lusted after her like a stallion after a mare in season. Why, when I heard that you carried her out of the salon, I actually pictured in my mind's eye a scene of you playing the stallion and she the rider, whipping your flanks. I've seen this coming for days now."

Andrew stopped at the cashier's box and took a few coins from his waistcoat pocket to purchase counters before turning back to Dash. "Theatrics. Nothing more."

Dash said nothing, just stared at Andrew as if he could unnerve him. Then he laughed. "Good God! You're being a gentleman!" He chuckled again before clapping him on the shoulder and saying, "What? Was she virgin? Bless me, no. Couldn't have been—an accomplished little tart like that."

Andrew merely shrugged his friend's hand off and went forward into the main salon.

"So you had her and then she refused to be your mistress? The heartless wench! Shall I talk to her for you? Or would you rather carry out the punishment?"

"Nothing happened between us. Now keep out of it, Dash, or you and I will come to blows."

"Wouldn't want that, would we, dear boy? Well, never fear. You know I can keep my mouth shut. Have for eight years now, haven't I?"

Andrew clenched his jaw. Yes, Dash had kept his secret, but he never lost an opportunity to remind him of it. And of how much he owed Dash for that favor. Damn.

"Then if you are not here to devil our Lady Lace, come out with me and Henley. I swear, that lad has endless ideas for entertainment. Were you not saying that you wanted something different? Exciting? Something to make you *feel* again?"

Andrew spied Bella across the room standing at a *vingt et un* table beside a tall man. She turned to the man, and even in profile, he could see her smile at him. A knife twisted in his gut. The man was tall and dark, and because of that, he was going to be kissed. Oh yes, Andrew was feeling again. It did not matter that he knew what she was doing and why. Wycliffe had sworn him to secrecy, and he could not talk to her about it unless she confessed it.

"Easy, Drew," Dash, close to his elbow, murmured.

He unclenched his fists at his sides, cursing himself for a fool to have betrayed himself in so obvious a manner. "Ignore me, Dash. I am out of sorts. Not enough sleep."

"So it seems." He offered Andrew his glass and Andrew shook his head. "And here I was going to ask you to come out for late entertainments of the sort you were quizzing Hank about."

This was interesting. He turned away from his study of Bella to face Dash. "Have you found something?"

"Imagine my amazement to learn of your interests. We are men who…well, walk the fine edge, so to speak, but I did not suspect you were looking for more."

"Yes, I know. You've already said you thought me more conventional. Sorry to disappoint."

"Never think it! Why, this opens new territory for us, does it not? And Henley is just the man to find fertile fields. He is out beating the bushes for a hint of excitement."

"I say, did I hear my name?"

They turned to find Henley adjusting the sleeves of his jacket and looking rather smug. He winked at Dash and snagged a glass of wine from a passing tray. "Remember the Whitcombe Sabbath last week? Well, I've found another like it. But I'm told 'tis more daring."

Andrew glanced toward Bella and then back at Henley. "When?"

"Tonight. Past midnight."

"Where?"

Henley shook his head. "You will not be admitted if you come without a member."

"No problem there." Dash straightened his lapels importantly. "Between us, we know damn near everyone. Shall we sally forth, lads, in search of an invitation?"

"I'll catch up to you later," Andrew said with another glance in Bella's direction.

Henley, already halfway to the door, spoke over his shoulder. "Meet us at the Lion and Bear at midnight sharp."

Andrew watched them leave and smiled. As contentious as his friends could be, they were always willing to join him in a debauch.

Bella had been aware of Andrew's presence almost from the moment he'd entered the grand salon. Her stomach burned as she waited for him to accost her or make a scene, but he kept his distance instead. Every time she turned in his direction, he was watching her intently, unnerving her and driving her insane. This new tactic was almost worse than a direct confrontation.

She tried to provoke him by going into one of the alcoves for which

Belmonde's was famous, with one of the men who'd been clinging to her elbow all evening. But nothing. He was standing at the *rouge et noir* table and raised his glass to her when she exited, another man eliminated. But there was still one more man who'd been paying her attention, and one more opportunity for Andrew to flex his muscles.

From the corner of her eye, she noted that he was watching her again when she led the second man toward the alcove. And still watching when she came out several minutes later, having kissed the man, then politely refused more. Heavens! He must be planning something devastating for her. She turned toward the refreshment table and took a glass of wine.

Two sizable swallows had her feeling a bit better before he stood beside her and said, "I see you are still working on that drinking problem, m'dear."

"You will have noticed by now that I never give up, Mr. Hunter."

"Aye. A trait that once annoyed me endlessly. Now, however, I find it annoying for entirely different reasons."

"Do tell!"

"I see what it does to you, Bella. Each time you kiss a stranger, you loathe yourself a little more. I see it in your eyes and you betray it with your glass."

He inclined his head toward her drink, and she put the wine down. She hated that he could read her moods so easily.

"And since it causes such loathing, I wonder why you do it. Again, Bella—why? Tell me. I will not judge you."

How could she tell him why she kissed men if he would not kiss her? If he had been the one— She glanced toward the door, wondering if he'd follow her to Thackery's, but she would not meet his gaze.

He took her by the elbow and led her toward an alcove. Would he finally kiss her? Oh, pray that he would taste as sweet as cherries and never, ever lick his lips afterward. When he sat her down, she folded her hands in her lap. She knew that, this time, she would have to let *him* kiss *her*.

He closed the curtain and sat beside her. "Bella, do you know how much you are asking of me when you expect me to stand idly by while you kiss strangers?"

"I have wondered from the beginning, Mr. Hunter, why you care about what I do. It can mean nothing to you. How many times have you told me so?"

"I have never told you so."

"Not in those precise words, perhaps, but in your every action and demeanor. You blame me for Mr. McPherson's death. You are convinced I am a tart bent on making fools of men. You have tried everything you can, including…well, everything you can think of to stop me and to be rid of me. No, sir. I haven't the faintest notion what I am asking of you. Prithee, what?"

The silence dragged on so long that she finally looked up at him. There was something in his eyes that told her he was as confounded by her question as she. Instead of answering, he turned the question back on her.

"What is it costing you, Bella? I see you reach for a glass of wine when you have finished with one of them. I see your shudders. And I see that none of these men means a whit to you. So what does it cost *you?*"

"A piece of my soul, Mr. Hunter. Each and every one." She answered before she could think better of it, then felt herself coloring with the confession. But it was too late to call the words back now. "And that is my business."

"It has become mine." He took her hand in his. "I will have to kill any man who kisses you henceforth, Bella. Do you want that on your conscience?"

"I am not even certain I have a conscience." Tears burned the backs of her eyes. Surrender her soul to forge on, or surrender her honor to turn her back on her promise to her sister? She looked down at their clasped hands. "You told me you would not interfere with me again."

"I thought I could honor that promise, Bella. But I cannot. Nor can I walk away. There is too much at stake. Too much we have not settled between us."

"There is nothing to settle."

"You are mistaken. Think, Bella, about the potential consequences of what I did to you the other night."

"What consequences? That I can never marry now? That I can never go about in society? That I am ruined?" She paused to give a rueful laugh. "Oh, I believe that was the case long before you carried me to that room. I have ruined myself rather effectively on my own."

"Those were not the consequences I meant."

"No? Then I cannot think what you mean, Mr. Hunter."

He released her hand and placed his over her stomach. "Think again."

Her heartbeat stilled with shock and surprise that he would mention such a thing. *Enceinte?* Impossible. Her monthly flux had only just ended. She looked up to catch a fleeting smile cross his face. Did he find this amusing? "You…you… cannot think…"

"Why not? It is possible, after all. We will not know for some weeks. Meantime, I would be severely out of sorts to find someone else planting on fields I had plowed."

She stood and took two backward steps. "*Plowed?* I am a field to you? What is it you fear? That I will give my favors to another man, perhaps one who *kisses* me, and that you will never know whose baby I bear? *If,* indeed, I bear anyone's baby?"

"Hush," he urged with a glance at the curtain. "You do not want this conversation overheard."

"Oh, of course not. Because we have been so circumspect in the past. 'Twould never do to cause gossip." She lifted her chin and crossed her arms.

He looked torn between amusement and anger as he stood and pulled her into his arms. "You want a kiss, Miss O'Rourke? Would that calm you and win your cooperation?"

A lump formed in her throat as she nodded. The moment was finally at hand, and she was alarmed to realize how desperately she needed him to be innocent.

He smoothed a wisp of hair back from her face as she tilted it up to him, and her heart nearly broke with the tenderness of that gesture. Slowly, with maddening deliberateness, he lowered his mouth, his lips barely touching hers. "On my terms this time, Bella," he whispered. "I want to taste this last forbidden part of you…"

That reference to their night together weakened her knees and she nearly sank, but his left hand, splayed at her waist, pressed her tighter against him while his right hand cradled her cheek, ensuring that she could not turn away. He played with her, denying anything deeper than the light fluttering of his lips as he nibbled hers. When he finally deepened the contact, it was not in a single kiss, but in a series of smaller insistent kisses—coaxing her mouth open, testing her.

Somehow, she found herself responding to his wordless urging, opening to him, allowing him access to her inner heat and tasting his. She closed her eyes, the better to experience the sensations he was evoking. His mouth was warm and sweet, and reminded her of brandy and...and mint?

She moaned, and he surrendered her lips long enough to say, "Well said, Bella."

And then he kissed her again—really kissed her, deeply and oh, so thoroughly. She found herself drifting on an endless sea and lost track of time. She slipped her arms around his neck, partially for support and partially to draw him closer. She fondled the cool silken curls at the nape of his neck and marveled at his slight shiver and faint groan.

He gathered her even closer, until there was not a particle of space separating them, and continued the kiss. She did not want it to end. There was something so very intimate about it, so caring, so deeply soulful.

She was incapable of moving, or of ending the kiss, and when Andrew finally relinquished her mouth, he did so with a series of smaller kisses to the corner of her mouth and along her jaw toward her ear. She opened her eyes again and watched him struggle for control. When his eyes opened, she caught her breath at the emotion they betrayed. He looked raw, vulnerable and hopeful all at once.

And he did not lick his lips. Not once. "Thank God," she whispered.

Luminous tears filled Bella's eyes and he breathed a sigh of relief. He had prayed that, whatever trait her sister's killer had betrayed in his kiss, he did not share it. And her little prayer, offered up without explanation, had been her admission of that.

"Thank God," he agreed, fighting the urge to kiss her again. If he did, he would not accomplish anything else tonight.

He took her hand and opened the curtain. "I am taking you home,

Miss O'Rourke. I have business to be about and will not be able to keep my eye on you."

He was relieved when she did not defy him and only stood with a bemused expression when he draped her cloak over her shoulders at the door. He tossed Biddle a coin and stepped onto the street to summon a coach. It was barely half past eleven, early yet for London, but Dash and Henley were waiting at the Lion and Bear. And this could well be the lead he'd been looking for.

He glanced at Bella on the seat across from him—he dare not sit beside her or he'd give in to another of those remarkable kisses. She gave him a small smile and his heart twisted. He'd give anything if only Wycliffe had told him about Bella sooner. What he had thought to be defiance and brazenness had really been valor and determination. Single-handedly, and as a result of Wycliffe's manipulations, she had taken on the impossible task of finding her sister's murderer in the only way Wycliffe had been unable.

Damn Wycliffe and damn his unconscionable strategy! If Bella even got close to the villain, her life would be in grave danger. Andrew hadn't seen any sign of the "covert agent" Wycliffe claimed was watching her.

"Andrew?"

Her voice was so soft that he barely heard it over the clatter of the horses' hooves and the rattle of the harness. He leaned across the distance and took her hand. Though she'd drawn her gloves on, he could still feel her warmth. "Yes?"

"You realize that kiss changes nothing, do you not?"

He kept his disappointment hidden. He hadn't dared think she would forgive him, or that her kiss had meant anything more than what it had been—a test of his innocence. "Yes, I know, Miss O'Rourke, although I had hoped it would change a few things."

"I...I will still go on kissing others."

The tears shimmering in her eyes nearly undid him. "Why?" he asked, and prayed she would answer this time so they could have it in the open.

"If I do not, who will?"

He tensed at the pain and resignation betrayed by that simple question. "I will," he said.

She blinked and then began to giggle.

"Though it is unlikely that I will have your success," he warned.

"Thank you for your generous offer, but—"

"Nothing generous about it, Bella. I have quite a bit to atone for, and I would think this would pay my account in full."

"And I...but that is not possible."

He tightened his grip on her hands. "I do not think you understand. The choice is no longer yours."

She tugged her hands free and sat back against the leather squabs. "I surrendered a kiss, sir, not my free will."

"Not to put too fine a point on it, my dear Miss O'Rourke, you surrendered *everything* to me *but* your free will, and I now consider those things to be mine. Sadly for you, I do not share."

"You promised you would not interfere with me."

"I lied."

"Then everything is the same as it always was."

"Not everything. You now have my cooperation and whatever assistance you require. Everything, in fact, but my willingness to stand by and watch you kiss other men. I know I've given you little reason to trust me, Bella, but you have my vow that you can. If you could bring yourself to believe that, things would go easier between us."

He watched the expressions flicker across her face and knew she was struggling with herself. God knew she had no reason to trust him, and less to believe his word that she could. And yet he hoped, for the sake of that one kiss, that she would manage it.

"There is a man," she began. "I will know him only by his kiss. I must find him."

It was a start. "What will you do when you find him?"

"I shall report him to the authorities."

"Why?"

"He is a murderer."

He leaned forward again. "How do you know this, Bella?"

Her pause was longer this time. He could only imagine how difficult this was for her. "He...he murdered my sister."

He gave her a look of deep sympathy, relieved that she had finally bridged the gap that had separated them. "May I assume my kiss has exonerated me?"

She closed her eyes and the dark fans of her lashes were spiked with unshed tears. "Yes."

He reached across the distance and touched her face, stroking her cheeks with the pads of his thumbs. "I wish I'd kissed you sooner, Bella."

She nodded. "I tried."

He groaned, remembering those times. "You have my apology for my ungentlemanly behavior."

"But you see now, do you not, that I must continue? The authorities have given up, and if my sister is to have justice, it depends upon me."

Blast Wycliffe and his lies! If it were not for the other murders, he would tell her everything. "I shall find another way. I cannot allow you to trade your honor for your sister's."

"What honor?" The question had been delivered more like an accusation, and she looked immediately contrite.

He took a deep breath. "Another thing we shall remedy once this is over."

"Do you know of some potion to drink? A magical spell that will restore it?"

"I know a ritual that will set things straight."

Her expression of disbelief did not change. Either she did not realize he had just proposed, or she chose to ignore him. Well, perhaps that was best for the moment. She already had enough to think about.

They reached the corner of James Street, and the coach pulled up as Andrew had instructed. He hopped down and turned to lift Bella to the street. She braced herself with her hands on his shoulders and when he set her on her feet, she looked up at him. Faith! She was so beautiful, so vulnerable. How could he let her go?

He held her at arm's length. If he gave in to temptation, he'd miss his appointment at the Lion and Bear. He wasn't doing this for Wycliffe now, but for Bella.

"I'll wait until I see you are safe inside," he whispered, turning her around and giving her a little push in the right direction. "I will meet you tomorrow at Belmonde's."

Chapter Fifteen

The Lion and Bear was located on a dark street in the rookeries of St. Giles. Even at midnight, there was no cessation of crime, noise, commerce or drunkenness. Andrew had dodged a pickpocket, refused a street doxy and turned down the purchase of a jeweled snuff box from a street urchin by the time he reached the tavern and pushed his way through an unwashed crowd to find Dash.

But Dash and Henley were not alone. Somewhere along the way, they had collected Jamie, Elwood, Charlie and Throckmorton. Dash waved him to their table near the back of the public room.

"Here you are at last," Henley said. He poured a measure of wine into a waiting glass. "You've got some catching up to do, Hunter. No one goes sober, I'm told."

Andrew cast a suspicious glance at the rest of them. Elwood and Throckmorton appeared deep in their cups, Dash and Jamie did not seem much the worse for wear, but Charlie and Henley looked to be well on their way to oblivion. He lifted his glass, took a drink and winced.

"For the love of God, Henley, did you bring a special brew?" He studied the bottle, but it looked like any other wine bottle. "I can understand the salacious appeal of brimstone at a Sabbath, but why imbibe the concoction before we must?"

"To put us in the mood, my good man. Come, there is not so much in the wine as last time."

Andrew couldn't say. He had only a fuzzy memory of the last

Sabbath he'd attended. Could it be only little more than a week ago—the night he'd met Bella? "I daresay they will give us more to drink once we begin," he murmured, taking another cautious sip.

"Aye, there's always free-flowing wine at such events," Jamie agreed as he finished his glass and shuddered.

Dash merely sipped his and smiled, and suddenly Andrew wondered if he could be Wycliffe's covert agent. Why not? He was frequently around, had taken more than a passing interest in Andrew's supposed flirtation with Bella, and had seemed as interested in blood games as he had. The thought amused him because, after the questions he'd asked, Dash would be wondering if he was the man the Home Office was looking for.

"You look like the cat who swallowed the canary," Dash said.

"Not quite, but I believe I'm creeping up on the cage."

Dash laughed and raised his glass again before pulling his watch from his waistcoat pocket. "Drink up, lads, and there'll be time for another before we must be off."

Andrew tipped his chair back on two legs as Dash filled their glasses. "I am curious, Henley. Where did you learn of this event? It has been kept on the hush, from what I hear."

"This one? Why this one is just a—" He broke off with a frown. "Should be amusing," he finished.

Dash poured a little more wine into Henley's glass. "Tell us the rules, Henley."

"We are to enter through a secret door, don black robes and keep the cowls raised to protect identities. When we enter the chamber, we are to cease talking and remain silent but for the chants."

"Gads!" Jamie gave Henley a belligerent look. "Who do these people think they are? Seems like a lot of trouble over a lark."

"I do not believe this is a lark to them," Dash said. "They seem to be quite serious, do they not?"

"They're some kind of secret brotherhood or something." Henley took another sip from his glass and shrugged. "I wouldn't ask them too many questions, were I you. We are only allowed because of Hunter and Dash."

Brotherhood? Andrew straightened in surprise. There it was again, the reference to a secret brotherhood. *Blood Wyvern Brotherhood.* He covered his surprise and shrugged. "What? Do I know these people?"

"They know you and Dash by reputation, so they think they can trust our group. I wouldn't want to disappoint them."

Dash grinned and ruffled Henley's hair. "Why, Henley! Are you afraid? Or merely jealous?"

"Neither, you dolt." He held up one hand for silence. "There's more."

Charlie groaned and rolled his eyes. "If I drink much more of this wine, I won't recall a single rule."

"At the beginning of the ceremony, there is an oath of fealty and secrecy. After that, we're to follow the chants, and drink from the chalice each time it's passed around the circle. You're to watch the master and do as he does."

Throckmorton snorted. "Master? We are supposed to swear fealty to some oaf in a monk's robe? Lord, this is rather more amusing than I'd thought."

"Sounds satanic," Jamie said.

"More like a witches' coven." Andrew forced down a bit more of the bitter wine. He looked around the table and wondered which of them, if any, were involved in this. "One o' yer friends," Wilson had said, and that warning had been echoed by Devlin Farrell.

Dash stood and dropped some coins on the table while Henley corked the wine bottle to take with them. "Witches, Satanists, mysterious brotherhoods—it's all nonsense. Mere taradiddle to lend cachet to the proceedings."

Andrew silently agreed with him. Whatever was going on at the ceremony tonight was not likely to have anything to do with worship of any kind and was far more apt to be sponsored by some tonish dilettante rather than the group he was looking for. A large number of clubs participating in lewd ceremonies and orgies had sprung up of late.

They entered the street, and a surge of excitement coursed through him. Whatever was to come of this night, it was bound to be interesting.

Charlie sneezed. His words were slurring together when he asked, "Where you taking us?"

Henley glanced over his shoulder as he led the way. "Not far, if we cut through St. Giles churchyard."

They walked in silence for a time, then cut across the churchyard as Henley suggested and found themselves at the door of a warehouse. The lack of a more conventional location bothered Andrew. The "passion plays," as he thought of the salacious ceremonies, were almost always held in ruined abbeys, mausoleums or tombs beneath deserted churches. Warehouses were easily changed—easily converted and easily vacated. And harder to find. He'd be willing to wager that this location would never be used again after tonight.

Henley knocked three times and the door was opened by a robed figure. The cowl was deep and drawn far forward, so Andrew couldn't tell if their host was male or female. The figure swept one hand toward the interior where a single candle burned, the light swallowed by a yawning darkness.

Following previous instructions, no one spoke. They were led to a small anteroom where another single candle burned in a lantern suspended from the high ceiling and black hooded robes were hung on pegs along one wall. The candle flickered and Jamie stumbled, disoriented by the shifting light. Andrew began to feel slightly dizzy himself.

Charlie leaned against one wall as he shed his jacket and struggled to pull a robe over his head. If Andrew was any judge, his brother was quite a bit the worse for drink. There would be more wine during the ceremony and Andrew looked forward to it. The bitter brew from the tavern had left him thirsty. He hung his jacket on a peg and struggled into a robe, then took the bottle from Henley so he could do the same. Before he realized what he was doing, he'd pulled the cork and taken a deep swallow. By the time he glanced around again, he could not recognize a single one of them. Their robes guaranteed anonymity.

Another robed figure appeared to lead them down a steep flight of uneven stairs. He nearly tumbled headlong when someone ahead of him stumbled, and he threw himself backward to compensate.

The room below had been a cavernous storeroom. Now it was empty but for an altar draped in a crimson cloth and a dais behind it with a raised throne. Upon the throne sat a woman dressed only in filmy white gauze, which hid nothing. Every curve, every subtle shade, was clearly visible. The woman's chestnut hair was unbound and fell in waves all around her—truly her crowning glory. She appeared nervous but unafraid. There was something oddly familiar about her and he tried to recall if he'd met her before or had seen her in passing. But then she smiled and exposed a few broken teeth. No, he would have remembered such a thing. She blurred in his field of vision and he shook his head. There was something he couldn't quite grasp, something just out of reach—

Their host led them in a circle three times around the altar, and Andrew noted two wickedly sharp blades laid crosswise at the long ends of the altar. Behind them, a brazier blazed to life, adding to the dark magic atmosphere. Incense permeated the air and Andrew realized that whoever had produced this passion play was a dab hand at showmanship.

Throckmorton's giggle, an absurd sound in this setting, came from somewhere behind him. A new figure clad in a robe as crimson as the altar came forward out of the darkness. This must be the "master" Henley had told them about. He held a large chalice in both hands and lifted it to the woman on the throne, who drank deeply and gave it back. Then the chalice was handed to the man closest to the master to begin the ritual passing of the cup to symbolize their brotherhood. Their robes made it impossible to identify any participant, and Andrew had lost track of where Charlie and Jamie were. The diminutive size of some of the participants hinted that they might be females.

The woman on the throne stood and spread her arms wide, the filmy gauze draping from her slender figure like some present-day Egyptian princess. "Drink deep, My Lords, before laying claim to me, your vessel."

There it was again—that out-of-place feeling of familiarity. He narrowed his eyes and peered at her again. Through the gloom and the rising smoke from the brazier, she looked like…almost like…Bella?

"Malaise?" Lady V. repeated with an elegant lift of her eyebrows. She glanced around at Lilly and Gina, too, as if to include them in her annoyance. "You haven't time for such niceties. As I have repeatedly told you, your entire future depends upon making a favorable impression this season."

Bella put her teacup aside and smoothed the fabric of her napkin over her lap. A glance at the parlor door, slightly ajar, told her that Nancy was eavesdropping and would probably report to Mama. "I am grateful for your concern, Lady Vandecamp, but I do not feel in the least amusing or engaging."

"I understand your loyalty to your sister, Isabella, but you mustn't squander the scant time left to you. You must pull yourself together and make appearances."

"Surely I will not attract attention when I am in such a funk."

"That is not so. Why, I have had an inquiry about you already."

She tried to think what man from Lady V.'s dinner or Lord Lockwood's small party could have had the slightest interest in her. None of them had made a lasting impression on her—at least, not lasting enough to be recalled now. "I…think you must be mistaken, madam. No one has paid me more than passing interest. Perhaps you misunderstood and it was Eugenia or Lillian they inquired about."

Lady V. sniffed. "My mind is not gone yet, child. I think I know who I have had discourse about. And I give you fair warning that I have granted Mr. Franklin permission to call upon you. Properly chaperoned, of course."

"Mr. Franklin? Our factor?"

"Yes. It seems he finds you sensible and intelligent. I have had my husband make inquiries, and he is quite well off. He could make you very comfortable, Isabella, and your mother, too, if she should choose to reside with you. I would not dismiss him out of hand when he comes to call."

Her head swam. Mr. Franklin? But they had never exchanged a single social sentence. They had only discussed business. The man was presentable, for all that he was at least twenty years her senior. But… But he was not up to the standard against which she measured men. Andrew Hunter.

"There, there, Isabella." Lady V. leaned forward and patted Bella's hands as they lay in her lap, still smoothing the napkin. "He is not such a bad match. I think you might be able to do slightly better, but Mr. Franklin is settled. He has need of children, and you are young enough to give him that. You could do worse than a man who would cosset and spoil you. Only give him a chance to woo you. Then, if you cannot bear the thought of marriage to him, I will not press you, though your mama has already given approval of the match."

"You have not told him that, have you?"

"No, of course not. But I have given him permission to call upon you this afternoon. I will expect you to receive him and to be civil. Eugenia, you will chaperone, of course."

Gina's lips twitched as if she were trying to keep a straight face. "Of course," she agreed.

"And you, Lillian," Lady V. said, turning her attention away from Bella for the moment. "I've had inquiries about you, as well. But I think you can do better. Thus far, Lord Olney is the only one I've given permission to address you. He is the Duke of Rutherford's heir. Just think! You could become a duchess. Do be on your best behavior, Lillian."

Bella nearly choked when she saw Lilly give Lady V. one of her innocent smiles. "Always, Lady V. But, as Lord Olney is nearsighted, he will likely be pleased if he can just see me."

Lady V. sniggered. "Now, Lillian, he is not as blind as all that." She stood and drew on her gloves. "Isabella, I will excuse you from tonight's activities, but I will expect you to be up to form tomorrow, do you understand?"

Oh, she understood, well enough. She'd need to think of another excuse for tomorrow. "Yes, madam."

"Good. Now, Lillian, if you would see me out? I would like a few private words with you regarding Lord Olney."

Gina waited until they were gone, then closed the parlor door. "Shh. I do not want to be overheard."

"Please do not tease me about Mr. Franklin, Gina. I am not in the mood."

"I did not intend to tease. You have not told me about last night. What happened?"

"I have eliminated a few others. And Andrew Hunter."

"Oh! You kissed him at last? How was it, Bella?"

Wonderful. Entrancing. Breathtaking. Compelling. "I believe he has some experience in the art."

Gina giggled. "That good, eh?"

"I have no intention of discussing Mr. Hunter's kiss with you."

"I wonder if his other brothers kiss as well as he."

"Do not even think it, Gina!"

She giggled. "I am teasing you, Bella. Where have you left your sense of humor?"

In a ward at Middlesex Hospital. "Is that all you wanted to know? Because—"

"No. You asked me to tell you if I recalled anything else from that night. I feel so awful that I can barely remember. I have never been so besotted with drink before. I still cannot imagine what it was."

"What is it you remember, Gina?"

"I have some rather spotty memories. One of the men asked me where they might find me, but I believe I only shook my head and refused to answer. Then—oh, I am certain I am imagining it—but I vaguely recall Mr. Henley asking if I was virgin. Heavens! Why would anyone ask such a question?"

Bella felt as if someone had hit her in the stomach. She braced herself with one hand on the back of a chair. Henley? But he was blondish and shorter than Papa. How could he…but he was Andrew's friend. Who else was in that group? Andrew's brothers—all of them—and Lord Humphries, and Mr. Throckmorton.

"Bella? Are you ill?"

"What…how did you answer that question, Gina?"

"Why, with the truth, of course. Though I do not know if they believed me. After all, when you consider my boldness in joining them—"

She seized Gina's arms and squeezed as tight as she could to convey her urgency. "Listen to me, Gina. It does not matter that you did not tell them where to find you—in the end they brought you home. They know! You must not leave the house unless you are with Lady V. And do not allow Lilly to leave, either. *They know where we live,*" she repeated.

"Why does that matter, Bella? They will not come calling."

"I…I do not know. I…it is just a feeling I have. Caution will cost us nothing. Please, promise you will keep safe."

Gina's face softened and she pulled Bella into her arms to give her a comforting hug. "You are overwrought, Bella. 'Tis only natural after losing Cora and going about kissing men. But of course I will keep safe."

* * *

Andrew sat on the edge of his bed staring down at the clothes he'd worn last night. Somehow, he'd managed to get home and undressed by himself. His standing order to Edwards was to not wait up and not to disturb him unless he rang.

His temples throbbed and he could not rid himself of the taste of brimstone. What the hell had happened? He had no memory beyond Bella…no, not Bella, but somehow Bella. A woman who looked like her? She'd stood from the throne at the head of the altar and issued some kind of invitation as if she had rehearsed the words. Then… there were bits and pieces just out of reach, but mostly a black void. The night was lost to him. He was certain he hadn't had that much to drink. And he'd begun to feel the effects long before the Sabbath began. Blast! The wine at the Lion and Bear had been drugged. Add to that the wine at the Sabbath, and it was a wonder he could remember anything at all.

"Christ have mercy!" He stood and staggered to the washstand and splashed water on his face, hoping to dispel the last of the cobwebs from his mind. His headache was eerily like those he'd had when he'd taken opium.

His stomach churned as he bent to examine his clothes. They smelled of the sickly sweet incense and there were drops of something dark and stiff on the bottom of his trousers—the only part of his clothing that had been exposed beneath the black robes. He touched it, and knew it was not mud or tar. He'd seen enough blood, wet and dried, to know it now. But how had he gotten blood on his clothes?

A quick glance at his boots told a similar story. Damn! If his head did not ache so much, perhaps he could remember something. And yet he dreaded knowing. It was enough to know what he was capable of—and he was easily capable of killing.

Jamie and Charlie! Bloody hell! He needed to find them.

Unshaven, bleary-eyed and wrapped only in a woollen robe, Jamie entered his study. The relief Andrew felt at finding his brother faded quickly with his words.

"Have the decency to leave us to our rest, Drew. How the hell do you do it? Carousing all night and still up in the morning?"

"Charlie? Is he here?"

Jamie's hand shook as he reached for the wine decanter. "Aye. But he's considerably the worse for wear."

"Coffee," Andrew suggested.

His brother replaced the decanter and shook his head. "I've never felt like this, Drew. I swear I didn't drink so much as to be so thoroughly foxed."

"Not foxed. Drugged."

Jamie slumped into a chair and buried his head in his hands. "Damn," he mumbled. "Knew it had to be something like that. Why aren't *you* home with a big head?"

"Experience. The headache will ease but leave you craving more. I'd advise against it."

"Have you warned the others?"

"Dash will recognize the headache. Throckmorton and Henley—" he paused and shrugged "—will fend for themselves. I needed to know that you and Charlie were home safe."

"Odd choice of words. I just assumed…well, if not you, who got us home?"

"Likely we got ourselves home, or someone tumbled us into a coach and gave our addresses. What do you remember, Jamie?"

"Precious little." He raked his fingers through his tousled hair. "The Lion and Bear is fairly clear, though I recall feeling a bit lightheaded. Could just have been the noxious wine."

But if the drug had been given to them at the Lion and Bear, and if the sulfur had been added to disguise the opium, then Henley…

"Tell me everything you remember, Jamie, no matter how inconsequential."

"I recall walking to the warehouse, cutting through St. Giles churchyard, but once we were there, things began to go out of focus. I remember changing into the black robes. I remember someone leading us down to the storeroom, and how the place had been made into a makeshift tomb. I am certain we marched around an altar and drank more from the chalice. And…was there not someone in a red robe we all hailed as the master?"

Andrew nodded, relieved that Jamie's recollections agreed with his own. "I thought I saw Isabella O'Rourke there."

Jamie's eyes widened. "No! I do not recall that at all. There was a woman, though. She might have…yes, she looked like Miss O'Rourke. Same color hair and slender build. But this woman was clearly a tart hired for the occasion."

"How can you be certain?"

"She had a coarseness about her. And no sense of modesty. It was clear that she was offering herself to the participants of the ritual. Something about being our vessel. Your Miss O'Rourke would never have behaved in such a manner."

And this was where Andrew's memory failed him. Pray Jamie remembered more. "And then?"

"Then things blurred. I recall stumbling and someone catching my arm. Thought it was you, but it was impossible to recognize anyone in those damn robes."

It could have been him. If the amount of opium was carefully controlled, one could remain in control of one's body, but all sense of propriety and morality, along with memory, would be gone. He nodded for Jamie to continue.

"I can see her standing on the altar, and then dropping that filmy thing she was wearing. Then there was a monotonous nonsensical chant we were all forced to repeat. Then I began to lose all sense of reality. 'Twas like…like being in some sort of trance. Our 'vessel' knelt and did obeisance to the master. And then…I do not remember anything. I just remember thinking that I did not care who had paid her, or how much, I did not want to participate in that part. Never have liked sharing my women. I cannot think how I used to find these things amusing, and now they are just…silly."

Pray it was no worse than silly. But there was still the blood to account for. "Examine the things you wore last night, Jamie. Have Charlie do the same. Let me know if you find anything unusual."

"What are you thinking, Drew?"

"I am thinking we had better stick together in this. If anyone asks, we just say we drank too much and cannot remember anything. And, meantime, trust no one. No one, Jamie."

"Do you not think it is time for you to tell me what you are doing? I know you are up to something."

"I'd rather not say at the moment. Just let me know if you find any-thing. I have some other people to see. I will find you later."

Jamie gave him a sardonic smile. "Much later, if you please."

Chapter Sixteen

Clearly, Mr. Franklin was not accustomed to wooing. He appeared awkward and ill at ease, and stumbled over his words. She found that he'd been ever so much more entertaining in his business environment. There was, it seemed, a very good reason Mr. Franklin was unmarried. He had no social skills.

Bella poured him another cup of tea while Gina sat near the fire, her back to them as she read a book. Every once in a while her shoulders would shake as she suppressed a laugh at the awkward conversation. She wondered how much longer Mr. Franklin would stay, considering that he'd said little and merely cleared his throat for the past five minutes.

"I...er, am glad your family has decided to stay in London until September, Miss Isabella."

"Yes, well, the weather has been obliging. I do long for the coolness of the countryside, however. I have been trying to persuade Mama to take a little jaunt for her health. Do you ever visit the shires, Mr. Franklin?"

"My family hails from Devon. I visit them twice a year. My sisters are situated there, and my nieces and nephews."

The bell rang and Bella prayed for some timely interruption. Anything to spare Mr. Franklin from her own awkwardness. Perhaps if they talked about leases and the family funds?

Nancy opened the parlor door and gave Bella a reproving stare.

"There is a Mr. Hunter here to see you, Miss Isabella. I informed him that you were engaged, but he says he will not leave until he sees you."

Gina came to her feet and turned toward them. "Do show him in, Nancy."

Bella could scarcely catch her breath. Which Mr. Hunter? And, heaven help her, if it was Andrew, why had he come? He knew Lady V. had excluded him from her "acceptable" list.

Nancy turned and gave a little exclamation when she collided with Andrew Hunter. He had not waited at the door, but had followed her. Nancy slipped around him and hurried off in a huff—to tell Mama, no doubt.

Mr. Franklin stood and Bella followed suit. Andrew's face, when he noted her caller and the teapot, registered astonishment. He removed his hat and gave a polite bow. "I am sorry to interrupt, Miss Isabella, but I needed to see you."

"I, ah, I should be going," Mr. Franklin said with a brief glance between her and Andrew. He turned to Bella and bowed. "I shall come again at a more opportune time, Miss Isabella. Please tell your mother I asked after her health." They all stood suspended in time as Mr. Franklin made his exit and closed the parlor door behind him.

Andrew came forward, looking as awkward as Mr. Franklin had been. "I, literally, needed to see you."

Her heart fluttered. How touching to have him in her parlor instead of a ball or a gaming hell—so ordinary, and yet so foreign at the same time. She couldn't think what to say or do.

Gina filled the void. "Tea, Mr. Hunter?"

"I cannot stay long. I am sorry if I interrupted."

Gina laughed. "We are in your debt, sir. Now, I hope you will forgive the impropriety, but I must chase after Nancy before she arrives at Mama's door."

Alone, Andrew came to Bella and searched her face with an almost desperate expression. "I had a dream…no, I was confused. I thought I might have seen you last night after I brought you home, and I needed to assure myself that you were well."

"Where did you think you saw me?"

"You do not want to know, Bella. But thank God you are safe." He breathed a deep sigh and looked out the window. Mr. Franklin's gig was pulling away from the steps. "It never occurred to me that you were spoken for."

"This is the first time Mr. Franklin has called. Lady Vandecamp gave permission. I gather, from the look he gave you as he departed, he will not be calling again."

Andrew grinned, not in the least contrite that she could tell. "That does not disappoint me, Bella, though I realize he is far more acceptable to Lady V. than I could ever be. I cannot help but wonder if your taste in men is the same as hers."

She shrugged. "I do not think she cares about my taste in men. Her goal is to find us husbands. Apart from that, she has not asked us our preferences on anything."

"I am asking, Bella. What do you prefer?"

Her cheeks burned and she looked down at the toes of her slippers. How could she tell him she preferred him? Apart from the kiss she had begged for him to prove his innocence, he had not so much as kissed her since their night at Thackery's. Though he now felt responsible for her, she was left to conclude that he no longer wanted her in *that* way.

He glanced at the door again and then leaned closer and lowered his voice. "Listen well, Bella. I want you to stay home and out of trouble. You are in far more danger than you could imagine. Whatever must be done, whoever is to blame, I will handle it."

"I will not stop now. I will see this through or die in the effort."

"That, my dear, is exactly what I fear."

There was a clamor in the corridor and several female voices were raised at the same time. Bella groaned. Gina, Nancy and someone else. Pray it was Lilly and not Mama. She stepped away from Andrew, hoping to preserve some decorum despite the fact that they were unchaperoned.

"Tonight," he whispered as the door burst open and everyone crowded through the opening.

Heavens! It was all of them—Mama, Gina, Nancy and Lilly. Her mother hadn't even paused long enough to smooth her gown or arrange her hair. She looked like a middle-aged general leading her battalion. "What is this?" she asked.

"Mama, may I present Mr. Andrew Hunter? He is the Earl of Lockwood's brother. Mr. Hunter, may I introduce my mother, Mrs. O'Rourke?"

"Hunter?" she asked with an imperious lift of her voice. "Hunter? He is not on Eleanor's list."

"He...I..."

Andrew stepped forward, took her mother's hand, bowed and lifted it to his lips. "Mrs. O'Rourke. Of course. I would have known you anywhere. 'Tis easy to see the family resemblance and where your daughters acquired their fine looks."

"Oh? Well...yes, all my girls are lovely, are they not?"

"Indeed. And please do not blame Miss Isabella. I was, ah, bringing her something she dropped in the park the other day when I saw her walking."

"Dropped?" She turned to Bella and fixed her with a stern expression. She hoped Mama would not embarrass her with a tirade about her inadequacies. "What did you drop, Bella? Have I not warned you repeatedly that you are too careless?"

"I...I..."

"She was not careless in the least, Mrs. O'Rourke. She was escorting her sisters, and her attention was somewhat diverted." Andrew reached into his waistcoat pocket and brought forth a little square of lace-edged linen and presented it to her with a bow. "Your handkerchief, Miss Isabella."

She accepted the handkerchief, breathing a sigh of relief and a prayer of thanksgiving that Andrew Hunter was so brilliant at deceit! "Thank you, sir."

Mama gave him a begrudging look of approval. "Well, as long as you are here, Mr. Hunter, you may as well stay for tea."

"Thank you for your kindness, Mrs. O'Rourke, but I have another appointment. Perhaps another time?"

"Yes, perhaps," she allowed. She waved Bella back as she followed Andrew to show him out.

"That was close," Gina whispered in her ear.

Bella looked down at the handkerchief. Emblazoned across one corner were the initials C O. Cora! Her fingers trembled as they traced the letter. *How had Andrew come into possession of Cora's hankie?*

Andrew was on his third cup of coffee and reduced to reading the classified section of the *Times* before Wycliffe arrived in the salon of his club on St. James Street. He helped himself to a cup of coffee from a sideboard near the door before taking a seat with a casual air. The only other occupant of the room was an elderly man dozing in his chair by the fire.

"Have you got something?" he asked in the low tones associated with the club.

Andrew hardly knew where to begin. "I think I am on the trail. If I am right, the ceremony is moved each time."

"That would explain why we have been unable to locate it. Just when we think we have a lead, it disappears into thin air. Tell me more."

"There was a ritual last night, but I cannot be certain who is behind it."

"Did you talk to Wilson?"

"He was less than cooperative. In fact, I wouldn't be surprised if he has put a price on me. He did not like me asking questions, nor did he believe that I was merely curious. Nevertheless, I would lay odds that he sold those girls for use in the rituals. There are more than you know about. Farrell's people found them and buried them quietly. He did not want attention from the authorities."

"There were more bodies than those we found?"

"According to Farrell, eleven, including Miss O'Rourke. And he recognized the markings."

"Make that twelve. The night watch in St. Giles parish found a body near dawn. Same markings, same mutilation."

Andrew felt the bile rise in his stomach. His blood-splattered shoes! God, no. This was his worst fear. He took a deep breath. "Do you have her description?"

"Yes, but no clues there. They've been all sorts. Short, tall, blonde, brunette, common prostitutes mostly, until Miss O'Rourke and a few governesses."

"But the one last night. What did she look like?"

"Dark brown hair, smallish, slightly built, fair complexion."

He closed his eyes and shook his head. He couldn't think about it now. Whatever he'd done, his head was clear now and he had to find a way to end this butchery, even if he was a part of it. He looked up at Wycliffe. "There's to be another Sabbath—ritual, actually. Friday the thirteenth."

"And I've come into news of something being referred to as the thirteenth rite."

Friday the thirteenth. The thirteenth rite. The thirteenth sacrifice? "Tomorrow, then. I believe we have very little time if we are to prevent another murder."

Wycliffe's eyes widened and he glanced at the door as if to make certain they couldn't be overheard. "You *believe?*"

"That would explain the escalation, would it not? The previous murders…could have been mere rehearsals, especially if this has all been leading to this 'thirteenth rite.'"

"How can we find out?"

"Farrell. If anyone has heard rumors, he has. I asked him to discover where it will be held. He made no promises, and now we know why—they move the damn thing to keep the location secret."

"Sooner or later someone will talk. I cannot believe it has been kept secret so long."

Andrew shrugged. "Perhaps that is not so odd. I was drugged last night. There was laudanum in the wine, and the taste was disguised with sulfur. Jamie and Charlie were there last night, too, and they have no more memory than I. But I recall a woman. Some nonsense about her being our vessel. Then I am blank until I awoke at home this morning."

"Who else was there?"

"We wore robes with deep cowls. I did not recognize anyone beyond our own party. Me, Jamie, Charlie, Henley, Dash, Lord Elwood and Throckmorton."

"How many were there?"

Andrew rubbed his temples. Every time he tried to recall specifics, his head began to throb. "At least a dozen, maybe more. And the woman."

"You have no recollection of how you got home?"

"None," he confirmed.

"Where was Miss O'Rourke?"

He went blank for a moment, remembering that terrifying dream of Bella on the altar, then collected his thoughts with a deep breath. "I took her home before I met the others. Wycliffe, you have to stop her. You cannot continue to use her when her very life is in danger. Blast it all, *you've* put her in danger! And do not give me that twaddle about your covert agent. I've seen no trace of him. And certainly of no one protecting Miss O'Rourke."

"*You* are protecting her," he said. "And my other man is in place, ready to step in if needed."

"You will understand if I doubt you, Wycliffe. Miss O'Rourke has come to harm already."

"What sort of harm?"

Andrew shook his head. For his part, he'd admit his error and atone for it in any way required of him, but he would not compromise Bella's reputation without her permission. He used a diversion instead of an answer. "Have you ever heard of the Blood Wyvern Brotherhood?"

Wycliffe frowned and stirred his coffee. "That would fit the markings, would it not—the wyvern drawn in blood? I must say, I do not care for the name. Are these the men you think are behind the murders?"

"Aye. And it fits what I've learned from Farrell. All the others have been found in the same condition. I just...cannot imagine why they take the patch of skin from the forehead. What can they want with such a trophy?"

"Who can say, when this must come from the workings of a demented mind."

"Several demented minds, I would think. I know we were drugged, but there must have been those who were not—at least not to the degree we were. This was not the first time I've been drugged. Two weeks ago—before you asked for my help—I went to a Black Mass where sulfur was added to the wine. I had a suspicious loss of memory the next day. Last night, again, I hadn't had much to drink."

"Who gave you the wine last night?"

"Henley, though I do not know where he got it. Before...I cannot recall. But I was with all the same people both times, Wycliffe. Last night, because of the robes, I did not know anyone beyond my own party. But the ceremonies were nothing alike. The one before was like so many others. Salacious. Brazen. Scandalous. But I cannot recall worse crimes than drunkenness and adultery that night. Last night, I suspect much worse occurred. And with another body…"

Wycliffe was silent for a few moments before he nodded and sighed deeply. He tapped his finger against the side of his coffee cup as he thought. "If you are concerned about your complicity in last night's events, unless you woke covered in blood, do not be. I saw the body. Whoever inflicted the damage was drenched in it. Being there, being drugged, does not make you guilty."

Andrew released a long-held breath.

"So, if the rumors are true, we have until tomorrow night to find and stop these curs," Wycliffe said.

Andrew's stomach turned. "Tell Miss O'Rourke what you are doing, and that you haven't given up on her sister's case. Put her out of the path of danger and I will do anything you ask. Anything."

Wycliffe gave him a sympathetic glance, then looked away. "I wish I could, Hunter. Unfortunately, she may be our only means to solving this mess. She can identify the killer in a way that none of us can. And if they should discover who she is and what she is doing, so much the better. They will come for her, and we will be ready."

Andrew crumpled the newspaper and stood, containing his rage with difficulty. "You'd sacrifice her to solve this, wouldn't you?"

"To my shame, yes. It has to stop, no matter what the cost."

The cost wouldn't be Bella. He'd damn well see to that.

Angelo's was overflowing this late in the afternoon and Andrew had managed to work off some of his frustration and all the effects of the brew from last night, though he'd been sluggish and fuzzy-headed until he found his concentration. He'd won all but the first bout with the club champion.

He'd been about to go home, bathe, meet Bella at Belmonde's, and persuade her in any way necessary to stay home until Saturday, when Daschel found him and begged him to stay for a quick match. He wiped his forehead on his sleeve as Dash threw his jacket to Henley and blunted the tip of his rapier with a small cork ball. He had never liked using the academy's blunt swords.

After saluting with the blade to his forehead, Dash took the offensive as he launched into conversation—his usual tactic to distract and disadvantage his opponent. "I see you are none the worse for wear today. You have an inhuman capacity, Hunter."

"How did *you* fare?" he asked as he parried Dash's advance.

Dash laughed, holding his blade straight out toward Andrew's heart. "I must have had a good time. I can still feel the effects in my blood and bones, though my memory of it is somewhat impaired. What a ghastly headache!" He lunged.

Andrew parried. "You seem to have recovered quickly enough."

"Not until half an hour ago. And you? What do you recall of the festivities?"

"Beyond the comely wench standing on the altar, nothing."

"Ah, yes. I do recall her." Dash chortled. "Quite a sight, was she not? I conceived that she looked remarkably similar to your Lady Lace."

Andrew blinked, disconcerted by the thought that others might have noted that resemblance. Could the girl have been chosen for just such a reason? Dash used the brief advantage to press the cork against Andrew's heart.

"Hit," Andrew acknowledged, dropping the tip of his blade and rubbing the spot. Dash had made contact rather more vigorously than necessary. "Did you take me home last night?"

"Me? Though I'd love to take credit for it, I must admit that I have no idea how *I* got home." He turned to Henley on the sidelines. "Was it you, Henley?"

But Henley spread his arms wide and shook his head as if to disavow any knowledge of the event. Andrew studied his face and wondered if the man knew more than he was telling. "Who else was there?" he asked.

Dash saluted again and assumed the *en garde* position. "Damned if I know. Must've been Throckmorton who got us home."

Highly unlikely. Throckmorton had been stumbling even before they left the Lion and Bear. He'd been showing more ill-effects from the wine than the rest. Andrew brought his blade up and saluted Dash. "Notice anything unusual this morning, Dash?"

His friend grinned. "Aside from the foul taste in my mouth and the thundering headache? No."

"You, Henley?"

"Nothing. I barely recall arriving at the warehouse."

Andrew suspected that was a lie. He lunged at Dash and caught him off guard, quickly scoring a hit to his sword arm. Dash acknowledged the hit and stepped back, rubbing his shoulder as if Andrew had actually injured him.

"Well," Dash drawled, "whatever happened, it must have been interesting to have started so conspicuously."

"Damn, what's the point if we cannot remember? I can stay at home and drink myself insensible. I was hoping for something different. Something exciting, or at least something that would stir my blood. All I've found is more of the same."

"We shall have to see what we can do about that. Are you certain you are ready for it?"

Andrew nodded as Dash advanced on him, forcing him backward, and it was all he could do to fend off the blows. The cork popped off the tip of Dash's blade, but he was so intent on his advance that he seemed not to notice. He and Dash scored hits simultaneously.

Dash threw off the side of Andrew's blade with the back of his arm and looked shocked when a slash of red appeared on Andrew's right bicep. Andrew gritted his teeth against the sharp ripping pain, his sword clattering to the wooden floor.

"Good God!" Dash's eyes widened as Andrew gripped his arm over the cut. "Bring the medic kit," he yelled to Henley.

A moment later, Andrew had been bandaged by an attendant and told to rest the arm for a month to prevent permanent damage to the muscle. Henley held his jacket for him as they made their way to the nearby livery where they'd left their horses.

"Thank God you are not opposed to a little blood," Dash said. "I will find a way to make this up to you. Henley, here, would have passed out had it been him."

"You know damn well that is not true, Dash. I hold my own with the best of them. Why last—"

"Come now, Henley. I was jesting."

Andrew would have liked to hear the end of that sentence. His arm was beginning to tingle by the time he mounted and looked down at his friends. "This will not put me off my game, Dash. If you hear of anything…"

"You will be the first to know. I swear it, Drew. No more games."

He nodded as he reined into the street. His arm was the least of his problems. The suspicion that Dash and Henley were somehow involved in this grew. Had his first instinct been right? Was Dash Wycliffe's covert agent? Or was he involved with the dark rituals?

Bella's pulse quickened at the now-familiar sounds of gambling. Belmonde's.

Biddle took her wrap. "Mr. Hunter has not yet arrived, miss. Perhaps you would like to await him in a private salon?"

Heat infused her cheeks. "No, I shall just look around, Mr. Biddle. Perhaps I will see someone I know."

"As you wish, miss." He gave her just enough of a bow to avoid insulting her.

She was wondering if this was the sort of veiled disapproval she would have to deal with for the rest of her life, when Lord Humphries intercepted her midway across the main salon.

"Well met, my dear Lady Lace. *Bella,* is it not?"

She hesitated. She did not mind Andrew using the familiar form of address, but hearing it from Lord Humphries assumed a familiarity they did not share. Was this yet another indication of her lowered status? First Biddle and now Lord Humphries reminding her of her "place?" "Yes, it is. But I would prefer not to be addressed as such in public."

He took her arm and led her toward the punch bowl. "Ah, a reputation to protect? Very well. I can be most discreet, my dear."

She was still trying to decide if there had been a hint of something salacious in his assurance when he handed her a cup of rum punch. "Thank you," she said.

"Are you meeting Mr. Hunter here tonight?"

"I expect to see him at some point this evening," she allowed.

"I gather you and he have…er, reached an understanding?"

"Not the sort you are hinting at, Lord Humphries."

"Egads! Still unattached? That is a piece of good news. Call me Dash, as I expect we shall soon be better acquainted."

She arched an eyebrow, hoping that would discourage him, but he only chuckled in amusement.

"Our last chat was cut short when Hunter arrived. I hope we shall not be so importuned this evening. Come, sit with me."

The other thing that had been interrupted that night was a kiss. She still had not excluded Lord Humphries as a suspect. Oh, but the mere thought of kissing anyone after she'd known Andrew's kiss was loathsome. A bit reluctantly she took Lord Humphries's arm and allowed him to lead her to one of the alcoves. When he began to draw the curtain, she stopped him.

"Please, sir, I do not like surprises. I want to see anyone coming this time."

He laughed. "Oh, I am sure you do, Bella. But come. Drink up and I shall fetch you another."

She merely smiled and took a judicious sip of the rum punch. She was not about to allow Lord Humphries to get her drunk. "Are you trying to seduce me, my lord?"

His grin was really quite charming. "Alas, I am too transparent by half. But since you are not obligated to Hunter, I must assume that you are open to other offers."

"That would depend upon the offer."

"That would depend upon *you,* my dear." He took a sip from his own cup and settled on the bench beside her. "It is not often that someone of your…caliber comes along. Beauty, charm, wit, intelligence and confidence in your own self-worth make you rather irresistible. So it might make more sense for me to ask you how much you are willing to yield."

She liked the way he put the question to her. It assumed nothing but hinted at much. "That remains to be seen, sir."

"I never assumed you would come easily, Bella. Or cheap."

"Thank you for the compliment," she said. "At last I have found a man who understands."

He beamed. "Then I am right? Excellent. I sense that you come from quality. Tell me about yourself, m'dear."

"As you have previously guessed, sir, I am new to London. I am yet getting my bearings and finding my way though the maze of society here."

"Was it so provincial where you came from?"

Oh, dear. She had not meant to give so much away. If only she knew how much Cora had told her suitor. "Is not everywhere provincial when compared to London?" she quipped.

"Indeed. Then your family did not go about much in society?"

She glanced down into her cup, marveling at how well she had learned to lie. "Not often. After all, in our reduced circumstances, we were hardly able to afford the necessities for the season."

"There are more than you? How glorious to think of more like you waiting to be discovered. How many more, Bella? I could pray you have a plethora of sisters. And are they virgin, like you?"

Virgin? She swallowed hard. As wrong as his assumption about her was, it was still insulting to be asked such a question. Ah, but if she truly were from a family fallen on hard times and with no money for dowries, perhaps she would be looking for protectors for her sisters. If she had sisters. She fiddled with the mauve ribbon that trimmed her neckline. "I fear I have given you the wrong impression, Lord Humphries. When I said 'we,' I meant my mother, father and brother. I do not have sisters."

He looked crestfallen and sighed theatrically. "And here I had got my hopes up. You mustn't tease like that, my dear. But tell me, does your father not object to your activities?"

"He passed on several years ago."

"But your brother—"

"Is gone in service to the crown. He is in His Majesty's Navy."

"What a great pity that you have no male family to see after your needs."

Or her safety. "But I am a boring topic, Lord Humphries. Pray, tell me about *you.*"

"Ah, a sad tale, that." He paused to finish his punch. "I was an only child. My mother and father both passed on whilst I was posted on the peninsula. By the time I had word of their illness—rancid food, I believe—it was already too late to go to them. We were difficult to reach, you see. I am not certain Hunter would have allowed me to go, in any event. Those were…difficult days." His dark eyes took on a far-away look. "Amazing how fragile the human creature is. How, and the many different ways, they accept the moment of death…"

Bella shuddered, not wanting to think about that, and about how Cora had begged for justice. But what had he said? "Mr. Hunter was your commanding officer?"

Lord Humphries blinked. "He outranked us, and someone had to keep order in the midst of the chaos. Even someone who was completely crazed." He literally shook off his pensiveness. "But let us not speak of such unpleasantness. I'd much rather think of you, m'dear. Of us."

"M-Mr. Hunter was crazed?"

"Why, yes. Looking back on it, I suppose we all were. It was not easy to hold a gut-shot friend as he died, or to look down your rifle sight, stare the enemy in the face and pull the trigger. But it got easier as the days drifted on. One eventually loses one's humanity. Once the lust for blood takes over… Hunter, I suppose, was the worst because he also carried the burden for the rest of us. A pity, really, because now he is capable of… anything."

Andrew was capable of anything? *Anything?* She shivered, wondering if she could have misjudged him.

Lord Humphries noted her shiver and took her hand. "Ah, and here I was hoping to steal a kiss, and instead I have upset you. I am sorry, my dear. I warned you we should not speak of war, did I not? Now drink your punch and I shall fetch you another."

"Yes, but I did not realize—that is, I have not seen that side of Mr. Hunter. He seems so gentle, despite his gruffness."

He laughed. "Aye, 'tis why we call him Lord Libertine. One moment all moroseness and remorse, the next all mischief and mayhem. One can never predict what he will do next."

She had seen that side of him, and the thought that he might, under certain circumstances, be capable of mayhem troubled her. His anger was never very far from the surface, and she had provoked it in a way she doubted his friends had, and yet he had never done her harm. Well, not physical harm. And nothing she hadn't participated in.

"And I see we have chatted just long enough for your would-be swain to arrive. I want that kiss, Bella. Will you meet me here to-morrow night?"

She glanced toward the foyer, where Andrew had emerged and spotted them. Almost desperate, knowing he would stop her, she leaned toward her companion. "Kiss me now, Lord Humphries."

"And irritate him? I think not. 'Tis one thing to kiss you, and quite another to do it in front of Hunter. I do not relish that prodigious temper of his. I already had a taste of that this afternoon. Say you will meet me here at nine o'clock tomorrow. Oh, and it would be best if you did not mention this to Hunter. He would likely find a way to foil us."

Chapter Seventeen

Bella remained seated when Lord Humphries stood and intercepted Andrew. They exchanged a few words, then Lord Humphries went on to the foyer and Andrew came her way. She finished the remainder of her punch and prepared herself for his usual challenge.

Instead he sat next to her and tilted her chin to look into her eyes. "Dash tells me you were expecting me?"

"Is that not what you meant when you whispered "Tonight" in my parlor this afternoon?"

"I had hoped to find you at home."

She gasped. "You did not disturb Nancy or Mama, did you?"

He laughed. "After meeting the venerable woman, I concluded that she was the last person you would want to know that you were not at home. No, Bella, I met your sister on the street. Miss Eugenia. She told me you had already left for the evening."

"Gina was out?" A cold knot of suspicion began to twist in her stomach. Had Gina lied to her?

"Aye. She said she was on her way to sit with a sick neighbor."

Oh, the minx! Where had she really gone? How would Bella find her?

"That disturbs you?" he asked, reading her agitation.

"Only because it is a lie. We haven't any sick neighbors. She has got it into her mind that I need help. She wants to assist me in finding Cora's killer."

Andrew's expression turned to one of concern. "Do you know where she's gone?"

"No. She has only done this once before, but all she said was that she'd fallen in with a group outside a theater."

"Then there is not much you can do, Bella. Go home and wait. Come, I will take you."

"I am not ready. I haven't…"

"Kissed anyone?" he finished. "I am relieved to hear that, my dear. In fact, I would be quite out of sorts to hear anything else. Did we not decide that you were to cease that particular aspect of your investigation?"

"No, I do not believe we decided anything of the sort."

He surprised her by bringing her to her feet and escorting her toward the foyer. "This really is not open to argument, Bella. I told you that I will not tolerate you kissing men—strangers for the most part—and most especially, Bella, not my friends. Never my friends."

"What possible difference could that make?" she asked as he took her wrap from Biddle and draped it over her shoulders.

"Because I won't have them comparing their experience and lying to best the others. I won't have them talk about you as if you were some sort of…of…"

"Doxy?" she finished as he led her outside, where a gentle rain had begun to fall. He lifted the hood of her cloak and arranged it over her hair. His knuckles brushed her cheek, and she drew in a sharp breath. Odd, how that gentle sensation could affect her more deeply than if he'd struck her.

"No, Bella. We both know you are not a common doxy."

"An uncommon one, then," she snapped.

He hailed a hackney, handed her up and gave her address before joining her. "You are not any sort of doxy," he said as he settled beside her.

"How many times must I remind you that you swore not to interfere with me?"

"As many times as I must remind you that I changed my mind. Surely you must see that I can never honor such an oath. You are asking me to sit on my hands whilst you put yourself in danger and deliver yourself over to any man for the price of a kiss."

"Must you put it that way?"

"Prithee, what other way is there?"

He had a point. In fact, he'd been more delicate in his wording than she would have been. "But Gina—"

"Is not a child, despite your posture as her mother. You cannot control her any more than I, evidently, can control you."

"She could be in danger."

"As are you."

"I never should have told you about my sister's death."

"Too late for that lament now, Bella."

The coach lurched as the driver veered to avoid a pedestrian and Bella was thrown against Andrew. He winced and gripped his upper right arm.

"Did I hurt you?"

He shook his head. "No, Bella. 'Twas just a fencing accident from this afternoon. 'Tis nothing."

She placed a hand on his knee to balance herself and regain her seating and heard him make a sound that was almost a groan. He covered her hand with his own and moved it slowly back to her own lap. When she looked back at him, the heat in his eyes nearly set her afire.

Struggling to regain her composure, she looked away again. "I…I must do something, Mr. Hunter."

"Andrew. And there is nothing you can do. If you do not know where she is, you would likely spend the whole night traversing London and never finding her. The only thing you *can* do, Bella, is to go home and wait."

She said nothing, but she settled back against the leather seat and sighed. "I am painfully aware of the dangers awaiting an innocent female in London."

"Bella, please be reasonable. There is nothing you can do."

"There has to be something. My honor, my loyalty to my family, demands that I do more than sit at home while one sister is missing and another sister's killer walks free."

He turned her toward him and cupped her face. Then slowly, giving her more than ample time to protest, he lowered his lips to hers. She closed her eyes as she surrendered. Oh, thank heavens he had kissed her. This was the only thing that made sense in this wasted night.

The hackney pulled up to her house. Andrew opened the window and gave the driver a new address.

Damn! Andrew had to go. He had to meet with Farrell and pray the man had found news of where and when the next Blood Wyvern ritual would be held. That, and that alone, was his best chance of keeping Bella and her sister from harm.

But when, in the dim light of the hackney, he watched the stubborn jut of her chin, he knew she would leave the moment he was out of sight. If only Wycliffe had not sworn him to secrecy, and if he could be certain the knowledge would not make her reckless, he would tell her that no one had forgotten Cora O'Rourke. And that others were actively searching for the killer.

The moment they'd drawn up in front of Bella's house, he knew he couldn't leave her. He'd have to take her somewhere and keep her until morning and she was safe for another day. He'd wend his way through the rookeries then, roust Farrell from his bed, if necessary. He'd catch a few hours' sleep in the afternoon and then return to the hells and rookeries until he found the demented men who had killed Bella's sister and so many more.

"Where are you taking me?" she asked.

"Where you cannot get into trouble." He answered more gruffly than he'd intended and she tightened her jaw, a sure sign that she was angry. Too bad. Better angry at him than dead on some sacrificial altar.

She sulked until the coach drew into the courtyard of an inn on the outskirts of London. He paid the driver extra to wait, handed her down and led her into a deserted public room. Henderson, the proprietor, peeked out from a back room and then came forward with a wide grin.

"Ah, Mr. Hunter, sir. 'Tis been awhile since we've seen ye. A room, sir? And the usual?"

He ignored Bella's sharp intake of breath. "Yes, Henderson. Thank you."

"A pleasure, sir." He took a key from a peg on the wall behind the counter and brought it to Andrew. "I'll bring the rest in a moment, sir. 'Tis quiet tonight. You'll not be disturbed. If you've need of anything, just ring."

Andrew nodded, took the key and guided Bella down a narrow passageway. He could feel her tension through her stiffened elbow. She was not going to make this easy.

The moment she entered the room, she whirled on him, hands on her hips and eyes narrowed. "Is this where you bring all your doxies, Lord Libertine?"

Where the hell had she heard that nickname? He held his tongue until, a moment later, Mr. Henderson brought a tray with a bottle of excellent wine, a bowl of fruit and a plate of bread and cheese. He placed it on a low table between two chairs facing an unlit fireplace, then went to the wide mullion windows, unfastened the latch and swung them open.

"'Tis a lovely night, sir. The rain has cleared and the garden smells especially sweet."

"Thank you, Henderson. That will be all. We shall be leaving early, so no need to wake us."

"Aye, sir." He backed out the door and Andrew locked it behind him.

Finally alone, he turned to Bella. "Never doxies, Bella. I only bring women of quality here. Women who have need of discretion."

Her cheeks burned livid pink, whether with anger or indignation, he could not tell. "Married women, you mean? And women you do not pay for sex?"

"Precisely. And if you expect me to apologize for that, you will have a long wait, my dear. What I did and who I saw before I met you is none of your affair. And if you expect an explanation for all of them, we'll be here long past next week."

"I…I did not mean to suggest that you owed me an explanation. Just that I do not intend to be one in a long line of…of…"

"Lovers?" he supplied as he poured two glasses of wine. "I did not imagine you would. Nor would I subject you to such a dire fate. You are correct in believing you deserve better."

"That is not what I meant."

He handed her a glass and lifted his in a toast to her. "To better days, Bella."

"Goodness, yes!" She lifted her glass and drank deeply.

A soft breeze stirred the draperies framing the window and the rain-washed air filled the room with the scent of roses and honeysuckle. He watched her as she leaned on the sill to gaze at the moonlit garden.

The simple act of observing her was sheer torture, and he was mystified by the bittersweet irony. He had longed to feel again. Now he felt. He loved. And he ached because of it. Yet he would not change it. Loving Bella was all that gave his life meaning now. She might not love him in return, she might not even want him in her life, but her mere existence had lifted him from his mire of self-indulgence and desolation.

She turned from the window and sighed, a look of resignation on her face. "Then if you do not intend to seduce me, Lord Libertine, why have you brought me here?"

"To keep you safe, though you may not believe that. Your flirtations could eventually cost you more than a kiss."

She shrugged. "It would appear, Lord Libertine, that it already has."

"Stop calling me that, Bella. What happened between us the other night was regrettable, but it would never have happened if I'd known the truth. I doubt there is a single man at Belmonde's or Thackery's who would have believed that you were virgin. Of course, that does not excuse my behavior, but you might have spoken out at some point during my dastardly seduction."

"Would you have believed me?"

"No." Of course he wouldn't have. He would have thought it was a laughable ploy to stop him. The real question was, would he have stopped? He sighed. Probably not. He would simply have used his knowledge of lovemaking, of what makes a woman pliant and malleable, to persuade her. As unconscionable as that was, it was also a testament to how badly he had wanted her. And how few scruples he had when it came to her.

She accepted his denial without comment and changed the subject.

"At least this place is clean." She glanced toward the bed—an imposing four-poster with a deep down mattress and crisp linens—and sighed. "How long do you intend to keep me here?"

"Until it is too late for you to traipse about London kissing men."

"Dawn."

"Or very close to it."

"And do you intend to do this every night?"

"If I must."

She shook her head. "I do not understand. Why do you care?"

"Perhaps it is me that I care about. I would likely go to gaol or hang for killing the men you kissed. I would prefer to avoid that."

She gave him a smile, her first of the night. "That is a hollow threat, Mr. Hunter."

"Try me."

"I've told you everything. I've been as honest as I know how. Why can you not do the same for me?"

Would that he could—damn Wycliffe, anyway! "I am afraid for you, Isabella O'Rourke, and I do not want anything bad to happen to you. And that is God's own truth."

For the first time that night, she looked completely disconcerted and at a loss for words. He went to her and lifted her light cloak from her shoulders. She shivered in another breeze from the open window. "Shall I close the window, Bella?"

"I rather like the smell of flowers and rain. It reminds me of home."

"Do you miss it so much?"

"I wish we had never left."

"I can imagine," he answered a little wistfully. Cora, of course, and his seduction. He had no doubt she'd turn back time if she could.

He turned his attention to slicing an apple and cheese into wedges and placing them on a flowered dish, then poured a bit more wine in her glass.

"If you'd like to get some sleep, Bella, go ahead. I will sit here." He indicated one of the chairs.

She glanced at him over her shoulder, cocking a suspicious eyebrow. He laughed. "It would be better if you could trust me. I swear I will not ravish you in your sleep."

"I have lost my trust since coming to London, Mr. Hunter."

"Damn! Can you not call me Andrew? At least when we are in private?"

She looked down, and the delicate fringe of her dark lashes lying against her flushed cheeks awoke a need in him. He was ashamed of that. Bella, it seemed, had to do little more than sigh and he was aroused. For all that he'd indulged his passions before, he'd never been governed by them until now.

"Andrew," she said, barely above a whisper, "how did you come to be in possession of Cora's handkerchief?"

"Cora's?"

"The hankie you gave me in the parlor this afternoon."

"You dropped it the night you left Marlborough House. I retrieved it."

She sighed and tension drained from her shoulders. She had not quite trusted him, but at least she had asked the question. He finished his wine, shrugged out of his jacket and laid it over the back of the chair. He didn't know how much longer he could act the platonic protector when she smelled like lilacs and fresh rain and just stood there, looking lost and lonely.

She came closer and took a wedge of apple from the plate. "Mr. Henderson seems to know your tastes quite well."

"He is a most attentive host."

"And are all your women the same? Do they have the same tastes, as well?"

There was something veiled in Bella's voice. Was she wondering if she was like all the rest? "I think Henderson is safe enough with wine, fruit and cheese. Actually, I think he believes you are a cut above the others. You are the first he has brought fruit."

"How would he know what sort of person I am?"

"He is a quick judge of character."

"But I am not actually one of your women."

More than she knew. "No doubt he thinks you are too good for me."

She smiled. "Ah, but we know better, do we not?"

He took her hand and turned her toward him. "Do not do that,

Bella. Do not belittle or diminish yourself. You are the only person I know who is working without self-interest here. You have nothing to gain in finding your sister's killer, and everything to lose."

"It was my fault that Cora—"

"It was not your responsibility. Cora was a grown woman and acted without your knowledge. I doubt you could have prevented her in any case. What troubles me now is what this has done to you. There was more than one victim the day your sister was killed, Bella. There was you.

"We are more alike than you might imagine, my dear. I went to war. You came to London. We both lost what was left of our innocence and joy—our belief in a happy future and our ability to trust. But, unlike me, you turned to duty rather than pleasure. I wanted to find whatever comfort, whatever enjoyment or gratification I could, because I believed there would be few tomorrows. I had seen too much of the savagery of men, and so I sought the things that would help me forget. You, Isabella O'Rourke, saw the same, but you nurtured the pain of losing your sister. Where I have become shamelessly self-indulgent, you have thrown yourself on an altar of self-sacrifice. Not a pretty thing, my love. A decision as poor as mine, in fact. But I am here now, I understand, and I intend to save you from yourself."

Her eyes sparkled with unshed tears. She touched his arm, and a shock went through him. "I am still determined—"

He threw his hands up in exasperation. "And so am I."

"I know that I am in danger, and that if...*when* I find the man I'm looking for, I could pay with my life. But I cannot let that stop me. I want you to stay out of this, Andrew. If you should come to harm because of my resolve—I could not bear that."

He had only one more argument. "Though you have no reason to, I am asking you to trust me. Give me tonight and tomorrow, Bella. Stay home. Stay safe. After that, I will..."

"Allow me to do as I please?" she asked.

"I will not block your way." He lied as smoothly and unremorsefully as he ever had. He'd have promised anything to keep her out of the way until after the thirteen Sabbath, and after what he believed would be the thirteenth sacrifice.

"I do not believe you. There is something you are not telling me, Andrew. What will change after tomorrow?"

He pulled her into his arms to silence her the only way he could—with a kiss. He expected her to push him away, to beat his chest or stomp on his foot, but she surprised him by matching his passion with an innocent urgency that shook him to his core.

He struggled with the wave of undiluted lust that swept over him. He pulled her arms from around his neck and stepped back. "Bloody hell, Bella! Just when I want to be noble, you make it impossible! Can you not see what you are doing to me? How can I ask you to trust me when I cannot trust myself?"

"I do not want you to be noble, Andrew. I want you to touch me and make me forget who I am and what I've become. I want to pretend that there is no tomorrow, that there is nothing beyond us and tonight. I want to close my eyes and believe that you...want me, too."

He groaned. She wanted him. How could he deny her anything knowing that? He slipped his arms around her and held her so tight that she gasped. "Believe it, Bella. You can always believe that. I will want you until the day I die."

She tilted her head up to him and he accepted the invitation. When her lips parted, he was lost. The very earth could have shaken and he would not have been able to stop.

Before he was quite aware of what he was doing, he had undressed her and lifted her to rest against the pillows of the massive bed. As he shed his own clothes, the candles guttered in a breeze, leaving them veiled in the shadows of the moonlit room.

She reached out to him as he came down on the bed beside her. Her hand skimmed his arms and stopped at the bandage. "Did it hurt?" she asked.

"Only for a moment," he whispered, running his tongue along the rim of her ear. It would cause him far more pain to stop what he was doing at this very minute.

Her fingers resumed their exploration, tracing the muscles of his chest, and he shuddered at the delicacy of her touch. If she continued lower, he'd be lost. He captured her hand and moved it to his cheek, then turned his face to kiss her palm.

"Keep that kiss, Bella, and know that there is an endless supply

awaiting you," he whispered. "Wherever you go, whatever you do, I
stand ready to give you more."

She smiled and she was even more beautiful by moonlight. "What
gift can I give you?"

"This," he said, nibbling one earlobe. "And this." He found the spot
where her pulse beat at the hollow of her throat.

She raked her fingers through his hair and held him closer as she
squirmed against him.

"And that," he groaned, making a Herculean effort to slow himself down. This time he would not cheat her. This time he would be
certain she found pleasure.

He kissed a path down from her throat and cherished one firmed
nipple. She moaned and lifted one knee to skim along his leg and hip.
She was open to him now, vulnerable in a way she had never been.
He slipped his hand along the curve of her bottom toward her center,
trailing one finger along the moist cleft.

"Drew!" she gasped.

He grinned. "Hush, Bella. I am unwrapping my gift."

"But…"

"Too late to take it back. I've already made it mine." He found the
tight bundle of nerves and caressed it with a sure and gentle touch.

She gasped again and stiffened. "What…"

"An interesting discovery, eh, pet?" He created a gentle rhythm
until he felt her relax and begin to open to his touch. He realized that
she had been too innocent, too frightened, the first time, and he had
been too caught up in the urgency, to fully appreciate what he was
doing. Poor pet. He would make up for that now. "What other secrets
do you hide?"

"I think…you know that better than I," she admitted in a breathy
sigh.

He chuckled as he dipped one finger lower, finding her damp and
ready. He invaded her, savoring her sweetly naive response.

He relinquished her breast with one final nip and kissed his way
to her navel, where he traced his tongue in a circle. Her thighs began
to tremble. She was near…so near. But not yet.

He opened her wider and trailed his tongue and his kisses down to
the delectable mound of his final destination. Holding her hips steady,

because he knew she would protest in maidenly shock or twitch with surprise, he found her with his tongue.

She arched and made a soft keening sound that sent shivers up his spine. She was panting now and he knew she was near. Oh, but not yet. Not until—

"Please, Andrew! Please. I cannot stand much more," she begged.

He raised himself above her and fit himself to her. She was so aroused, so ready, that he entered her easily. She stiffened, but not with shock or pain. Her internal muscles rippled and clenched around him, gripping him in an erotic tightness that was insanely pleasurable. Before she could recover from her first orgasm, he began moving again, finding her pace and taking her with him to a higher pinnacle.

Still, he held back until he knew that she had reached her own release. And then, in a rush of dark explosive pleasure, he seized his own completion. And he found Bella waiting for him on the other side, her eyes closed and her cheeks glowing, a smile curving her kiss-swollen lips, fully a woman in every sense of the word.

He recognized her languor. She had fallen into a swoon, *la petit mort*. Yes, he'd satisfied her, and that was the greatest gift of all.

He eased his weight from her and pulled the coverlet over them. He'd let her sleep yet awhile, then wake her to take her home before dawn.

And then he'd meet Farrell and find Cora O'Rourke's killer.

Chapter Eighteen

Dawn was staining the eastern horizon a pale pink by the time Andrew left Bella at her doorstep. He had straightened her hood and kissed her forehead, evidently unconcerned that anyone might see but the early tradesmen with their carts of fruits and vegetables fresh in from the countryside.

"Stay home tonight, Bella. I will call on you Saturday afternoon and we shall settle your future."

"My future? But—"

"Hush. Do not argue with me so early in the morning. I have business to tend."

With that admonition, he departed and reality set in. She wanted to think about his hint as to her future, but there was something more pressing she had to deal with. She turned the key in the lock and slipped through, closing the door with a faint click behind her. The house was silent, but Nancy would be down soon to begin her chores.

She hurried up the front stairs and paused at Gina's door. It was ajar and she pushed it open. Nothing. Not a single wrinkle on her coverlet, not the faintest sign of a presence. Panic welled in her chest and she nearly screamed her anxiety. She would have to raise an alarm, and her head spun at the thought of Mama's hysterics and Lilly's tears.

She went to her room to leave her cloak, and there, in the center of her bed, sat Gina. She leaped off the bed and flew into Bella's arms.

"Oh, Bella! Where have you been? I've been waiting forever."

Relief washed over her. Thank heavens Gina was safe. "Where

were *you?* Mr. Hunter told me he intercepted you when you left the house last night."

"Oh, that." Gina released her and stepped back, affecting an air of nonchalance.

"Yes, that. We agreed that you would stay at home and keep watch over Mama and Lilly."

"No, Bella. *You* agreed. I merely remained silent. Just because you are the oldest, you think you can tell me what to do. Well, I miss Cora, too. I want to find her killer as much as you do. And I am terrified every time you leave the house that I will not see you alive again. I remember Cora…and I fear that is what you will look like when I next see you."

Bella's heart twisted. She had never considered how her activities might affect Gina. The memory of Cora's ruined face haunted her sister's dreams, too. She sank into the chair and watched as tears sprang to Gina's eyes. "I am so sorry. I swear, I shall keep safe. Give me another day or two and, whether I find the man or not, I shall stop."

Gina looked doubtful. "You swear?"

"Upon my life." She said a silent prayer she'd be able to keep that promise.

Gina sighed and her shoulders sagged as the lines between her eyes softened. "Thank heavens. I have been so afraid for you. And, then, tonight…"

"What happened tonight?"

"I went back to the theater and found some of the same people. Mr. Henley was there, and he remembered me. We all fell in together and went to a…a…oh, Bella! Men and women were posing on a dais. Mr. Henley called it a *tableau vivant*."

Bella had heard of such performances, where participants dressed in costume and enacted a scene from a famous painting or some historical event. "What scenes did they portray?"

"There was one of the painting of Ares discovering Aphrodite with Adonis." Gina lowered her voice as if someone might overhear them. "And they were completely *naked!*"

She blinked. "Gina, you must not go anywhere with Mr. Henley again. I do not think he is of good character."

"Faugh! You think I did not know that? But he is the sort who might know what happened to Cora. And the last scene the actors portrayed was an example. I do not know the painting. Perhaps it was a scene from a story, or a drawing from Dante's *Inferno,* or a variation of the sacrifice of Isaac. But when the curtains were opened on the last tableau and the lights came up, there was a girl, naked I think, lying on a table draped in red to look like an altar. In the background, there was a large triangle where a cross might have been. Inside the triangle was a circle with the outline of a dragon. A man dressed in red robes with a black dragon on the chest stood over the girl with a curved knife lifted above his head as if he were about to strike."

Triangle! Cora's forehead! Bella leaned forward. "What else, Gina? What else did you see?"

"The man struck! Blood ran everywhere. I nearly cast up my supper, but then the girl stood and bowed with the man." She closed her eyes and shuddered. "I thought it was real until that moment. Mr. Henley said it was a trick with a sheep's bladder, and that when the priest struck with the knife, he cut the sheep's bladder and released the blood. Oh, 'twas awful."

It was more than awful. It was terrifying. And it was surely what had happened to Cora. "Who was the priest? Did you recognize him?"

"He never unmasked. He was tall. Taller than Papa. As tall as your Mr. Hunter. And his laugh…'twas frightening. Almost mad."

"Can you remember anything else, Gina?"

She looked down. "Mr. Henley said that, if I found that tableau titillating, I might like the real thing. He asked me…"

"What, Gina?"

"Nothing. I…everyone was talking at once. I couldn't hear."

Bella's mind whirled. This is what she'd been looking for. Something that would link the ton to Cora's death. Certainly there were too many details in common to be mere coincidence. "When? Where do you meet them, Gina? Outside which theater?"

"Covent Garden," she said. "The Royal Opera House. Before the performance."

Then tomorrow night *she* would be outside the Royal Opera House at approximately eight thirty, before her meeting with Lord Humphries at Belmonde's. If Mr. Henley did not acknowledge her, she would speak to him. She would do whatever she must to get an invitation to the same event, and hopefully to the "real thing." And then she would send word to Lord Wycliffe. And Andrew. She would discover who the robed man was, and if he had anything to do with Cora's death.

But first she would have to make certain that Gina did not interfere. "Listen carefully, Gina. You must promise me to stay at home until this is over. Swear you will not meet Mr. Henley tomorrow."

Her sister glanced away and sighed deeply in resignation. "I swear."

This was not the first morning Andrew had found himself in Whitechapel at dawn, but this was the first time he'd observed that the rookeries looked better by night than in the harsh light of day. Some things, he mused, were better left in shadows.

Patrons of Farrell's had been expelled for the morning scouring. Andrew barely dodged the contents of a mop bucket as he approached the entry.

"'Ere now, chappie, we're closed, we are," the toothless scouring woman told him, trying to close the door in his face.

"Get Farrell," he told her as he shouldered his way past and slipped her a shilling for her trouble.

"Ain't receivin'. 'E's just gone up."

"Good. Then he will not be in bed yet. Where are the stairs?"

She stared at him in mute surprise. Evidently, one did not disturb Mr. Farrell once he had "gone up."

"Come now," he urged, tossing her another coin. "I will not tell him you sent me up."

She tilted her head to the left, and Andrew went in that direction. He found the narrow stairway behind a closed door and followed it upward to another closed door. He tried the knob, but it was locked. He gave three sharp raps and waited. Whatever he'd expected, it wasn't the shabby but proper valet who answered his knock.

"Sir?" he asked.

"Mr. Farrell, please. Tell him Andrew Hunter is here to see him."

The valet inclined his head and closed the door, leaving Andrew on the dimly lit landing.

Devlin Farrell was full of surprises. Who would have suspected a valet in apartments over a gin house? Was this pretension? Or necessity?

The door opened again and the valet stepped back to allow Andrew to pass. "Mr. Farrell will see you, sir."

The rooms appeared to be spotless, and none of the sour smell of stale beer and rotgut gin carried up the stairs, thanks to the double doors and generous insulation between the floorboards. The furnishings were tasteful and of the highest quality—the best that money could buy—and completely unexpected in an apartment in the Whitechapel rookeries.

The valet led the way down a wide passageway and indicated an open door on the right.

The room was a study or gentleman's parlor. Gleaming, polished floors, heavy draperies to filter daylight for an occupant who slept days, overstuffed furniture and overflowing bookshelves gave the impression of a Mayfair town home. He certainly hadn't expected Devlin Farrell to have such refined taste.

"I feared I'd seen the last of you, Hunter. I looked for you all night, and when you did not come, I thought you'd been killed for your questions."

Andrew grinned. Farrell was holding a cup of coffee and indicated the pot on a sideboard with a wave of his hand. Andrew poured himself a cup and went to sit in a chair across a low table from his host.

"I was delayed," he said. "But after what happened to Hank, I am glad to see that *you* are still among the living."

"I've got more lives than a cat, Hunter."

"Did you learn anything?"

There was a long pause as Farrell seemed to consider his words. Finally, "Quite a bit more than I wanted, and yet not enough."

"That is a little too cryptic for me. Care to explain?"

"Aye. Have you heard that Wilson is dead?"

Andrew nearly choked on his coffee. He put his cup down and shook his head. "What happened?"

"Took a knife to the gut. Typically, no one saw anything, heard anything or knows anything, despite the fact that the killer would have had to walk down the passageway between the cribs."

"When?"

"Not long after you paid him a visit. Myself, I suspect a connection."

"Hank and now Wilson," Andrew mused.

"Quite a puzzle, is it not?" Farrell asked. "I would have suspected Wilson of ordering Hank put out of the way, but whose reach is long enough to end Wilson's life?"

Farrell's reach was long enough. "If Wilson knew anything, he did not give it away. He hinted at involvement from someone in the ton, but that is all I could get from him. Perhaps his murder was not related to my questions."

Farrell grinned and rubbed the dark stubble along his jaw. "Wishful thinking. Death follows close on your heels, Hunter. I'd say Wilson had to trust his killer to allow him close enough to strike. That would suggest a measure of trust and some sort of conspiracy, would it not?"

Andrew nodded. In truth, he was not sorry that a piece of dung like Wilson no longer walked the earth to sell women as human sacrifices.

Then the incongruity hit him. He looked at Farrell in astonishment. "But it should have been me, should it not? Why kill Wilson? Or Hank, for that matter? I was the one asking questions. Why wasn't *I* put out of the way?"

Farrell took another long drink from his cup before answering. "I have been wondering that myself, Hunter. And I believe I have the answer, though you will not like it."

"Out with it," Andrew growled.

"The killer is someone you know. Someone close to you. For some reason, he does not want you dead, but he doesn't want you to know what he is up to. Were I you, Hunter, I would watch my back and trust no one. I know I will."

Andrew wanted to argue, but the logic was so clear that he couldn't. He'd begun to wonder the same thing after his wine was drugged. He hadn't wanted to believe Henley had drugged them, but the evidence was compelling.

Henley had changed in the last months. He'd become sly and secretive, more prone to drunkenness. He and McPherson... McPherson? No. Surely not.

"Making a mental list of those you can trust?"

"Damn few. Tonight…" he murmured. "Someone else is going to die tonight if I do not find the answers to my questions."

"We do not have much time," Farrell acknowledged. "For all my questions, I've gotten precious little in return. I've heard more about the 'Thirteenth Sabbath.' Most of it is speculation, but there are a few tidbits that are more promising. I need more time, Hunter, to sort the wheat from the chaff. If I am right, I will have the information you need tonight."

"What have you heard thus far?"

"Midnight. A Mayfair location. An elite guest list."

"Are any women reported missing?"

"None in my strata. Yours?"

"None that I know. I will find out more this evening."

"I think the next victim will come from society, Hunter."

"Why?"

"*Virgin* sacrifice. That is the other thing I'm hearing. There are precious few virgins in the rookeries. And children are not in this particular pattern."

Andrew's stomach turned at the thought of children being used for such purposes.

Farrell stood and went to the sideboard to pour himself another cup of coffee. "The more I dig into this, the more I want to see an end to it, too. I have a few ideas. I know people. Highly connected people."

"So do I," Andrew said.

"Keep your name out of it, Hunter. The more questions you ask, the more danger you are in. And I think there may be someone else you need to protect?"

Bella! Damnation! She was too vulnerable. Too stubborn. If he did not watch her, she could stumble into the middle of this. "If I do not hear from you sooner, I will come here at nine o'clock tonight."

Farrell nodded and walked Andrew to the door. "By nine."

"Miss Isabella! Come down at once. Mr. Hunter is here, and he says he will not leave until you see him!"

Nancy's voice was bordering on hysterical, and Bella realized that Mama must already know they had a caller. "A moment," she called through her closed bedroom door. She paused long enough to check her appearance in her mirror. Dark smudges beneath her eyes bore testament to inadequate sleep, and the high color in her cheeks betrayed her apprehension. Something must be wrong. He'd told her he would come tomorrow. What was so urgent that he'd come today?

As she hurried down the stairs, Gina and Lilly fell in behind her. Oh, dear. How could she and Andrew talk when her sisters were hanging on every word? As if reading her mind, Gina gave a little shake of her head, as if to say she had no intention of leaving them alone.

Andrew was standing by the window, his hands clasped behind his back in an attitude of waiting. He turned and gave her that crooked grin that made her blush. She, Gina and Lilly all dropped a perfunctory curtsy. Her heart tripped a beat and she tried not to think of the things he'd done to her last night. Oh—or the things she'd done to him!

"Mr. Hunter, how nice to see you so soon again," Gina said, filling the awkward pause.

"Thank you, Miss Eugenia. And may I say it is good to see you looking so well this morning."

"We were just about to have our tea. Would you like to join us?" Lilly asked him.

"No, thank you, Miss Lillian. I just came to have a few words with your sister."

"Oh, it is no trouble at all, sir." Lilly sent a hovering Nancy away with a wave of her hand to fetch the tea, then sank into the middle of the sofa and folded her hands in her lap.

Gina settled in a chair and took up her embroidery hoop before casting a curious glance in Bella's direction.

Andrew gave her a helpless look and she almost laughed. He knew what to do in the most awkward situations, but he could not handle her sisters in a drawing room. The thought made her feel a bit calmer. She took a deep breath and gestured to a chair opposite the sofa before taking a place beside Lilly.

"It is a lovely day, is it not?" Lilly's expression was so completely innocent that Bella wondered where she had perfected such an art.

"Lovely...yes," Andrew repeated as he sat, looking at a loss. He cleared his throat and cast Bella a desperate look. "I wonder if you might consent to walk with me in the garden, Miss Isabella."

"I would..." A thumping gait on the stairs told Bella that Mama had collected herself and was on the way to sap any possible enjoyment from the gathering.

All eyes turned to the door and Mama entered, her hair mussed and her gown wrinkled. Bella would have groaned with embarrassment if not for Mama's unpleasant expression.

"Ah! Mr. Hunter again, is it?"

Andrew stood and offered a polite bow. "Madame."

"Come to call on Bella, did you? Has she mentioned the family is in mourning, sir?"

"She has, Mrs. O'Rourke. But there is a matter of some import I would like to discuss with her."

"Import? What is the chit up to?" Mama narrowed her eyes and gestured Lilly and Gina to the door with a shooing motion.

Lilly rolled her eyes as if to say she always missed the most interesting parts. Gina gave her a helpless shrug and closed the door behind them.

"Well, now," Mama said, looking between them. "Suppose you tell me what is afoot here, Mr. Hunter. You cannot have more than a passing acquaintance with my daughter. How has she encouraged your interest?"

Andrew stiffened and Bella realized he was offended on her behalf at the suggestion that she might have done something wrong or unbecoming for a lady. That fact caused her a confused mixture of pleasure and embarrassment. "Mama, I am certain that Mr. Hunter meant no insult. He merely—"

But Andrew's expression had hardened. A smile curved his lips, but Bella knew him well enough to know there was no warmth in the gesture. He went to her mother and took her elbow.

"As a woman of the world, Mrs. O'Rourke, I am confident that you know how quickly a man's interest can be engaged." He began leading her toward the door, ignoring the expression of astonishment on her mother's face. "Miss Isabella is easily the most comely of your daughters, so I know you will not be surprised when I tell you that she turns heads wherever she goes. Most certainly mine."

"Well, I—"

"But Miss Isabella and I must have a little time together to determine if we 'suit.'"

"But your name is not on the list of Lady Vandecamp's suitable—"

"And I shall be pleased to address myself to Lady Vandecamp at her earliest convenience. For the moment, however—" he paused to open the door and assist her mother into the passageway "—Miss Isabella and I have need of private conversation. I give you my oath that nothing untoward will take place. Should I misbehave, she can call to you."

"See here—"

"Thank you so much for understanding." And he closed the door in her face.

Bella covered her mouth to muffle her nearly hysterical giggle. "Oh, dear. I am so sorry for that."

He led her away from the door and lowered his voice. "I will handle your mother, Bella. Do not give her another thought."

She glanced back at the closed door, half expecting her mother to burst in and demand that Andrew leave at once. Instead, there was only silence and she could almost envision her mother and sisters with their ears to the door. Yes, he most certainly could handle her mother, and that thought warmed her clear to her toes. "I did not expect you until tomorrow," she said.

"I had to talk to you. I needed to be certain you and Miss Eugenia were safe and that you would stay at home tonight. Promise me, Bella. Do not go abroad."

"I have lectured Gina, and she said she will stay at home." But *she* had an appointment with Lord Humphries.

"And you, Bella? Will you stay at home?"

Drat! He'd seen through her ploy. "I wish you would not ask me to make promises I cannot keep. You must stop feeling responsible for me."

He cleared his throat. "I cannot help it. Surely you can appreciate my guilt over misreading your supposed lack of virtue. Had I known… I have never forced a girl before, Bella. I would not have started with you. And last night…"

She felt the heat rising to her cheeks and glanced at the door again.

"You did not force me that night at Thackery's, Andrew. I knew what you were doing, what you wanted, and I said nothing. I meant to, but I was carried away. The things you did…well, I had never felt such things before. I knew I could stop you. I nearly did. But, in the end, I think I wanted it as much as you did."

"That is the nature of seduction, Bella. I used my knowledge of a woman's weaknesses to overcome your good sense. You were innocent. You were not thinking clearly."

"Oh! Why must you contradict everything I say?" She nearly stopped when she saw his jaw tighten and a frown knit faint lines between his brows, but she lowered her voice and forged on. "Despite my behavior in society, I am not of such little consequence that I would allow myself to be swept up and seduced by the first handsome man to come along. Do you think so little of me as that? You must be addlepated!"

"Addlepated?" His dark eyes widened. "Think *little* of you? From the moment I met you, I have thought of nothing else. Allow me to demonstrate just how I *do* regard you."

She held her ground as he stepped closer and pulled her into his arms, his intent clear. "Why do you think I cannot countenance another man kissing you, Bella? Why do you think I am everywhere you go?"

"I thought it was because you disliked me and what I was doing. Because you wanted me to suffer for Mr. McPherson's death. Now I am not certain."

"Dear God, I am sorry for that. No, my dear, I follow you because I am captivated by you. No woman has ever engaged my interest so thoroughly. I am possessive of you because I cannot tolerate the thought that you might ever give another man the gift you've given me. Though you have every reason to loathe me."

"I do not loathe you."

"Listen carefully, Bella. We haven't much time before your mother's curiosity gets the best of her. Tomorrow, when this is over, I will come again and we will straighten this mess out. I want you to know that I will always provide for you. You need never worry over your future because of what I've done to you—ruining your prospects in such a vile manner."

"But—"

He bent his head and met her lips in a touch so soft that she might have dreamed it. He moaned and his arms tightened around her. She melded against him and slipped her arms around his neck, growing hot with the memory of last night.

With a muffled curse, he untwined her arms and stepped back mere seconds before the door burst open and her mother rushed in, Lilly and Gina fast on her heels.

"Here now! This is most improper. I must insist that you be chaperoned at all times, Mr. Hunter. At least until Lady Vandecamp has given her approval. And there will be no walks alone in the garden. Put that from your mind at once."

"As you wish, madam."

Bella watched as Andrew offered a small bow and skimmed by her mother on his way to the door. Thanks heavens he was gone! Another moment and she would have told him everything—what she'd learned, what Gina had seen and her plans for tonight. But he would have tried to stop her, and she had no intention of stopping so close to her goal.

Chapter Nineteen

Andrew leaned against the doorjamb of Wycliffe's office, his hand raised to knock. He wished he could wait longer for this particular interview. He'd spent years avoiding it, fooling himself that it would never come. But now, because of Isabella O'Rourke, he knew he had to make a clean slate of his life. Because of her. For her. To be worthy of her. For better or worse, his lies and secrets would end here and now.

He was tired of holding his sins inside, his guilt and his self-loathing. At first he'd told himself that it was for the good of Frederick's family. That they'd be happier not knowing what had really happened to their son and brother. Then he'd wondered if it was cowardice on his part—an unwillingness to face the consequences of his actions. Whatever the reason, the secret had poisoned him and nearly destroyed him. Prison, even execution, would be better than living with his damning secret another full day.

His only regret was Isabella. He had found the courage to confess because of her, but he would lose her in the bargain. He'd already made arrangements to transfer funds for an annuity to be paid to her. She would not live under reduced circumstances or take the role of poor relation because of what he'd done to her. The only thing that remained was to confess, and to finish his assignment. He took a deep breath and rapped on the door in three sharp knocks.

Wycliffe called entry and Andrew pushed the door open to find Wycliffe returning a stack of papers to a folder and looking up. "Come in and sit down, Hunter. Do not just stand there looking like you've lost your puppy."

Andrew grinned in spite of himself. He closed the door but he didn't want to sit. Restlessness, guilt and the old habit of standing at attention while addressing his commanding officer kept him standing.

"I gather you've got news," Wycliffe said.

"As we thought, the Thirteenth Sabbath is tonight. It will take place somewhere in Mayfair. Devlin Farrell is finding the exact place and time. He will have that information for me by tonight and I will pass it along to you."

"Excellent. I will alert the watch and call in my agents. The moment you send me word, I will dispatch them and—"

"I'd rather you didn't. The ritual will not begin until midnight or after. If they should get wind of anything unusual, or notice your men in the area, I suspect they'll either call it off or find another location. I am assuming you want to catch those responsible, not just those you might cast your net around in a general rout?"

Wycliffe sat back in his chair and nodded.

"Then I think our only choice is to allow the ritual to get underway before sending the charleys in. Catching those responsible while in the act should tell us not just who is involved, but who is in charge. I'd give a year off my life to know who that bastard is."

"That is risky, Hunter. If they've got themselves another sacrifice, and if the timing isn't right…"

"I'll take Jamie and Charlie with me. Pistols and knives in our boots."

"How will we know when to enter?"

"Get me a whistle from the watch. Keep your men hidden until you hear it."

"That should work. But I do not think I should call the entire watch. We need to keep this on the hush. The more people who know, the more likely word will get out."

Andrew rubbed his arm. Edwards had replaced the old bandage this morning and the bindings were a little snug. "I wish I knew how many will be there. I am guessing between twelve and twenty. I have no fear that my brothers and I could hold that many at bay until the watch arrives. We will have the element of surprise on our side. But if there is a delay—"

"There won't be."

He prayed Wycliffe was right, or there'd be three fewer Hunters in London come dawn tomorrow.

"I am curious, Hunter. Why have you not involved Humphries in this? Seems the sort of thing that would be right up his alley."

"You said you chose me because my friends were likely to know something, and that I should be discreet. As it turns out, you were right. I suspect some of them are in it up to their teeth."

"Yet your brothers—"

"Charlie and Jamie got caught up in the last Sabbath with me but they don't know the particulars. I trust them with my life."

"That's good enough for me. You've always been an excellent judge of character."

Even the thought of that made Andrew squirm. Had he truly been a good judge of character, perhaps Wycliffe's brother would be alive today.

He squared his shoulders and stood a little straighter. "As to that, Lord Wycliffe, I believe you are wrong. I've made many mistakes. Fatal mistakes."

Wycliffe blinked, a telling trait. He could not know what was coming, but he would know it was going to be unpleasant. "You have something to say, Hunter?"

"Long overdue."

Wycliffe emitted a sigh so deep that Andrew almost lost heart. "I think I know what you want to say, and it really isn't necessary."

"You haven't any idea, sir. And, believe me, it is necessary. I only hope that when I am done, you will allow me to finish this assignment before you—"

"For God's sake, Hunter! Spit it out, will you?"

Years of pain and guilt tightened his throat and twisted his stomach, threatening to hold back the words that would surely condemn him. They'd been a constant albatross, and harder to shed than he'd thought. "I killed your brother."

Wycliffe didn't even blink this time. He stood and went to his window to look out at the street, bathed in late-afternoon sunshine.

Andrew braced himself for a scathing denouncement or a spate of angry curses and questions, but Wycliffe's words, when they came, were soft and thoughtful.

"I know. I've always known."

He stared in stunned disbelief as Wycliffe turned back to him. "How…"

"The family knew what Frederick was. We always knew, though we never spoke it aloud. We hoped that sending him away to war would mature him. Perhaps awaken some virtue or strength of character in him."

"He—"

"He was the baby of the family, you see. Everyone from our mother to the maid spoilt him shamelessly. I doubt he'd ever heard the word no until he was sent off to school."

Andrew sat and stared at his hands, clenched from the tension in his muscles. "Why did you not tell me?"

"You were his commanding officer. I assigned him to you because I knew you would make a man of him or die trying. He admired you, you know. He fancied you were friends."

Andrew groaned. "We were, sir. Until we could not be."

"I blame myself, you see." Wycliffe turned and faced him. "I gave you the worst assignments, the most dangerous posts, knowing you were equal to them and hoping Frederick would learn from your example. When I sent you out that last time… our intelligence was faulty. I did not realize what you'd be facing, or I'd have sent the whole damn regiment."

"The slaughter…the rage…" Andrew shook his head, remembering. "I had never seen anything like it before. None of us were prepared."

"War is never a pretty thing, Hunter. It either brings out the best or the worst in a man. For Frederick," He shrugged, leaving the conclusion unspoken.

Andrew closed his eyes, seeing it again as if it were yesterday. "Valle del Fuego." His voice was raw and, now the worst of his confession was out, he could not stop. "I've seldom seen the enemy more savage. And our response was…worse. Frederick fought like a dervish that day. No one could stop him. Even after it was over, after the surrender, he was like one possessed. I called orders to him. Sanders seized his arm to stay him from slaughtering a woman who was standing in her doorway, calling to her child in the street. Frederick sliced his gut open and then finished the woman off. Blood lust. I could not get to him, the bodies were that thick in the streets. Sanders died quickly, but Frederick…still could not stop. I think he had gone mad—killed one too many men or simply seen too much blood. He'd dismissed the human element and only saw them as obstacles, much like a forest to be cut though."

He opened his eyes and found that Wycliffe's face had paled. "It was the baby that decided me, sir. The child saw his mother struck and was terrified. He went running to her as she fell. Frederick turned on him. He turned his bayonet on a toddler, sir."

"So you stopped him the only way you could," Wycliffe finished.

Andrew's hands began to shake. "He was my friend. He never should have been on that detail. I should have seen it coming. I should have seen the signs. I should have sent him behind the lines. Instead, I raised my rifle and—"

"You couldn't have known."

"I killed a friend and a comrade. I took a life that had been entrusted to me. 'Tis one thing to be killed by the enemy and another by your commanding officer.

"I thought it would be easier for you, for his entire family, to think of him as fallen to the enemy. I pray you will believe that that, and not cowardice or self-interest, is the reason for my long silence. The truth seemed so unnecessarily cruel. I swore that I would never raise my hand against a friend again, and I have kept that vow, but I have lived with the knowledge that it was I who ended Frederick's life, not an enemy's sword. That an English court of law would deem my life forfeit for what I'd done."

"You're wrong there, Hunter. You did what few men would have the courage and moral fortitude to do. In any case, I would consider it a personal favor if you would refrain from making this confession of yours public. Let sleeping dogs lie."

Andrew felt lighter, clearer than he had since the war, the burden of the wasted years and crushing guilt lifted from his shoulders. He nodded, but he had his own question. "How did you know what had happened? That it was me?"

"You wore your grief and guilt like a badge. I had no small amount of guilt over the affair, myself. And when I saw what it was doing to you…well, I should have spoken to you, but I suspected you did not want to expose my brother. I, too, believed that to be the best course for the family."

"What of the charges against me?"

"There will be no charges. It is over, Hunter. The war is over. The ghosts are laid to rest. Let that be an end to it. I would be indebted if you would never speak of this again."

He got to his feet as Wycliffe sat again.

"Now get on with you, Hunter," Wycliffe said without looking up. "I'll be waiting here for your instructions."

"Aye," he said as he turned to the door. "By midnight."

Boxes and boxes of new gowns had arrived from the dressmaker after Andrew had departed. Bella, Gina and Lilly had spent teatime trying them on and admiring one another. Lady V. had selected the colors to be as light and airy as possible without flying in the face of propriety for mourning. Not even the subdued colors had dampened their spirits for long.

After supper was over and Mama had retired to her room, Bella selected a luscious pale-gray silk trimmed in a mulberry Greek key edging for her stop at the Royal Opera House and her meeting later with Lord Humphries. She took time over her toilette, matching mulberry and gray ribbons. She hoped she would, at last, charm Lord Humphries into a kiss.

The clock on her dressing table struck the hour of eight with a soft chime, and Bella swept up the gray silk pelisse she'd laid out. There was not a rain cloud in sight and she would need nothing heavier tonight.

Bella tiptoed down the corridor and knocked softly on Gina's door. She knocked twice more before she turned the knob and peeked in. The wick of the lamp on her bedside table had been turned low, and Gina was nowhere to be seen. A quick look through Gina's boxes showed one new gown was missing, and a deeply fringed shawl.

Drat! Gina had gone out to meet her new friends again. She'd sworn! If she hurried, perhaps she could catch Gina at the theater. Bella would throttle her once she was safe.

She braced herself and knocked on Lilly's door. Her sister opened it quickly and her eyes grew round when she saw how Bella was dressed.

"Where are you going, Bella? Do Mama and Gina know?"

Bella slipped into the room and closed the door. "Gina is gone. She must have left no more than half an hour ago. I am going after her. I fear she may be in danger."

"What?" Lilly's eyes rounded in astonishment and tears welled in the blue depths. "Danger? Oh, Bella. Not…not…"

"No! Be calm, Lilly. I think she just went to the theater. I hope to find her there and bring her home. I wanted to tell you because…well, someone should know. Please do not alarm Mama. She would have apoplexy. But…but—"

"What?" Lilly's fingers bit into Bella's arm. "Oh, do not frighten me so."

"If, for some unaccountable reason, Gina and I are not home by morning, please go at once to Lord Wycliffe at the Home Office. He will know what to do."

"Oh, Bella! What have you and Gina got yourselves into?"

"Nothing. We just…" She sighed. Lilly deserved to know the truth. "We are looking for Cora's killer. I am afraid Gina may have got in over her head."

Lilly took a deep breath and squared her shoulders. "If there is anything else I can do, you must tell me. Do not concern yourself over me or Mama. Just find Gina and bring her back safely. I shall wait up, Bella. Knock when you are home."

Bella gave her a quick hug before hurrying down the stairs and onto the street. She hailed a passing hackney and was at the Royal Opera House before she could think twice. Alas, there was no sign of Gina or Mr. Henley. Gina must have whisked him away, knowing Bella would not be far behind. Oh, she would give Gina such a good dressing-down when she found her!

Belmonde's was not far and she walked there, trying to sort things out in her mind. Everything had become so terribly complicated with

Gina in the mix. Clearly, she would need help to find her sister. If only she knew how to reach Andrew. Whatever it was he had to do tonight, she thought he would put it aside to help her, if only she could find him. Perhaps Lord Humphries would know how to find him, or their mutual friend, Mr. Henley, and thus, Gina.

Mr. Biddle bowed and took her pelisse. "I have not seen Mr. Hunter this evening, madam."

"Thank you, Mr. Biddle. I am not certain if he will be coming. I do not plan to be here for long. Could I leave a message for him, should he come?"

"Of course, madam. You will find pen and paper at the desk in the foyer."

Bella returned to the foyer. She was scribbling a quick note to Andrew, informing him that Gina was missing and asking his help to look for her, when the man himself arrived. He looked startled and not altogether pleased to see her.

He took her arm and led her aside. "Did I not warn you to stay at home tonight?"

"Did I not tell you I must find my sister's killer?" she countered.

"What can one night mean to you? Let this one pass, and then I shall help you in whatever manner you wish."

She shook her head. "Lady V. expects me to participate in the engagements she is arranging, or she will send me back to Ireland. Every night is precious to me."

"Bloody damn hell," he muttered. Then he gripped both her arms and squeezed. "I do not have time for this tonight, Bella. If I am to accomplish anything, I need to know you are safe at home."

"And how shall I remain safe at home when Gina is not?"

He blinked and a dark look came over his face. "Where is your sister?" He eased his grip, led her into the main salon and to the nearest alcove, and sat her down. "Tell me what this is about, Bella."

"Gina has got it into her head that she must help me find Cora's killer. After you encountered her last night, I thought she would stop. She promised. But tonight when I went to her room, she was gone. I know that she had been invited to meet a group at the Royal Opera House tonight. I went there straightaway, but I was too late. There was no trace of her or Mr. Henley."

A muscle jumped along Andrew's jaw. "Henley?"

"He was the one she was supposed to meet."

He sank to the cushions beside her. "Damn Wycliffe and all his secrets! Bella, listen carefully, because I do not have time to repeat myself. Wycliffe never gave up on finding your sister's murderer. He only wanted you to believe that so he could use you as bait to find the killer."

She frowned. "No. He said—"

"He told you a pack of lies. Nearly two weeks ago he enlisted me to keep my eyes and ears open for any activities out of the ordinary. He pointed me toward witches' Sabbaths or satanic rituals. He said he was trying to solve a string of murders of young women who had either disappeared or whose bodies were found bearing certain markings. Cora was one of those women, though I did not know it then."

"Satanic rituals?" The horror of such a thing sent a shiver up her spine. To think of Cora at the mercy of such people! "But she had a suitor. Someone who abducted her."

"Yes. Someone she trusted." He gripped her hands again, pleading for her to understand. "It was not until you confessed why you were kissing men that I understood your involvement. I'd have told you then, but Wycliffe had insisted upon secrecy. He assured me that he had someone watching you, and that I should protect you, too. Regrettably, I learned this too late to protect you from myself."

"Then you've only known a few days?"

He sighed. "I am sorry, Bella. But you know everything now."

"How…how many more women are dead?"

"Twelve that we can trace. Before that, we can only guess."

Her stomach burned and twisted into a knot. "How can you be certain my sister was a part of this?"

"The markings left on her. The things that were done to her. Bella, I have come to believe that Henley has something to do with all this. In fact, I believe there is to be another ritual killing tonight. Friday the thirteenth, and a thirteenth victim. A virgin, our sources tell us."

"And Gina is with him? Oh!" Suddenly some of the odd things that Gina had told her made some sort of twisted sense. "She said that Mr. Henley took her to a tableau vivant last night, and that a ritual murder was enacted. She said that Mr. Henley had asked her if she was… was virgin."

The look on Andrew's face terrified her. There was a wild, almost feral, light in his eyes, and his mouth had distorted into a snarl. "Damn it, Bella! I am taking you home right now."

"But—"

"Do not quarrel with me. I will win and it will only waste time."

"But Cora said her killer was dark. And tall. Mr. Henley is neither."

"But Henley has friends who are. Listen carefully. I only came here to find my brothers. James, I see, is at the tables. I shall collect him and we shall find Charlie and be off. I have a lead as to where and when the ritual will be held. You will only get in the way and slow us down."

Bella's mind whirled, trying to think of any argument he would accept or anything she could do that he could not. But he was right. She was in the way. If worrying about her slowed Andrew down or cost Gina her life… "Go! Hurry. Save her, Andrew. I shall see myself home. I will have Biddle summon me a hackney. I will be safe enough."

He nodded, clearly relieved that she had accepted his terms. "I will come to you the moment I can. If Eugenia comes home in the meantime, keep her there, even if you must knock her over the head. Do you understand?"

"Yes! Now go."

He pulled her roughly into his arms and kissed her in the way he had the first night they'd met: raw, frantic, hungry. She returned that hunger, desperate for him to stay, and just as desperate for him to go. Then, without another word, he stood and called to his brother, and the two of them left without a backward glance.

Breathless at the revelations, she remained sitting until her trembling stilled. She could not make sense of half of it, but she trusted Andrew to find Gina. There was something else, though. Something nagging at the corners of her mind. Something that she should remember or know.

After a few moments, she stood and smoothed the skirts of her gown, then made her way to the vestibule. Mr. Biddle saw her and wordlessly turned toward the cloak room. At that moment, Lord Humphries entered Belmonde's. He saw her and his face split in a wide grin.

"I scarcely dared to believe you were here, my dear. I just saw Hunter's coach pull away as I arrived. I thought you might have gone with him."

"I...am not feeling well. I was just going home."

"What a pity." He took her elbow and turned her back to the main salon. "I hope you will have a glass of wine with me first. It will calm your nerves. Or your stomach. Or whatever it is that ails you."

"Really, Lord Humphries, I should be going."

"And so you shall, m'dear. As soon as you've had a little glass of wine. I have a special herb that is well known for its calming effect on the stomach."

She reckoned having a glass of wine was better than making a scene with Lord Humphries and did not protest as he sat her on the banquette and went to fetch them wine. After all, they were in a public place.

Good to his word, he was back in quick time and handed her a glass. "Drink up, Bella. You will feel better within a few minutes."

She took a sip and wrinkled her nose. "Odd," she observed.

"Just for the first swallow. It disguises the herb and improves with each sip."

Within a few moments, she was feeling better. Her tension eased somewhat and she managed a smile. "Thank you, Lord Humphries. I believe you were correct. I am feeling better. But I really must go on home."

"Quite. I have an appointment, m'self. Shall we finish our wine and go? I shall give you a ride."

"Not necessary, My Lord."

"Dash. I hope we shall become much better acquainted tonight."

She smiled, thinking how very smooth and charming he was. And then, because of the hint in his words, it occurred to her that he was expecting a kiss. She had been willing to kiss the devil himself for Cora. But now that she'd fallen in love with Andrew Hunter, it was too late.

Another swallow of wine for courage and then she looked up into dark eyes that were studying her rather too closely. "Lord Humphries, I hope you will understand, but I have, um, decided to mend my ways. I doubt I shall be going abroad much in the future. And I have kissed more men than I should. My reasons…well, shall we just say that things have changed?"

"Oh, I don't think so, my sweet." He grinned, and a chill raced through her. "You can mend your ways fast after I have got what all my friends have got. What Drew Hunter had."

Surely he couldn't be suggesting that she make love with him? No one knew about that but Andrew and her, and he would never tell. Would he? Or did Humphries mean a kiss?

"Ah, I see you have taken my meaning, Bella." He leaned closer. "We've been on the verge of it for days now, have we not? Are you not in the least bit curious?"

Was she? The wine was corroding her resistance. The subtle relaxation was turning to lethargy. What was wrong with her? She could not even move as Lord Humphries lowered his mouth to hers.

He hesitated the barest fraction of a moment as he slipped his left arm around her and cupped the back of her head with his right hand. Then he pressed his lips against hers. She gave a halfhearted push against his chest in a futile attempt to dislodge him. When she tried to speak, she tasted the bitter wine on his lips, and when he released her, he licked his lips.

Bitter. Bitter? She felt faint. Cold fear spiked in her stomach. *It was him!* Cora's killer! "You…you…"

"Me? Me, what, m'dear?"

She couldn't think clearly. Scream? But she could barely raise her voice beyond a whisper. "You…let me go."

"Oh, I don't think so." He held the glass to her lips and poured the remainder down her throat before he stood and pulled her up, supporting her with an arm around her waist. "Try not to worry too much, Bella. 'Twill wear off in a bit. You will have sufficient time to recover before the festivities."

"Cora."

"Ah, yes. Dear Cora. She was a gullible little thing. It took me a while to figure out who you were and why you seemed familiar. I finally followed you, and found where you lived. Cora's house. I used to wait for her across the street in the park."

Mr. Biddle frowned as they passed him on their way out to the street.

"H-Hunter," she managed over the thickness of her tongue.

She had no idea if he had heard or understood her. He turned away, as if he would go for her pelisse again, and then she was being pushed into Lord Humphries's coach, landing on the forward-facing seat. Lord Humphries settled himself on the facing seat and fussed with the folds of his cravat.

"I really must remember to send your mother flowers, Bella. How utterly thoughtful of her to bring three such delectable creatures as you, Miss Eugenia and Miss Cora to town. Hmm. I shall have to think of something equally entertaining for little Miss Lillian. I've always fancied sisters."

And with that, a deep darkness descended. Her last rational thought was that she wasn't a virgin. She'd cheat Lord Humphries of that, at least.

Chapter Twenty

Leaving Jamie to wait for Charlie in the common room, Andrew went to Farrell's private office. A bottle of excellent brandy waited on the desk between them, and Farrell poured them both a generous draught.

"Easy," Andrew told him. "I want to keep my wits about me."

"If you had your wits about you, Hunter, you'd keep as far away from this muck as possible."

Andrew grinned. "Then you've got what I want?"

"Aye, but before I hand it over, I want to know what your plans are."

"To stop it. End it once and for all."

Farrell heaved a longsuffering sigh. "I gathered as much. But how?"

"I cannot know that until we are in the midst of it. What we do will depend upon who, how many, where and what resources we have at hand."

Farrell accepted that explanation but did not look too pleased. "I'd advise going in armed to the teeth. Whatever you can carry in, do so."

"Planned on it."

Farrell retrieved a pouch from his desk drawer, Farrell tossed it to Andrew. "There's your invitations."

"Invitations? Jaysus! Who sends invitations to a sacrifice?"

"I do not know what is customary for such events. I only know that this one is rather exclusive."

Andrew opened the pouch and found two stylish invitations. They were printed on red parchment and folded in triangles. Inside the triangle was a circle, and inside that, a wyvern—confirmation that this involved the Blood Wyvern Brotherhood. He looked back at Farrell. "Only two?"

"Do you think these vermin wouldn't notice an army arrive? No, two, I think, is the most you can slip in. Choose your guest wisely. I'd take someone with a good right hook. And do you have any idea what those two invitations cost me?"

Andrew could only imagine. Considerably more than Farrell owed him, no doubt. "How?"

"I found the printer. Had him print those. He was terrified, but he, ah, saw reason. I found the others, too. Merchants with uncommon orders for wine and sulfur, tailors hired to make black robes to resemble those of monks, all paid in advance. I had them make two." Farrell retrieved a paper parcel tied with string from a drawer in his desk and slid it across the desk to him. "But the most telling evidence was a large purchase of opium. The scum will be needing it to ensure compliance and a modicum of silence during the ritual. Too much screaming would alert the watch."

Bile rose in Andrew's throat. He could not imagine the villainy required to conceive such a thing. He glanced down at the invitations. Eleven Thirty was printed in bold black over the emblem. "There's a time, but no address."

"That!" Farrell chuckled. "That was a bit more difficult to come by. We were right about the neighborhood. I found an estate agent who recently let the old Ballinger manor on the outskirts of Mayfair. Do you know it?"

Andrew nodded. He'd ridden by there many times. The gates and the house appeared to be in good repair, but the grounds were a bit overgrown.

"There is a small chapel behind the manor, connected to the house by a tunnel, and I'd wager that is where the ritual will take place."

"Who signed the lease?"

"The transaction was handled by mail. The rent was paid in cash, and the name is, no doubt, a sham—as was the name of the man ordering the wine and robes. Or do you know anyone by the name of Wyvernman?"

Andrew snorted. "Not even subtle."

"Whoever your man is, he knows how to cover his tracks. Cash, enough of it, buys consciences and silence."

"Is that how you acquired the information?"

Farrell shrugged. "A little cash and a lot of persuasion."

Andrew didn't want to think about what sort of persuasion Farrell had used to come up with this information. Surely Wycliffe's agents had tapped some of the same sources, but they had come up with nothing. Farrell's complete lack of scruples had come in handy.

"Is there anything else?" he asked.

Farrell shifted his considerable size in his chair and took a deep breath. "I know I needn't warn you that you are playing with some very nasty fellows, but I must caution you again that they could be close associates of yours. Friends, perhaps. Even…family."

Family? Good God! Did Farrell know more than he was saying? "Do not start holding back on me now," he said. "If there is something I should know, I'd rather hear it from you than be blindsided when I can least afford it."

"I merely wanted to impress the need for discretion on you." He shook his head. "You, of all people, know that the darkness in a man's heart is often secret. How much do you trust those closest to you?"

The man had a point. Andrew trusted very few men implicitly, but his brothers were among them. Lockwood, Jamie, Charlie—he would not hesitate to trust his life to any of them. Curious, he asked, "Whom do you trust, Farrell?"

A sardonic, almost cruel, twist of his lips said what words did not. He took another drink and pushed his glass away. "Be very careful tonight," he said again. "I'd hate to hear you'd been caught in your own trap. And have a care for those around you. In robes and cowls, you will not recognize most of them. 'Twould be a pity if you killed the wrong man, eh?"

"A great pity," Andrew agreed as he stood.

Charlie had arrived at Farrell's by the time Andrew made his way back downstairs. He found him and Jamie with their heads together in a corner of the common room, tankards of ale in front of them. He sat across from them and slipped the invitations across the table.

228

"Two?" Jamie asked when he saw them.

"That is all Farrell could safely get us. Along with two robes." He patted the parcel in his lap.

Charlie glanced at the parcel and back at the invitations. "Seems like extraordinary measures just to crash a party."

Andrew squirmed. He couldn't ask his brothers to help him when their lives could be at risk. They had to know what they were facing, or they had to stay out of it.

Jamie read his hesitation. "What's behind this, Drew?"

"Rumor has it that there is to be a human sacrifice tonight. Everything I've learned has led me to believe this," he gestured at the invitations, "is it."

Charlie blanched. "By God, Drew. What have you got yourself into?"

"More trouble than I can handle alone. Who's in?"

"Me," Jamie said without hesitation.

Charlie shifted his gaze from one to the other. "Me," he said at last. "What is our game?"

Andrew sighed in relief. "We are going to stop it. If possible, we are going to take the leaders into custody and turn them over to Lord Wycliffe at the Home Office."

Jamie smiled. "It won't be that easy."

"I anticipate trouble. I would be surprised if there is not violence. Whoever is arranging this is a killer. So far, twelve women. Perhaps more that we do not know about. In addition, I believe he had Hank and Wilson murdered when I started asking questions. Farrell will be next if we do not stop him."

Charlie snorted. "Farrell can take care of himself."

"I thought the same of Wilson. Apparently our villain has a long reach."

"Do we have a plan?" Jamie asked.

Andrew made a quick decision and hoped he wouldn't regret it. "Jamie will come in with me. We shall bring whatever weapons we can secrete in our clothes or beneath our robes once we are there. Charlie, you will wait outside in the shadows. Watch who comes in or goes out. Do you have a piece of paper and a lead?"

Charlie nodded and patted his waistcoat pocket.

"Make note of those you recognize. If something goes amiss, send straightaway to Wycliffe." Andrew handed him the whistle he had gotten from the Home Office.

Charlie took the whistle and frowned. "This whole blasted affair is 'amiss.' Why do we not send for Wycliffe at once?"

"Because they'd blunder in before we have the evidence. And there's too damn many of them to disguise. Sometimes I think the watch could not find their left hand in the dark. I want to stop these bastards once and for all, not just foil them for one night."

"Aye, well, how will I know if something goes amiss?"

"I am trusting your instincts, Charlie. Just have a care. If you call them too soon, we may not have the evidence we need to convict before the bench at Old Bailey. If you call them too late..." He shrugged.

"Meantime, I've made sure Wycliffe is in his office, waiting for word from me. But if you cannot get to him, summon the nearest watch and send him after Wycliffe."

They stood to go and Charlie slipped the whistle into his jacket pocket. He frowned and took out a folded and sealed paper. "Damn. Forgot all about this. Biddle asked me to give this to you."

"Biddle?" Andrew turned the paper over in his hand. There was no writing. He recognized the seal. Byron Daschel, Lord Humphries.

"Aye. He said Dash left it for you and that it was something you'd be pleased to have."

He popped the seal and unfolded the page. A red triangular parchment fell out. The design was growing all too familiar. *An invitation.* Dash's usual scrawl darkened the inside of the folded paper. "I believe this is what you've been looking for. Enjoy yourself."

"Dash was not there?"

"According to Biddle, he'd just gone. Ah, yes! That was the second part of the message. Something about Miss O'Rourke, if I recall correctly."

"What about Bella?"

"Biddle said she was about to leave when Dash arrived but stayed to have a glass of wine with him. Evidently she became ill. Biddle said she was quite incapacitated when Dash escorted her out. Left her pelisse, too. He wouldn't have bothered you with it, he said, if Miss O'Rourke hadn't called your name just before—"

But Andrew was beyond listening. His mind reeled with the possibilities. Bella had been hale and hearty when he'd left her. For her to become ill so quickly...

God! Not Dash. Henley. Henley was the one who'd drawn Eugenia along, accustomed her to meeting him, trusting him. It was Henley who had taken her tonight. Henley who'd drugged the wine at the last ritual. Henley whose appetites were known to border on the bizarre. But not Dash. It couldn't be.

"Anything else you forgot, Charlie?"

He looked wounded. "Of course not. Did you think you could spring a human sacrifice on me and expect that I'd take it in stride? The message has only been delayed a matter of minutes."

Andrew was torn between chasing Bella and Dash down and following through on his assignment. Yet how could he concentrate on the events tonight when he did not know what had become of Bella? "Charlie, listen carefully. Go to the O'Rourke home on James Street. Try to find out if Bella and her sister Eugenia are there without raising an alarm."

"What about you?"

"Once you've determined that they are at home, come meet us. We will be at the Ballinger Manor on the outskirts of Mayfair. If they are not..." then they were in grave danger, and the gravest danger was where he would be. "Fetch Wycliffe and come meet us."

"Does she have something to do with what is happening tonight?" Charlie asked.

"The sacrifice tonight is to be a woman," Andrew told them. "To be precise, a virgin." But no one would know that Bella was not a virgin. "Bella's sister is missing. And if Bella is missing, too..."

Charlie turned away and headed for the door without another word. Jamie threw some coins on the table and gave Andrew a grim smile. "One way or the other, we will find the O'Rourke girls. Do not doubt it. And do not let it distract you."

Nausea swept over Bella in waves as she opened her eyes. The smell of mold in the dank darkness compounded the sensation and made her roll to her side on the straw pallet. A single weak candle had been stuck in its own wax on the stone floor, revealing the small, square windowless room. A storeroom? A cell?

The voices that had wakened her were faint, as if coming from outside the door or an adjacent room. Lord Humphries and another vaguely familiar voice. She could not hear all of it, but she caught enough to realize her danger.

"…doubt she is virgin," Lord Humphries was saying. "After all, Hunter has been at her like a stallion in rut and he rarely fails. But she will make a nice little surprise for him, don't you think?"

"Aye, but what if he doesn't come? What if Charlie didn't deliver the invitation?"

"He will come, by hook or by crook. He's been looking for us for weeks now, and he'll finally join us tonight. He will be one of us again, just as we were in Spain."

The other man chuckled, sending a chill up her spine.

Andrew. Had he lied to her? Was he involved in this? No, else she would not be a surprise. Was he in danger because of her? Did he suspect his friend was a murderer?

"She hasn't come around. How much did you give her?"

"More than I ordinarily would, but I had to get her out of Belmonde's without her raising an alarm. 'Twould be a pity if she doesn't waken and we have to put her on the altar unconscious. I like them warm and squirming."

Bella shuddered, revulsion heightening her nausea. A key rattled at the door and she swallowed her rising bile. She closed her eyes and stilled her breathing, hoping to stall the time when she would have to deal with Lord Humphries.

Hinges creaked as the door opened, and then a long pause. Remaining motionless, she prayed that they would go before she could no longer contain herself.

"How much did you say you gave her?"

The toe of a boot nudged her hip. "Hmm. She should have come around by now. I might have miscalculated. She is small, and this was her first dose. Hope it was not enough to kill her."

"She's still breathing. What do you say we take her now? The others will not care as long as our little Eugenia is still virgin," the other voice replied.

Gina! Oh, it was true! They had her, and they were planning on killing her tonight. She felt a scream rising in her throat and struggled to keep it contained. Feigning unconsciousness was her only chance.

"As tempting as that idea is, we have things to do. Miss Eugenia has to be prepared. The guests are starting to arrive. I've got a sewer rat guarding the chapel door, taking invitations and directing guests to the vestry, but I cannot trust him to maintain order until the rites begin. You, Henley, will perform that service."

The door closed again but Bella did not hear a lock turn. Had they forgotten? Or had they been so confident that she was incapacitated that they had dismissed the possibility of escape? She remained still for another full minute before she moved and risked a peek.

Yes, gone, thank heavens, and just in time. A clammy sweat beaded her forehead and she crawled to the chamber pot in one corner to void her stomach. Pray she had also rid herself of lingering effects. She felt better almost at once when she found a water pitcher near the pallet to rinse her mouth.

She pressed her ear to the door but could hear no sounds, no trace of a guard. Cautiously she tried the latch. The door inched open with a faint squeak, and she peered into the corridor. She made out a staircase leading upward at each end of the dimly lit passageway, and another corridor intersecting this one, confirming what she had suspected. She was underground. Screaming would only alert her captors rather than summon help.

She closed the door and leaned back against it. She could not just blunder out and risk encountering Lord Humphries or Mr. Henley. She had to think—and quickly. Had to form a plan. She had to find Gina. Had to get them both out of here. But how?

With a muffled thud, the glass of a lower-story manor window cracked. Andrew pulled the fragments from the sash, dropping them silently onto the grass. Jamie, holding the parcel with their robes, waited while he climbed through.

There had been faint lights in the small chapel, but none shone in the manor. Andrew had a legitimate invitation now, and Jamie could follow a few minutes later. But it would be an advantage if they could sneak in unnoticed. The best way was to find the tunnel leading from the house to the chapel.

Jamie tossed the parcel through the window and followed a moment later. "Jaysus," he cursed in a theatrical whisper. "I'd think it would be easier to simply ask Dash if you could bring me along."

"I don't want him to know you are here. Until we see how the land lies, it is better to keep your presence secret."

Jamie nodded. "I pray Charlie gets here soon, and I pray he has good news."

"Wishful thinking." Andrew dismissed his brother's optimism with a soft laugh. "Now where do you suppose the kitchen is?"

"You're asking me? Faith. I do not believe I've ever seen one."

Andrew headed for the back corner of the house nearest the stables and found what they were looking for. He pointed to a door on the inner wall. "To the cellar, I'd wager." And he was right. A small lantern was hanging on a peg just inside the door and shone a weak light into the darkness below.

"Why are these things always held in some subterranean vault?"

"Closer to hell," he whispered, and Jamie grinned.

At the foot of the stairs, they turned in the direction of the chapel and made their way through empty wine racks to a door in the paneling. It stood ajar and another distant light beckoned them onward. Bless Devlin Farrell and his infallible information.

Andrew had gauged the distance from the manor to the chapel to be no more than two hundred feet, and he paced himself now to be certain the earthen tunnel did not lead off in a wrong direction. When they came at last to another door, Andrew put the lantern down and listened for a moment. Nothing. He took his watch from his pocket and read the dial. Nearly eleven-thirty. If luck was with him, any lingering guards would be on their way to the chapel.

He swung the heavy panel back and stepped through into another corridor, this one better lit and constructed. Arches and niches told him he was in the family vaults beneath the chapel. He motioned Jamie forward and whispered, "Put your robe on now. If we are found, I will tell them that you were escorting me to the chapel."

Jamie nodded and broke the string securing the parcel. Andrew left the extra robe on the floor behind the tunnel door while Jamie slipped the other over his head and lifted the cowl to obscure his face. He hoped he'd be able to pick his brother out of a crowd of like-garbed participants. If not, they'd arrange a signal.

Remembering to hide his weapon, Jamie pushed a long dagger into his boot and turned to Andrew. "Better give me yours, too, in case they make you leave them in the vestry."

Andrew handed over his knife. He hadn't bothered to bring a sword, knowing there would be no way to hide such a long blade. Whatever happened in the next hour, he could not even begin to hope it would not involve violence. It was far more likely that someone would die. Pray it was not Bella.

As she tiptoed down the corridor following the faint sounds of voices, Bella tried each of the doors she passed, but without success. Gina had to be here somewhere. What had Lord Humphries said? They needed to prepare her? What, in heaven's name, did that mean?

The sound of voices grew louder as she approached a bend in the passageway. One more door remained. She tried the latch and it gave without a sound. She slipped inside, feeling so vulnerable in the open passageway and glad of the respite.

This room was very like the one where she'd been held prisoner. A pallet, a single candle and a chamber pot. She turned and found pegs attached to the back of the door.

And from the pegs hung Gina's clothing. Everything. Gown, chemise, stays, drawers and stockings! But that meant that Gina must be…naked?

Bella gulped as her heartbeat skipped. She spun around to look at the pallet again, noticing the small pile of personal items for the first time. Gina's amethyst pendant, her reticule, her gloves. Then she froze, trying to comprehend what this meant. Where Gina was. What they were doing with her. And all the while Andrew's voice was echoing in her head. A ritual killing? *Human* sacrifice? Virgin sacrifice…

A hand clamped over her mouth while another circled her, pinning her arms to her sides and pulling her back against a hard, lean form. She tried to scream, but she could not make a sound. Lord Humphries had come back for her!

"Sh-h," a familiar voice whispered in her ear.

She went weak with relief and nodded her understanding. When he loosened his hold around her, she turned and threw her arms around his neck. "Andrew!" she whispered. "Oh, thank God! Where did you come from? Have you found Gina?"

"Hush, and listen carefully," he said. "Jamie is with me. He is waiting in the passageway. Follow me."

Bella had so many questions, but they would have to wait. She followed Andrew back down the corridor, James dressed in a monk's robe behind her. To make certain she did not bolt? Or to protect her? They came to a door at the far end, and Andrew pulled her through into a dark earthen tunnel.

He waited until James was through and then closed the door. "Bloody hell! I know what happened. Biddle sent me a message to warn me what Dash had done. Are you all right, Bella? Did he hurt you? Did he touch you?"

She shook her head. "He forced me to drink a bitter wine. I am certain now that it was drugged. I cannot recall anything from leaving Belmonde's to waking up here."

He pulled her into his arms and kissed the top of her head. "Thank God…thank God. But what am I going to do with you now? I cannot leave you here, and I cannot take you with me."

"There's no time to take her home," James said. "She'll have to come with me."

"No, 'tis too dangerous."

"Safer to send her home alone? Or to leave her alone in the tunnel? God only knows who might come upon her."

Andrew's eyes closed and a muscle jumped along his jaw. When he looked down at her, his expression was unreadable. "It seems I have no choice. Go with Jamie. Stay close by his side, no matter what happens. Say nothing."

"But—"

He bent and retrieved a bundle from the ground. "Put this on, Bella. Keep the cowl forward. And keep your hands in the folds. They are so obviously lady's hands." He lifted one to his lips and left a kiss in her palm.

"But where are you going to be?"

"I shall be there, too, but I will come in with the others." He turned to his brother. "Jamie, wait until the ritual has begun before you enter. If you must put the chalice to your lips, do not drink from it. I wager it will be laced with opium."

"Gina—"

"She is here somewhere, Bella. And I swear to you, I will let nothing happen to her. You must not cry out or try to go to her. Do you understand?" He squeezed her shoulders and waited for her nod before he set her away from him. "Now go. I have to present myself at the chapel door."

She watched until he disappeared into the darkness of the tunnel. Fear for him tightened her chest. She knew him well enough by now to know that he would risk anything, including his life, to accomplish his goal.

Chapter Twenty-One

The faint chime of a single bell carried from the chapel as Andrew climbed out the window of the manor house and headed across the lawns to the arched entry of the chapel. A robed man waited inside the vestibule and took his invitation.

"You are just in time. It is time to close the doors. 'Twould never do to have an interruption." He chortled as if he'd made a joke. Andrew knew he was deadly serious.

He peered closer beneath the cowl. "Henley?"

"Aye." Henley reached past him to swing the arched door closed, throw the bolt and drop a wooden bar between two metal brackets.

How would Wycliffe's men get in? He and Jamie, it seemed, were on their own. Against how many? Andrew said a quick prayer there would only be a few.

"Go to the vestry while I finish locking up. Dash left a robe for you."

He entered a door between the vestibule and the nave and found the vestry. The room was small, as befitting a family chapel, and the wall was lined with pegs and shelves above. A single bench stood in the middle. Judging by the jackets, hats and other trappings, there were going to be more guests than he'd thought. Most disturbing was the number of pocket pistols, daggers and swords left on shelves and hanging from pegs.

As if to confirm his thoughts, Henley came to stand behind him and said, "No weapons."

Andrew shrugged out of his jacket and hung it up. "I did not bring any. Why should that matter?"

Henley shrugged. "Once we begin passing the cup, some could become a bit rowdy. Dash doesn't want any mishaps."

Was Dash in charge? Not Henley? He didn't want to believe his friend could be guilty of such villainy or betrayal, and yet the evidence against him was mounting.

He sat on the bench, pulled off his boots, tipped them upside down to show Henley he was not concealing any weapons, then pulled them back on. Henley patted his waistcoat pockets to be certain he was not carrying a pocket pistol, and then stepped back to let Andrew pull on the black robe.

He tied the thick cord at his waist and lifted the cowl over his head. After a second glance at the shelf, he decided that Henley was watching him too carefully for him to secrete a weapon in his robe. He would have to depend upon Jamie. "Lead on, Henley."

"No names. And keep your cowl up at all times. Do not speak unless it is a part of the ritual. Identities must be protected."

Andrew was glad Henley could no longer see his face. The absurdity of protecting men who engaged in blood games was an irony lost on him, no doubt. And ritual? What ritual? The men gathered here tonight did not believe in anything but themselves, and in their own desires.

And, until very recently, Andrew had been one of them.

Henley led him into the nave and toward the altar. A red rug had been rolled back to reveal a trap door with a heavy metal ring to pull it up. As Henley did so, the sound of soft chanting carried up the stairs to them.

"They've begun," Henley whispered, a note of excitement in his voice.

Andrew looked down into a dark stone stairway that descended toward a weak yellow glow. He thought of Bella and her sister down there, at the mercy of these men, and a surge of anger coursed through him. Bella, at least, was safe for the moment. He hurried down the steps and only stopped when he reached the narrow antechamber at the bottom. There was a small closed door on one side and an arched doorway at the end. Andrew paused for Henley to catch up with him and tried to assimilate the barrage of perceptions assaulting his senses. Together, he and Henley entered the vault through the arched doorway.

The faint odor of musky incense blended with something more foreign. Something that both seduced the senses and burned the eyes. Hashish? The dank air was heavy with smoke and mist, lending a hazy dreamlike quality to the scene. A soft rhythmic chant that was oddly hypnotic filled the air. The flickering of small torches, confusing in what it alternately revealed and hid, offered the only light.

What was revealed in the vault gave Andrew a very bad moment. There were more people crowded into that room, milling and shifting, than he could count. They gathered in a circle around a stone slab that would have held an altar cloth in days gone by, or the body of a long-dead Ballinger ready for interment in one of the sepulchers that lined the walls. A brazier glowed in one corner, and from that rose the smoke of hashish. Beside that was a wine cask from which a flagon was being refilled. And, as he'd expected, a goblet was being passed. Between the opium, hashish and hypnotic chanting, they would soon be insensible, ready to participate in anything, no matter how bizarre or grotesque.

He stepped to the side, separating himself from Henley and trying to blend in with the others as he tried to discern which of the black-robed figures might be Jamie and Bella. Had they melded into the gathering yet? He spied the passageway to the tunnel in the right wall and knew such a thing would have been easy for them.

Where was Dash? He and Jamie were of a similar size, along with one or two others in the gathering. But Bella…surely he'd know that form anywhere, even in shapeless robes. A quick scan revealed a tall figure close to a smaller form. A barely perceptible nod told Andrew that Jamie had noted him, too. He would have to keep track of them so he would not lose them in the coming melee.

He had to bide his time, wait for Eugenia to be brought forth. If anything, anyone, betrayed them beforehand, Henley and his cohorts would have time to spirit her away.

Someone stumbled on the uneven stone flooring and another caught him by the elbow. The mishap had been enough to reveal a familiar profile beneath the cowl. Throckmorton. *God, how many more here would he recognize?* Half his acquaintances, no doubt. He was certain he could make out Lord Elwood, Booth and even…yes, the Duke of Rutherford. If not for Wycliffe, would he be among them? Ah, but he *was* among them, and precisely *because* of Wycliffe.

Henley had stepped up to the head of the altar, lifted a large flagon above his head and raised his voice above the others in a chant that sounded more like a broken hum than any actual words. Then, with a flash of showmanship Andrew hadn't suspected in him, Henley filled the chalice again and splashed the remainder of the flagon on the bare stone slab in a profane consecration.

Again, the chalice was passed from hand to hand, being refilled from Henley's flagon at intervals. It was nearly full again by the time it reached Andrew. He lifted it to his lips and feigned a long gulp before he passed it to the person next to him. He wiped his mouth on the sleeve of his robe, afraid that even the smallest amount would render him as senseless as the rest. As he had been not so long ago.

Jamie and Bella, he noted, did the same. Jamie moved closer to him, but Andrew tilted his head toward the tunnel. Jamie stopped but did not retreat. Andrew wanted them as far away as possible when the fracas began.

And there would be a fracas before this was over.

An insidious drumming resounded from the antechamber and they all turned toward the archway. Andrew remembered the door in the antechamber. Could that be where they'd held Eugenia?

He was unprepared for what happened next. There was a flash and the acrid odor of sulfur. Gunpowder, no doubt. A red-robed figure stepped out of the smoke, his arms open wide.

"Welcome, brethren!"

And the drumming reached a crescendo.

Dash—his staunchest friend, his greatest ally in a sea of enemies. The man who had saved his life and who had fought shoulder to shoulder with him. And who had kept his guilty secret all these years. Until just a day ago he'd suspected Dash of being Wycliffe's covert operative.

And tonight he realized that Dash's memories of Spain, of Valle del Fuego, had dragged him into even darker places than Andrew had gone.

More recent memories flashed across his mind. Dash's amusement at the unfortunate inmates of Bethlehem Hospital. The fight outside the gin house on Petticoat Lane—the savagery with which Dash had attacked the longshoreman had been almost frenzied. Yesterday, at the fencing school…

The obscene congregation began to chant, and the words were indistinct and slurred. Something about the "Red wyvern" and "Master." Andrew could almost smell the rising excitement and urgency. At least some of them knew what was coming, and they could not wait.

The red-robed man—Dash, he reminded himself—displaced Henley at the head of the stone slab. "You have come, brethren, on this most sacred of nights, to celebrate the brevity of life and the pleasures of the flesh. Live while yet we may."

A cheer went up and echoed down the tunnel, but Andrew knew it would not be heard outside or on the street. The trap door would contain all sounds, cheers and screams alike.

"From the blood of innocents, we take our strength," Dash continued. "From their flesh we renew our own."

A chill invaded Andrew's bones. He remembered his own ennui and how he had longed to feel again. But he'd never wanted this. Those witches' Sabbaths in the beginning had been titillating games to find amusement in an unamusing world. Simple ways to pass the hours before dawn. How had Dash taken it so far? And how had he become so jaded, so callused, that a life meant nothing to him?

"Come draw your lot for the privilege of first breach."

The men pushed forward eagerly. Andrew's head pounded. They were drawing for the first right to violate Eugenia. Had he ever drawn lots in his drugged delirium? God, no. He could never have forgotten such a thing. His fingers curled into fists but he pushed forward to withdraw a stone from a wide-mouthed urn. Black.

Several draws later, one of the brethren cried out and held a red stone aloft. He moved around the altar and stood at the foot, opposite Dash.

"And, because this is the thirteenth rite, I have brought you abundance. A second drawing!"

Bella. Dash was talking about Bella. He did not know she had escaped. He must not have had time to go back and check on her. That much, at least, was in their favor.

A frisson of excitement sparked in the gathering. Andrew was nearly wild with anger when the brethren now crowded forward vying for the right to rape Bella. First. The winner, if Andrew had been able to keep track of him in the crowd, was Henley.

He glanced in her direction and saw Jamie grip her arm and shake his head. He could only imagine what she'd been about to do. His Bella might occasionally lack good sense, but she had no deficit of courage.

Once again the chalice was filled and refilled as it moved from hand to hand. When it was passed to him, he noted Dash watching him closely. He tilted the cup back and pretended a gulp before he passed it on. He staggered slightly as he stepped back, hoping Dash would attribute it to the wine.

The smoke from the incense and hashish burning on the brazier created a heavy haze in the vault, increasing the dream-like quality of the scene.

"Hail, Blood Wyvern. Hail great dragon, master of secret desires. Praise be to thee." Dash spread his arms wide and lifted them as if to accept the adulation and embrace the brethren.

This was no satanic ritual, nor was it any form of witchcraft he'd ever seen. This was praise for a monster who had read the worst in mankind, understood their sickest desires and given them form and substance. And Andrew knew how this would have to end.

He circled slowly until he was next to Jamie and Bella. Understanding, Jamie passed him his dagger, and he tucked it into a fold in his robe secured by the corded belt.

"Take her back down the tunnel, Jamie. Get her out of here and away from this place. Then fetch Wycliffe."

"It will be over by then," Jamie whispered. "You cannot stop it alone."

"I cannot stop it if I am worried about Bella. Take her away. Keep her safe."

"I am not leaving until we have Gina," she said. Her voice was steady but the note of desperation told him that arguing was a waste of precious time and only increased their danger.

He had moved closer to the altar when there was another flash of gunpowder at the archway to the antechamber. When it cleared, two men in Egyptian loincloths came forward, Bella's sister between them. These must be hired thugs, paid for their silence.

Eugenia's hair was unbound and fell loose down her back. She was dressed only in a transparent white wrapper draped to give the same Egyptian impression as her escorts, and she had a vacant look in her eyes. From her bare feet to the top of her head, she was artfully exposed to the brethren—all reminiscent of the ritual in the warehouse.

Andrew was surprised. He'd expected Eugenia to be brought unconscious to the altar. But that might have spoiled the effect. Dash would want her to give the illusion of cooperation. And she did. Leave it to Dash to know the exact dose of opium to render her senseless. And helpless.

He glanced at Bella and, even from the distance, saw her shudder. Thank God she had not cried out. He turned back to Dash, knowing that if he acted too soon, he would not have the evidence he needed and he would endanger Bella and Jamie. He needed to see the weapon. The dagger that had slain the victims. And find the souvenirs the killer had taken.

Dash took a red cloth from the folds of his robes and rolled it out upon the altar. The costumed thugs then lifted Eugenia to lie upon the altar, and the chanting reached a fever pitch.

"Blood Wyvern, exalted dragon, grant us our secret desires."

Standing at her head, Dash again spread his arms. "Come forward, supplicants."

The man who'd drawn the red stone positioned himself at the foot of the slab, and more gathered behind him. Dash leaned forward to loosen the folds of Eugenia's wrapper and lay her bare to the crowd.

Andrew could almost smell the lust in the rasped heavy breathing of the men now besotted with wine and opium. He clasped his hand around the hilt of his dagger, careful not to let it show too soon, and moved closer to Dash.

Eugenia's escorts flanked the first man to lift him to the slab between her thighs. He had begun to hitch up his robes when Bella's voice rang out clear and true.

"No!"

As the brethren turned in her direction, Jamie pulled her backward toward the tunnel. Dash drew a curved dagger from a red pouch fastened to his robe and took a step toward them.

At last, the evidence, and in the perpetrator's own hand.

Andrew's cowl slipped back as he released his own dagger from his robes and stepped between them. "Let them go, Dash."

His friend pushed his hood back and grinned. "Ah, I wondered. Yes, I wondered. I should have known better, eh?"

"Wycliffe and the watch will be here soon. Charlie has gone for them."

"Charlie has been…waylaid."

Fear spiked in Andrew's chest. Did they have Charlie locked in one of the tunnel rooms? Had they killed him? No. It had to be a distraction. A red herring. Dash had always been good at drawing attention away from his transgressions, and this was considerably more than that. One thing was certain—the outcome of this fight was entirely up to Andrew. He tried his own distraction. "You are bluffing, Dash. The authorities have been notified. Everyone knows what you've done."

With an ugly snarl, Dash slashed downward to prove him wrong. The dagger grazed Eugenia's throat but she barely moved. The man above her dropped his robes, scrambled down and backed away from them.

Andrew lunged at his friend, hoping to disarm him, but his injured arm proved treacherous. He could barely hold Dash off, let alone launch a counterattack.

Before Henley or any of the others could disarm him, pandemonium erupted at the sound of shrill whistles from the antechamber. The watch! Charlie had brought the night watch.

They separated and circled each other as the brethren scattered, tearing off their robes and running in all directions, the charleys in pursuit. Some hid themselves in arched alcoves, others made for the tunnel. The watch ran after them, brandishing cudgels and shouting orders to halt. But no one stopped their duel.

"We are alike, Drew, you and I. Cut from the same cloth," Dash said, his gaze never leaving Andrew's knife. "'Tis our lust for life that has enabled us to survive. We're brothers under the skin. We can go to France. The world is ours for the taking. Remember Spain? We were life and death there. Gods."

He was insane, Andrew realized. Beneath the civilized veneer, Dash was completely mad. "We are nothing alike," Andrew said.

In a smooth motion, Dash removed his robe to unfetter his arms, and his smile changed to something feral. "You stopped me too soon, you know. I had a little surprise for you."

"Bella," he said. "I know." Andrew noted that Dash was armed with a sword. He wanted to look around to see if she was safe, if Jamie was still beside her, but he knew that was what Dash was waiting for.

"Ah. But do you know everything? Did she tell you we had a little... interlude?" Bella would have told him, wouldn't she?

"That is a lie, Dash. A real clanker."

He laughed. "How can you be so certain? She's a tart, that one. Wasn't even virgin. Did you know that?"

Concentrate. He needed to concentrate and not let Dash distract him. But Dash was at the end of his patience. He slid his sword from the scabbard and lunged, switching the dagger to his left hand. Andrew could have defended himself against a dagger, but would not have a chance against the longer reach of the rapier. He pulled the corded belt loose, whirled his robe over his head and twisted it over his left forearm as a shield.

"Hunter!"

He spared a quick glance aside and found Devlin Farrell, who tossed him a sword, hilt first. He dropped his dagger, caught it and turned back to Dash just in time to fend off a blow. The clash of blades vibrated up his arm and tweaked his wound. How long could he last?

"You can't do it," Dash said, reading his mind and redoubling his efforts.

Blow after blow fell, and Andrew gritted his teeth to parry them, feeling his arm weaken a bit more after each one. Behind him, he heard Bella gasp and he had a sudden vision of what it would mean to her if Dash won this fight—a vision of her at Dash's hands. A trickle of blood oozed down his arm. His fencing wound had opened. He did not have long, and he lunged again and again.

Dash looked worried now, as if the outcome was suddenly in doubt. "Can you kill another friend, Drew? Has anyone ever protected you like I have? Kept your secret? What would you do with me gone? What of your conscience then?"

"It will not trouble me at all."

"Big words for a wounded man."

In a quick exchange of blows, Andrew flicked Dash's sword aside and backed him against the altar, his blade against Dash's heart. Eugenia blinked and turned her head, seemingly unable to move or to register events around her. A steady trickle of blood puddled beneath her right shoulder.

"You don't have it in you," Dash panted. "You cannot do it."

Damn! He was right. He couldn't kill Dash. Couldn't kill another friend. *"Wycliffe!"* he yelled, hoping against hope that someone would hear and come.

"No, Drew. Not prison. Not the gallows. Finish it."

He shook his head and kept his blade at Dash's heart as he leaned into him. Where was Wycliffe, damn it?

"I'd have done it, you know. I'd have raped her there in front of you. I'd have killed her and her sister. Just like I've always killed anyone who got in my way. McPherson didn't commit suicide, you know. He balked after an incident the night of our outing to Bedlam and I had to put him out of the way. And the others from our detail. Even Henley has outworn his usefulness now. I'll do it again, you know."

McPherson? The others they'd served with who'd supposedly died in service or in duels? Hank and Wilson? Bile rose in his stomach.

"A moment ago, I'd have killed you, too. So do it, Drew. End it once and for all. You or me."

Andrew's pause cost him dearly. In that split second, Dash slashed upward with his dagger, opening a rip along Andrew's right flank. Pain erupted with hot intensity and warm viscous blood oozed down his side. Bella gasped and, from the corner of his eye, he saw Jamie restrain her.

Dash drew his hand back, preparing to deliver another slash. He laughed, a crazed unholy sound. "I knew you couldn't do it. You never had an appetite for killing. I should have been in charge. I'd have given my fortune for ten more men like Frederick."

Andrew's arm shook with the effort to keep his sword steady at his friend's heart. He looked into Dash's eyes and saw the madness there. Whatever humanity he'd clung to was gone. But he'd been a friend. Like Frederick had been a friend.

Dash bared his teeth as he propelled his dagger upward again. Regret, grief and resignation mingled with inevitability as Andrew pressed forward, the choice made.

Disbelief flashed across Dash's face. A cynical twist of a smile distorted his face. "You…always did…surprise me, Drew."

Andrew withdrew his blade and Dash slipped slowly to the stone floor.

Lord Wycliffe stood expressionless as he listened to the reports his men brought him. They'd only managed to capture seven or eight of the brethren. The rest had escaped down the tunnel or back up the stone stairway. Henley had gotten away clean. Daschel was dead. The Blood Wyvern Brotherhood was disbanded. It was over.

Or nearly so.

Andrew winced as Bella tied a length of cloth torn from his robe around his middle. A stitch or two would repair his wound, and the bleeding had stopped for the moment. Bella was safe. Eugenia was shrouded in Bella's robe, a makeshift bandage at the base of her throat, and Jamie holding her close to still her trembling.

"We should take you to hospital," Bella said, her voice soft and solicitous.

He eased his back against the stone wall and sighed. "I'll send for a doctor once I am home."

"But—"

"Our first order of business is to take you and Eugenia home. There is still time for you to get some sleep before you must face your mother."

Bella rolled her eyes, and he chuckled.

Devlin Farrell wiped the blood from his sword on his trouser leg and slid it back into his scabbard. "I ought to be getting back. The barkeeper is likely stealing me blind."

"Where the hell did you come from, anyway?"

"I was always here. I knew you might need help but wouldn't ask for it, so I had my own robe made. Couldn't let Humphries get away. I came through the tunnel behind your brother and Miss O'Rourke."

"I owe you my life."

"We're even. I had my own reasons for coming. Just do me a favor and keep my name out of it, will you? I'd be finished in the rookeries if word got out I helped the charleys."

Andrew nodded, and Farrell slipped away before Wycliffe could question him.

When the last watchman finished his report and walked away, Wycliffe turned to them and shrugged. "Wish I could say that all's well that ends well, but…it galls me that some of those vermin will go free. We may never know the half of them."

"I have some suspicions. And if we ever find Henley, leave him to me. I'll make him talk."

Wycliffe laughed. "Aye, well, I might be tempted by that." He turned to Bella and gave her a stiff bow. "Miss O'Rourke, would you mind seeing to your sister while I have a word with the Hunter brothers?"

She gave a reluctant sigh that Andrew found quite endearing, then went to relieve Jamie of his duty.

"How is Eugenia doing?" he asked when Jamie joined them.

"She's starting to become a bit lucid now that the opium is losing its effect. With luck, she will recover by tomorrow and not recall a blasted thing."

"That would be a great kindness. And her wound?"

"Dash missed the artery and anything else important. She will require a bit of stitching, and there will be a scar. The real damage will come if she remembers any of it. We may never know what was done to her before we arrived."

"We shall pray, then, that she does not remember."

Andrew nodded and braced himself. "Before I…before Dash died, he confessed that he'd killed McPherson when he learned too much. I think we can also presume that he is behind the killings of Hank and Wilson. We may never know the half of his crimes."

"I am beginning to realize that." Wycliffe tugged on his right ear and frowned. "Good thing you were working so closely with my agent."

"Your agent? Never saw hide nor hair of him."

Jamie grinned but said nothing, and Andrew realized he'd been hoodwinked. "How long?"

"A year or two," Jamie confessed. "Lockwood dragged me in."

Andrew stood and rubbed his arm. "Is there anything unfinished that will not wait until tomorrow?"

"This." Wycliffe reached inside his jacket and brought forth a small lacquered box with a decorated lid. He pulled the hinged lid back and showed the shriveled, discolored contents to them. It took him a moment to realize what he was seeing.

Jamie paled and Andrew curled his lip in disgust. The rest of the evidence. The small triangular bits of flesh were somehow the greatest violation of the victims. An unspeakable violation every time Dash had opened that box and savored them again.

"Daschel was completely mad. He should have been in an asylum long ago. Souvenirs? Reminders of the power he held over others?"

"What are you going to do with it?" Andrew asked. "Since Dash is dead, we will not need it for trial."

Without speaking, Wycliffe went to the still-glowing brazier, removed the grate, dropped the box on the coals and waited until it caught fire.

He turned back to them. "And that, at last, is an end to it."

Chapter Twenty-Two

Bella turned to the parlor door as Nancy announced, "Mr. Andrew Hunter to see you, Miss O'Rourke."

Her heart leaped to her throat when Andrew pushed past the maid and came into the parlor, his hat in his hand. He bowed stiffly. "Miss O'Rourke."

"Mr. Hunter," she acknowledged, scarcely recognizing her own voice. She glanced at Nancy's retreating back, knowing she was on her way to summon her mother.

Andrew closed the door, turned the lock and smiled. "You look beautiful today, Bella. And how is Miss Eugenia?"

Her cheeks tingled and burned. How odd that he could make her feel like an awkward country girl after all they'd been through. After all they'd done—all *she'd* done. "She is well. Nearly recovered, in truth. But she recalls nothing of the events of last night. Only waking in her bed this morning."

"A blessing," he murmured, coming closer.

"I...I have told her that she fell and knocked her head last night as she was carrying a glass of water, and that is how she injured her neck. Nancy brought the doctor very early this morning, and he stitched the gash."

"You feel bad about lying to her."

She nodded. "Though I know it is for the best."

"And Miss Lillian?"

Lilly? She lowered her voice. "Mama woke last night, and Lilly laced her tea with laudanum. She only rose an hour ago. Lilly, it appears, is surprisingly resourceful."

Andrew laughed. "I can see that."

"And you? How are you this afternoon?"

He tossed his hat onto a side table. "Quite well, so long as you do not punch me in the stomach."

She went to perch on the edge of the settee and folded her hands in her lap. "I must thank you, Andrew, for all you've done for my family. Finding Cora's killer, saving Gina. And me. The O'Rourkes must have been a great trial to you."

His lips twitched as if he were trying to hold back a laugh. "That is something of an understatement, my dear. But I would have it no other way. Still, I could almost sympathize with your mother. The poor woman will never know that two of her daughters were kidnapped, meant for human sacrifice, and that her other daughter drugged her so she would not wake up and find them gone." He paused and shook his head in mock despair. "The O'Rourkes are going to mean a great deal of trouble. No doubt of that."

"We…we shall try to stay out of your way."

"That was not my meaning, Bella." He sat beside her and took her hand. "I will gladly take on the O'Rourkes if you come with them, though I would do you no favor by marrying you. You were meant for finer things than marriage to a rogue."

"M-marriage? But, no. The letter from your solicitor arrived this morning, saying you'd settle a sum on me so that I would never be a poor relation or at the mercy of others, and even that I must refuse."

He took her left hand and held it between his. "You are right to dismiss me, Bella. I've been nothing but a wastrel most of my life. But I dared to hope I might persuade you to save me from myself. I even acquired a license yesterday, after our night at Henderson's inn. We do not have to wait for banns to be read. We can be married whenever you're ready."

"Andrew, how can I marry you? Why, I've kissed half your friends. How could you go about in society, endure the whispers, knowing that?"

"Easily, by knowing I would be the object of much envy. And I would hate to tell you, m'dear, how many of the women you will be meeting that *I* have kissed."

"But the night we met, you told me that no respectable man would marry a woman who'd kissed half his friends."

"Just our luck, then, that I am not in the least bit respectable."

"I must doubt—"

"And you are entitled to your doubts. All but one."

She looked up and met his dark, welcoming eyes. He released her hand, cupped her face and spoke against her lips, "'Doubt that the stars are fire, doubt that the sun doth move, doubt truth to be a liar, but *never* doubt I love…'"

The quote from one of Shakespeare's sonnets brought tears to her eyes. He loved her…and that changed everything. Warmth and wonder seeped through her. "Are you certain you will not be ashamed of me?"

"You can only improve my lamentable reputation."

A sudden thundering shook the parlor door. "Bella! Bella, are you in there? Is Mr. Hunter with you? What are you doing?"

She started to rise, but Andrew pulled her back. "She will keep, Bella. And I will handle her when we are ready. For now, I am waiting for an answer."

"But—" The latch rattled as Mama tried to open it, then the pounding renewed. Andrew smiled, and suddenly none of it mattered. "Yes," she said. "I will marry you, and I will know I am the envy of every woman you ever kissed."

He laughed, standing with her and taking her into his arms. "Then a kiss to seal our bargain before we go, Bella? Just one kiss?"

"Will one kiss satisfy my Lord Libertine?"

"Never," he promised.

* * * * *

LADY PRISCILLA'S SHAMEFUL SECRET
Christine Merrill

As a ruined woman, outspoken Lady Priscilla has vowed never to marry. But needing a successor, the Duke of Reighland is not to be dissuaded. Once he sets his sights on this captivating woman, he will do anything in his power to claim her!

RAKE WITH A FROZEN HEART
Marguerite Kaye

When impetuous Henrietta Markham is attacked and then accused of theft, the notorious Earl of Pentland is the only one who can clear her name. Since the failure of his marriage, ice has flowed in Rafe St Alban's veins, but meeting the all-too-distracting governess heats his blood to boiling point…

MISS CAMERON'S FALL FROM GRACE
Helen Dickson

When mistaken identity leads to devilish Colonel Lord Stephen Fitzwaring unwittingly seducing respectable Delphine Cameron, the only way they can avoid scandal is to marry! Now Delphine must decide between a life of chastity…or succumb to her husband's irresistible temptation…

SOCIETY'S MOST SCANDALOUS RAKE
Isabelle Goddard

When apparently innocent beauty Domino de Silva meets wickedly handsome Joshua Marchmain an overwhelming force draws them together, but all is not what it seems and there are those in society who would stop at nothing to keep them apart…

Mills & Boon® Hardback Historical

*Another exciting novel available
this month:*

DANGEROUS LORD, INNOCENT GOVERNESS

Christine Merrill

THE DARK LORD'S ULTIMATE TEMPTATION

Daphne Collingham is convinced that her beloved cousin died
at the hands of her husband, Lord Timothy Colton, so decides
to masquerade as a governess in his home to discover the truth.
What Daphne hasn't bargained on is how the brooding Lord
will make her feel under his dark gaze…

Lord Colton is suspicious of the alluring new governess—and
with the scandal surrounding him he must control his passion.
But a man has his limits, and the delectable Miss Collingham
is pure temptation…

HIST0312 HB DLIG

Mills & Boon® Hardback
Historical

*Another exciting novel available
this month:*

CAPTURED FOR THE CAPTAIN'S PLEASURE

Ann Lethbridge

PREDATOR BY NAME, PASSIONATE BY NATURE

Captain Michael Hawkhurst relishes his fearsome reputation—
for he lives only to wreak revenge on the Fulton family, who
so cruelly destroyed his own.

Spirited Alice Fulton knows a ship is no place for a lady, but
she is determined to save her father's business…

When fate delivers him Fulton's virginal daughter as his captive,
Michael faces a dilemma—should he live up to his scandalous
name and find revenge with sweet Alice, or will his honourable
side win out...and win the girl…?

Another exciting novel available
this month:

BRUSHED BY SCANDAL

Gail Whitiker

WHAT WILL SHE RISK FOR LOVE?

Lady Annabelle Durst may be beautiful, but at four-and-twenty she's firmly—and contentedly!—on the shelf. She's learnt there's *nothing* more important than protecting her heart against the perils of love.

Then Anna's family is embroiled in the scandal of the season, with only Sir Barrington Parker to turn to. He has a reputation for exposing society's most disreputable secrets, and to save her family's honour oh-so-sensible Anna will do *anything*—even risk her reputation—to persuade this dangerous man to help...

HIST0312 HB BBS